Dee Williams was born and brought up in Rotherhithe in East London, where her father worked as a stevedore in Surrey Docks. Dee left school at fourteen, met her husband at sixteen and was married at twenty. After living abroad for some years, Dee moved to Hampshire to be close to her family. She has written several previous novels including *This Time For Keeps*, *All That Jazz* and *After the Dance*.

Visit Dee's website at www.deewilliams.co.uk

DEE WILLIAMS

A MOMENT TO REMEMBER

CHARNWOOD
Leicester

First published in Great Britain in 2010 by
Headline Publishing Group
London

First Charnwood Edition
published 2012
by arrangement with
Headline Publishing Group
An Hachette UK Company
London

British Library CIP Data

Williams, Dee.
   A moment to remember.
   1. East End (London, England)- -Social conditions
   - -20th century- -Fiction. 2. Domestic fiction.
   3. Large type books.
   I. Title
   823.9'14–dc23

   ISBN 978–1–4448–0982–4

Published by
F. A. Thorpe (Publishing)
Anstey, Leicestershire

Set by Words & Graphics Ltd.
Anstey, Leicestershire
Printed and bound in Great Britain by
T. J. International Ltd., Padstow, Cornwall

THIS IS FOR ALL MY FAMILY.

For my lovely daughter Carol and my clever son-in-law Gez. I am so lucky to have them as they are always there for me when I need them.

Also my two lovely, clever granddaughters, Emma and Samantha. Both have university degrees and I am very, very proud of them.

For my sister Christine who is on the other side of the world and who I miss a lot.

For my brother Roy; although we don't see a lot of each other, he is in my thoughts.

And all my nieces, nephews and cousins too numerous to mention by name.

Acknowledgements

The Red Cross and St Dunstan's for the help and information I needed and received.

Thank you.

1

October 1908

'And where you bin?'

Milly stood and looked down at her well-worn black button-up boots.

'Well answer me, gel.'

Her father was sitting in the room they used for everything. It had a table and three mismatched chairs; one had the back broken off. That was what her father did when he was in one of his frequent rages. They only possessed one armchair, which stood next to the fire. Nobody dared to sit in his chair. He moved his bulk and, picking up the brass poker, pushed it into the few paltry coals sitting in the grate, causing them to burst into flame.

'Yer mother's bin trying ter feed the kids while you've bin out gallivanting.'

Arthur Ash stood up. He was a tall, well-built man with a shock of black hair. His dark eyes were penetrating, and as he was still holding the poker, Milly cringed as she stepped back. She had felt the force of her father's hand many times and stood waiting for the blow that would send her reeling across the room.

'Lorst yer bleeding tongue, 'ave yer?' He leaned towards her.

'Milly, please answer your father.' Ivy Ash was a pale, thin woman who, after having ten children in twelve years and trying to feed her family on the pittance her husband gave her, looked worn out.

'I got caught up with all those women with banners and policemen; they was marching along the road and I couldn't get through.'

'What?'

'There was lots of people and policemen and I couldn't get past.'

'Leave her be, Arthur. She couldn't help it.'

'I've seen those silly cows outside the docks carrying on about votes fer women. I ask yer, what the bloody 'ell d' they want ter vote for? Wot der women know about fings like that? They should be 'ome looking after the old man. Don't you let me find out yer wiv 'em, otherwise yer get another pasting. I can soon knock that rubbish out o' yer.'

Milly looked at her mother. 'Honest, Mum. There was such a lot of people and I just got caught up in 'em.'

Her father grabbed her arm.

'Please, Arthur, leave it.'

'I bet she was flinging herself at 'em, hoping ter join 'em. She's nothing but a dirty tramp.'

Milly began to cry, and four pairs of eyes looked anxiously up at her from where her younger siblings were sitting on the floor. She was the eldest of the eight surviving Ash children.

What was the point of trying to talk to her father when he was in one of his moods? Not that she could ever talk to him. She didn't like him or the way he treated her dear mum. Milly,

2

who was thirteen, knew what a bully he was and wondered why her mum kept having babies, babies that she couldn't look after.

Milly herself had helped to deliver the last one. That day she had been terrified her mum was going to die. Old Mrs Grant, the woman who was with her mum, called for Milly to help. She had held her mother's hand and mopped her brow, and all the while her mum had tightened her grip on Milly's hand and cried out in pain. Milly had stood wide-eyed and speechless when the baby came into the world. Mrs Grant handed her the silent scrap covered with blood and instructed her: 'Wrap her up in that old towel, hold her close and keep her warm and make sure she don't stop breathing.' Terrified, Milly did as she was told and held the baby close. Baby Helen was a tiny, fragile little thing who had fought for her life; now, seven months later, she was a frail, sad little girl with big blue eyes and a lovely smile.

'Milly love, did you get the milk for Helen's bottle?' asked her mother, who was sitting on the hard wooden chair nursing her baby.

Milly knew she was trying to ease the tense situation and she just nodded. 'I'll go and warm it up.'

She hurried to the outhouse that was attached like a carbuncle to the back of the terraced house. The Ash family occupied the ground floor, which comprised a kitchen plus two rooms; the children all slept in one and Milly's mother and father and baby Helen slept in the other. Her parents had a bed, but the children slept on the floor on a lumpy mattress that at times had the odd bug or two crawling in it. They shared the outhouse with a Mr and Mrs Booker and their four children, who lived upstairs. The Bookers had the same layout, two rooms and a kitchen. Even with four children under four, they were very quiet. Mr Booker was an accountant, and he often said he wanted to move from Rotherhithe to a better place, but he never did. Milly worried that her father wouldn't be able to find the rent for the whole house if the Bookers moved. Mrs Booker was a quiet, thin lady who hardly ever spoke, and her children were very well behaved. They kept themselves to themselves and the only time the two families met was in the outhouse. As there wasn't any water upstairs it had to be taken up in buckets and the slops brought down to the outside lav, which they also shared. The water came from the tap over a large white sink where they all had to do their washing. Cooking for both families was done on a black stove that stood in the corner and had to be fed with wood and coal. It had an oven and two holes on top that would be uncovered when a kettle or a pan needed to be heated. The outhouse was a cold place and at times the inside of the brick walls ran with water, especially when the women were doing their washing and boiling it on the stove. When it was icy outside, they had to scrape the ice off the inside of the window to be able to look out on the very small back yard.

Milly sat on an upturned wooden box and thought about the morning. She had been so excited when she heard the band playing and the women came marching along. Everybody was shouting and women were throwing flowers. When she was able to find a newspaper, she would take it home and with the help of her mother they would read all about everything that was happening in the world. She knew that these women were called suffragettes and they wanted women to have a vote. Not that she knew why they wanted to vote, but her mother tried to explain that they hoped to make things better for women. Milly knew that her mother, along with her Auntie Doris, her mother's elder sister, had been very well brought up and properly educated; she also spoke differently to her dad and people who lived round here. Milly loved her mother dearly and often asked her why she'd married her father and didn't work in a big house like she had told them their Auntie Doris did. Her mother always gave a soft smile and said that she loved him. Milly couldn't see how anyone could love and marry a bully, but her mother said that he wasn't always like that; he used to be kind and gentle but then he had an accident and injured his leg and couldn't get regular work, so they had fallen on hard times. Milly could never remember her father being kind and gentle. Their mother had told them about how Doris worked in a big house, but they had never seen her, and she had never been here. Was Mum so ashamed at how she had finished up?

The milk boiling over brought Milly quickly to her feet. She silently prayed that her father wouldn't come through to go out to the outside lav, as that would mean another smack round the head if he thought she'd been daydreaming.

The back door slammed back hard against the wall and two scruffy-looking boys came in laughing and pushing each other.

''Allo, Mil. All right then?' asked Billy, who was eleven.

'He in?' asked Daniel, cocking his head towards the kitchen door.

Milly nodded. She loved all her brothers and sisters, but somehow she could talk to Dan and he always seemed to be able to confide in her. Even at ten years old he had a very sensible head on his shoulders, while Billy was more of a bruiser, his fists ready for anything and anyone. She knew her father would have to watch his step in years to come when Billy was a man. 'Did you manage to get some wood?' she asked.

'I should say so,' said Billy proudly. 'Bin down the railway sidings and got hold of some logs and a bit of coal.'

'We think someone hid 'em and put 'em away till later,' said Dan.

'And we pinched 'em,' said Billy gleefully.

'Let's hope whoever it was don't find out it was you two,' said Milly, testing baby Helen's bottle on the back of her hand.

'Na, they're in the yard and the cart's covered over.' Billy cuffed the dewdrop that was hanging from his nose. 'Fink somebody's bin using our bog again, it don't half stink.'

There was a narrow alley that ran along the back of the houses in Winter Street, and like

6

most of the tenants the boys had made a hole in the wall to save coming through the house, and blocked it with wood to try and stop people coming in. Not that it did.

Milly smiled. These two were very enterprising. They had made a cart out of an orange box they'd got from the greengrocer for running errands, and found a couple of pram wheels. Getting the wood and chopping it up into sticks meant they could sell the small bundles. That and finding coal was Billy and Dan's job. Everybody had to help in this family if they wanted to survive.

'I'll just take Helen's bottle in and then I'll tell you about the women I saw today.'

When Milly returned to the outhouse, the boys were sitting on the cold flagstone floor in front of the fire.

'Come on, then, tell us about the women, Mil,' said Dan eagerly.

'They was marching along the street and they looked lovely in their white frocks and big white hats. Ever so many people was there. Some of the ladies was carrying big banners that had Votes for Women painted on 'em and others threw flowers. It was ever so exciting.'

'I'd love to march along the street,' said Dan.

Billy laughed. 'You'd look silly in a white frock and big 'at.'

Dan pushed his brother. 'No, daft. I'm gonna be a soldier when I grow up.'

'There won't be a war so they won't want soldiers,' said Billy. 'Now me, I'm gonna go in the navy. Gonna go on a big ship and visit all

7

those far-off lands and make me fortune.'

'Mil, you still wanna find Auntie Doris and see if you can go and work with her in the big house?' asked Dan.

Milly nodded. 'I'd really like that. If we knew where it was and how to get there, I'd go and ask her.'

'Yeah, but Mum won't tell yer, will she?' Billy jumped up and rubbed his bum, then kicked his shoes along the flagstones, making the studs spark. 'It's bloody cold sitting there.'

'That's cos you ain't got no seat in your trousers,' said Dan.

Milly laughed.

'Why won't she tell us, Mil?' asked Dan.

Milly shrugged. 'I think she's ashamed of us.'

'We can't help it if our old man can't get proper work,' said Dan.

'He could do more for Mum than he does,' said Billy. 'He's only interested in getting enough money for a pint, and bugger us.'

'Billy, don't you let Mum hear you swear,' said Milly.

'Or Dad, or you'll end up getting another pasting,' said Dan.

Both boys had felt their father's belt more than once.

'One of these days I will go and try to find Auntie Doris,' said Milly wistfully.

'I dunno why she don't come and see us,' said Dan.

'When I ask Mum about that, she says they fell out years ago, and I don't think she wants Doris to see how she's finished up.'

'She must be a bit of a stuck-up cow,' said Billy. 'Cos it ain't like Mum to fall out with someone.'

'Mum don't go out to talk to anybody,' said Dan.

'She talks to Mrs Booker,' said Milly.

'I know, but she don't go out now, does she?'

'No. Not since Helen was born.'

'Why's that then, Mil?' asked Billy.

'Dunno.'

After that they fell into a comfortable silence. They often talked about what they were going to do when they grew up, but they knew that whatever dreams they had, they were just dreams. For as much as their mother tried to help them, they knew that without a proper education they would only get poorly paid labouring jobs like their dad, if they were lucky. Going to school cost time and money, and their father would never allow that. Everybody in this house had to work in one way or another for their survival.

2

'Now come on, put this paper away before your father comes home,' said Ivy Ash the following day. She was sitting nursing Helen. 'He was hoping to get some work in the docks today. I'll help you finish sewing those buttons on while there's still a bit of light and we don't have to waste pennies on lighting the gas mantle. Go and wash your hands, we don't want to get the shirts dirty.' She put Helen into the drawer that served as a cot and looked at her eldest daughter. Milly was growing into a beautiful girl, with pale skin and straight dark hair tucked behind her ears. Her dark eyes reflected her feelings and could change so quickly with anger or with love. But what was her future? There were times when Ivy wished that she was still in touch with her sister, then perhaps Doris could find Milly an interesting post, but she knew her sister would never come to see her. They'd fallen out many years ago and there were times when she wondered if Doris was even still alive. Ivy was proud of all her children. Billy and Dan were always looking for ways to make a few pence, and now Milly had been along to the shirt factory and managed to get some outwork sewing buttons on shirts. It wasn't well paid, but it helped.

As Milly folded the newspaper and tucked it into the drawer in the dresser, she hoped that if her father had a made a few shillings today that would put him in a good mood — that was if he didn't stop off at the public house and spend it all on drink before he got home.

But when he returned home later that afternoon, he was clearly in a foul temper. Although he'd had a few hours' work and been to the pub, he was annoyed when they threw him out. He must have been trying to scrounge drinks, Milly thought.

'If you can spare a few coppers for Milly to pop out and perhaps get some potatoes, I can make a meal,' said Ivy, smiling up at him.

He searched his pockets and threw tuppence on the table. 'And don't waste it. I've bin working bloody hard all morning for that pittance.'

Milly grabbed her thin coat from off the nail behind the door and hurried down the street. As it was late in the afternoon she hoped that she would find something the shopkeeper wanted to get rid of.

She was in luck. First she went to the market and managed to get a few potatoes and carrots, then, as the butcher was taking in his wares, she heard him talking to the young lad who worked for him on the stall outside the shop.

'Might have ter throw out those scraps. Can't see anybody wanting 'em now, seeing as how they've been out all day.'

'How much do you want for 'em?' asked Milly as she stood and watched the boy bundling up the sad pieces of meat.

The butcher looked at her. 'Give us a penny.'

Milly could have hugged him. Tonight they were in for a treat.

'You must be hard up to buy that lot,' said the butcher's boy.

Milly tossed her head. 'It might be for me dog.'

'I've seen you a few times and you ain't got no dog.'

'Come on, Jack, stop talking ter the girls and get this lot inside.'

As Milly walked away, the young lad gave her a wink. That made her smile and put a spring in her step. Today was her lucky day. She had some meat to boil up, and with a few veg, that would make them a lovely warming broth. Her thoughts went back to the butcher's boy. He had said he had seen her before, and he'd winked at her. He was rather nice-looking, with a ruddy face, a shock of ginger hair and a cheeky grin. She would have to go and see him again.

★ ★ ★

Jack worked mostly on the stall outside the shop, and since the day she'd bought the scraps, whenever Milly walked past he called to her. One day she stopped, and found him very nice; easy to chat to, just like Dan and Billy. She was buying a few bones to boil up when Jack looked around, then cleared his throat.

'Fancy coming out termorrer? We could go to the zoo or somethink.'

Milly blushed. He wanted to take her out. 'I'd like that, I ain't ever been to the zoo, but I can't.'

12

'There's no such word as can't; you can do anyfink if you make up your mind. Look at me: I wanted to go to work and learn a trade. Not bad for a kid wot was born in the workhouse. I know you can't go out to work, cos of yer poorly mum.'

Milly smiled. When she had told him that her mother never went out, he thought that she must be ill. 'I would really like that. My mum went there once and told me all about it.'

'Well that's it then.'

'I'd love to, but I have to help me mum. My little sister's got the croup and Mum's up day and night putting bread poultices on her poor little chest.' Over the brief time they had talked, she knew she could tell him anything.

'I ain't taking no fer an answer. You come here tomorrow and then you and me will go ter see the animals.'

'I'll ask me mum.'

'Right. I'll see yer at nine.'

Milly smiled to herself as she walked away. Jack wanted to take her out. It would be lovely if she could go. This might be a once-in-a-lifetime experience.

★　★　★

'So could I, Mum?' asked Milly when she told Ivy what Jack had said.

'I don't know. Your father wouldn't be happy about it and you could be gone all day. Besides, poor Helen needs a lot of care, and don't forget your dad will be home and there's the others to see to. Then there's your homework. The factory will want that lot back on Monday. I'm sorry, Milly, but I can't give you a hand, not with Helen so poorly.'

'I know,' said Milly. She went into the outhouse to put a pan of water on top of the fire. How could she go and leave her mother to cope? All she wanted was something out of life like Jack. She so admired him for going out in the world and getting a job. He had told her he had a future and was going to make something of himself.

Many times she wished she could go out to work instead of helping her mother with the children. She had never told Jack that she was doing homework, sewing on buttons. The pay was very poor and she couldn't always finish the order on time. Sometimes she worked late into the night, till the gas ran out and they didn't have any pennies to feed the meter and it was too dark to see. Why did life have to be so cruel?

* * *

The following day when Milly woke up, the sun was streaming through the thin piece of material that served as a curtain. What a lovely day to go to the zoo. She sat up and looked at the other children, who were all still asleep under their odd assortment of bedding. She knew that she would go to the zoo with Jack. Carefully she stood up and stepped over them.

'Where you going?' whispered Dan.

'To the lav,' Milly said softly.

'What's the time?' asked Billy.

'Shh. Keep your voice down,' said Milly. 'I thought I heard the church clock chime six.'

'Come on, Dan, we've gotta get up.'

Dan and Billy carefully manoeuvred themselves between the sleeping children.

In the outhouse, Milly put a pan of water on the stove. 'Go and get some wood, Dan, I need to get the fire going.' The sun shining had helped to make up her mind. She would worry about the outcome later.

'We don't want any tea,' said Billy, pulling on his boots.

'I ain't gonna make tea,' said Milly. 'I'm gonna have a wash.'

'Why? You going out?' asked Billy.

'Yes.'

'Where're you going, Mil?' asked Dan.

'The zoo. Where're you two going?'

'Just out scrounging, down under the railway arches.'

'Who yer going with, Mil?'

'Jack.'

'Who's this Jack? Does Mum know about him, and what — ' Dan didn't finish what he was saying.

They had all their backs to the door and were taken by surprise when their father came into the outhouse.

'What's all this then? What you lot doing up?'

'We're gonna get some wood before everyone else does,' said Billy defiantly, looking straight at his father.

'What about you, miss?' He quickly pushed

15

past Milly. 'I'll talk ter you when I git back.'

Milly stood silently and looked at his back as he rushed outside to the lav.

'What you gonna do, Mil?' asked Dan, looking very worried.

'I dunno. I didn't think he'd be up yet.'

'Look, why don't you come with us now?' Billy stood at the door, ready to go.

'I can't.'

'Why not?' asked Dan.

'I wanted to make meself look nice.'

'Why?' asked Billy.

'Jack's from the butcher's, and he asked me to go out with him.'

'Christ,' said Billy. 'Don't let the old man hear that, otherwise you'll be in for a right pasting and so will Jack. Come on, Dan, let's scarper, 'fore he comes out the bog.'

Dan looked at Milly. 'Please come with us.'

'I can't.'

'I'm sorry, Mil,' he said, and with that they both left.

It was no use her going off with the boys now that her father had heard about their plans. But just how much had he heard? She stood terrified, waiting for him to come back.

3

Ivy held her daughter close. The young girl's sobs were racking her body. She looked up at her husband. 'Why did she need punishing, Arthur?'

'Did you know she was planning to go out with some boy?'

Ivy slowly shook her head. 'Just that she wanted to go to the zoo.'

Milly looked up at her mother, but could see the fear in her eyes.

'She said she was going orf with 'im. She don't 'ave ter go to the bloody zoo, there's enough animals round 'ere.' He had a smug look. 'I heard 'er and the boys talking before they scarpered. Would 'ave thought she's got better fings ter do round 'ere than stand gawping at a load of animals.'

Milly's sobs slowly subsided and she raised her head again. How could her father think this way?

'What yer got to say fer yourself, then, girl? Yer turning inter a right trollop. Not surprised, it runs in the family.'

Milly buried her head in her mother's lap again.

'Come on. Speak up.' He dragged her up by her arm, making her wince with pain.

'Milly, for goodness' sake answer your father.'

He was still holding on to her arm, and now he pushed his face into hers. His dark eyes were narrowed and menacing.

'I just wanted to go to the zoo,' she said softly between sobs.

'What about this boy?'

'He asked me to go with him and I didn't think it would do any harm.'

'Well yer fought wrong, didn't yer?'

Milly nodded.

'Arthur, I think Milly's been punished enough.'

'You would. I'm going out, and I'll be back when I'm good and ready.' He took his jacket from off the nail, put his cap on his dark hair and left.

Milly waited till she heard the front door slam, then she jumped to her feet. 'How could you?' she shouted at her mother.

Ivy Ash looked at her daughter in amazement. Milly had never spoken to her like this before.

'Why did you let him hit me like that?'

'I'm so sorry, Milly, but what could I do? He's a very strong man.'

'You could have said you knew I was going out and didn't mind.'

'And what good would that have done?'

Milly shrugged. She knew her mother was as afraid of him as she was. 'What did he mean when he said it runs in the family?'

'Nothing. I don't know what he's talking about.'

'If I knew where Auntie Doris lived, I'd run away.'

Ivy Ash looked up with horror on her face. 'You wouldn't leave me, would you?'

Milly slowly shook her head. She knew her

18

mother was a weak woman who couldn't stand up to her husband. What if she did leave and he injured her, or worse still, in one of his rages he . . . Milly couldn't even bear to think about that.

'Please, Milly, I beg you. Please don't leave me.'

'Why are you so afraid of him? Why don't you leave him?'

'Where would I go?'

'We could go and find Auntie Doris.'

'And who would want to look after a penniless woman with eight children?'

'Billy and Dan and me can look after ourselves.'

'But what about Helen? She's such a poor helpless little thing. You know we could all finish up in the workhouse.'

Milly couldn't answer her mother; she knew it was hopeless.

★ ★ ★

For the rest of the day Milly was very subdued, and she went about her chores with a heavy heart.

That evening she was in the outhouse when the boys burst in laughing and pushing each other.

'Did you go out, Mil?' asked Billy.

She shook her head. 'No.'

'Why didn't you go?' asked Dan. 'What's wrong?'

Milly wiped the tears that had trickled down her cheeks with the bottom of her overall. 'He was listening at the door when you was asking me who I was going with.' She gave a heart-rending sob. 'He took his strap to me for wanting to go out with Jack.'

Billy's face filled with fury. 'D'you know, I'll swing fer that bloke one of these days.'

'Billy. You mustn't talk like that.'

'What did Mum have to say about all this?' asked Dan.

'Not a lot really. I said I wanted to run away and find Auntie Doris, but she begged me not to. She's really afraid of him.'

'I know,' said Dan.

Milly was deep in thought. They knew they couldn't do anything about the situation. Not yet.

'We'll do somethink about it one of these days,' said Billy, as if reading her thoughts.

Milly gave him a weak smile.

*   *   *

That night as Milly lay on the mattress looking at the red stains on the wall where the bed bugs had been squashed, in her imagination she could see patterns. She was trying hard to sleep but her thoughts kept returning to her mother. What if she did leave home and got a job so she could send money back to Ivy? That way her mother could lead a better life without the fear of the workhouse. But what sort of job could she get to earn that kind of money?

In the next room Ivy Ash was also awake, trying to think of ways to make life better. Why

20

had Arthur turned out like this? Things had been so different all those years ago. Her sister was always coming to see them after they got married, and they would all laugh and joke together. Then, when Ivy was expecting Milly, Arthur began to change. She always thought it was something to do with her sister, but she could never find out what. When she asked Doris if she knew anything, she flew into a rage and had never been to see them since. Was Arthur angry about all the children he had to support? It wasn't her fault that she kept having babies. If only she could stop. Many times she had been tempted to go and see the woman who was supposed to be able to help women like her, but she had been afraid her husband would kill her if he found out. In his strange way he always loved the babies when they were first born, but was that because he was proud of what he'd done?

He turned over. Please God, Ivy prayed silently. Don't let him demand his rights again tonight. She was worried that she could find herself with yet another baby next year.

It was November the tenth and Milly's birthday. Today she would be fourteen. Only her mother would wish her happy birthday. She had never had a present or cake. It must have been lovely to have a cake with candles on it.

Upstairs the Bookers were preparing to move out; they were going over the water to the Isle of Dogs. Her father was in a rage over it and everybody tried to keep out of his way.

'How we gonna manage, Mum?' asked Milly.

'I don't know.'

'Please tell me where Auntie Doris lives so I can go and ask her for help.'

'I can't.'

'Why are you so proud?'

'It's a very long story. Besides, I don't know where she lives.'

'Do you think we might be able to get another lodger to help with the rent?'

'I don't know.'

Milly wanted to shake her mother. She just sat in her own world and seemed to have lost interest in all that was going on around her. Milly picked up Helen and tried to soothe her. She was such a poorly baby, who cried a lot. She knew she had to go out and get something for them to eat. She looked at little Iris, who was four and was sitting on the floor rocking backwards and forwards. She had sores round her mouth and was permanently wet.

'Pammy, could you keep an eye on Helen for me? I must go and try and get some bread.'

Pammy, who was seven, looked up at her with her big blue eyes. 'All right,' she lisped as she wiped her runny nose with the back of her hand. 'But don't be too long.'

Milly wanted to cry. They were such a sorry-looking bunch. What would become of them all?

★　★　★

As she wandered round the market, like the other snotty-nosed kids Milly was looking for anything that got tossed away. There was so much poverty all around her, children without shoes and ragged hand-me-down clothes. She was miserable and so full of her own thoughts that she didn't hear Jack calling her.

'Blimey, you look down in the dumps. What's up?'

With that Milly burst into tears.

''Ere, steady on. It can't be that bad, can it?'

'Today's me birthday and I'm so miserable.'

'I can see that. Look, hang about, and when I've packed up I'll take yer fer a cuppa. How's that sound?'

She gave him a tear-stained smile. 'I wish I could, but I've gotta get back. The kids want their tea.'

'Look, Mil, I know things are bad at home, but I'm sure it will be all right one day. You wait and see.'

As much as she wanted to stay with Jack, she knew she would have to go. 'I'd better get on home.' As she picked up the bag holding half a loaf, a few potatoes and some speckled apples, Jack put a few meatballs in a paper bag and tossed them in too. 'Jack.' She looked quickly around. 'You mustn't do that. You'll get the sack.'

'No, it's all right. I'll spin old Percy a line.'

'I can't take them.' She held them out to him, but he grabbed her arm.

'I said leave it. Call it a birthday present. Now go on.'

She walked away, then turned mouthing her thanks. Jack was such a nice boy. She really would like to go out with him. After the day they were supposed to go to the zoo, he said he'd waited an hour for her and was disappointed when she didn't turn up. She never told him how her father had hit that day. She still winced at the thought.

4

Early one morning, two weeks after Milly's birthday, Ivy Ash's screams woke everybody. Milly lay terrified in the silence that followed. What had happened? Had her father hit her mother?

'Milly, come in 'ere.' Her father's voice was harsh.

Slowly Milly pushed open their bedroom door. The gas had been lit and Milly could see her mother rocking backwards and forwards, clasping baby Helen. She looked up at Milly with a tear-stained face.

'She's gone. Our baby's gone,' she whispered.

Milly squatted down beside her mother and gently took Helen from her. She looked into the waxen face and kissed the blue lips. Somehow Helen was extra special to Milly.

'Take 'er out of 'ere,' said her father, who was seated with his back to them, his head in his hands. He looked up and added softly, 'And wrap 'er in that bit o' blanket.'

Milly looked at her father. Unless she was seeing things, there was a tear in his eye. Silently she wrapped Helen, who was very cold, in the blanket and left the room.

Billy and Dan were waiting in the passage.

'What's 'appened, Mil?' asked Billy.

'Helen's dead,' she said softly as they moved into the kitchen.

'What happens now?' asked Dan.

'I don't know,' said Milly, still holding Helen close. She wanted to warm her and bring her back to life.

'D'you wanna box or somefink to put her in?' asked Billy.

Milly nodded as her tears fell on the small bundle.

Billy rushed from the kitchen and came back with a cardboard box. 'We got this one yesterday.' He placed it on the table.

Gently Milly placed the delicate baby inside and tucked the blanket round her, leaving her face exposed. She was standing looking at her when Pammy came in.

'What's Mum crying for?' lisped the little girl.

'Baby Helen.'

Pammy scrambled up on to a chair. 'What's she doing in this box? Come on you, wake up.'

'Pammy, stop it,' cried Milly, as her sister began shaking Helen.

Dan lifted Pammy down on to the floor.

'Why don't she wake up?' she asked.

Billy took her hand. 'Helen will never wake up again. She's dead. She's gone to be with Jesus.'

'Oh. All right.' With that, Pammy walked away.

It was then that their father walked into the room. 'Take yer mother in a cuppa, Mil.'

'I'll go and get some wood to put on the fire,' said Dan.

Milly walked slowly into the outhouse and filled the kettle. She shuddered. It was very cold. 'What do we do now?' she asked Dan, who was stuffing pieces of wood into the stove.

'Dunno. He'll have ter see ter things. Mum

26

can't, she ain't bin out fer years.'

'She'll have to be buried.'

'Me and Billy will make a cross.'

Milly gave her brother a half-smile.

When she took the tea in, she sat on the bed and gently shook her mother, who had her head buried in the pillow. 'Mum, 'ere's yer tea.'

Her mother raised her head, then slowly sat up. Her grey hair was a tangled mess and her dark eyes had almost sunk into their sockets.

'How did it happen?' Milly asked gently.

'She been crying and . . . ' Ivy stopped and brushed away her tears with the flat of her hand. 'So I brought her in here with me.' She let out a long, deep sob. 'I didn't know. She was so cold when I woke up. Milly, please help me.'

Milly put her arms round her mother and held her close. 'Mum, you've got to look after the others. They need you as much as Helen did.'

'I can't.' With that, she lay back down and covered her head.

Milly stood up and looked at the pathetic figure. 'You must, Mum. I can't do everythink.'

There was no reply.

'Please, Mum.'

'Go away.'

Milly was angry. How dare her mother leave her to do everything? She walked out of the room, slamming the door behind her.

★　★　★

It was bitterly cold as Arthur Ash, with just the eldest of his children, made his way to the cemetery. He carried Helen, who was in the cardboard box; Ivy Ash had refused to join them. Billy carried a spade. Dan carried the rough wooden cross he and Billy had made; they had burnt Helen's name on it with the poker. Milly had managed to get some flowers. They weren't very fresh, but they were all she could afford with the money she had from her sewing. Slowly they walked into the damp, misty graveyard. Their father had been to see the vicar, who had told them where Helen could be laid to rest. The ground was very hard as Billy and Dan took turns to dig the hole, and then, very carefully, their father placed Helen in it. Milly wanted to ask, was this where his other babies had been buried? She had tears running down her cheeks. She had never seen her father so gentle. Perhaps he did love his children in his own way. She placed the few pathetic flowers on the little mound. She had dearly loved this little girl who she had helped into the world, and she would never, ever forget her. The vicar said a short prayer and made the sign of the cross.

As they left the cemetery, Arthur Ash put his arm round his daughter's heaving shoulders, but she shrugged him away. Even if he was looking sad today, she could never forget or forgive him for some of the things he had done to her. How dare he try to be nice to her in front of the vicar?

As they walked home, Milly made up her mind. Her mother didn't have an excuse not to go out now Helen was no longer around — she could look after the children again. Milly would run away. She wanted to get away from all of them; she wanted to live her own life. Somehow she knew she had to find out where Auntie Doris was.

★ ★ ★

For the rest of the month Milly did the shopping as usual, as her mother still refused to leave the house. Even when Milly came home and told her about the Christmas decorations in the shop windows, Ivy always made some sort of excuse. She said she didn't have a coat, or her shoes hurt or let in water.

'Why won't you go out, Mum?' Milly asked one afternoon when they were busy sewing buttons on shirts.

'I can't.'

'You must have a reason, and not just cos you ain't got shoes or a coat.'

'I can't face the outside.'

'That's daft.'

'Is it?'

Milly could see that this conversation was upsetting her mother.

'For years I had to look after the children, and when you started running errands, somehow I just got out of the habit of going out. Now the thought of it frightens me.'

'Look, why don't you and me go out one day? We can take the kids with us.'

'No, they'll be too much of a handful. I'll look after them here; you go out and get what we need.' She smiled. 'You know, you're very good at making a little go a long way.'

Milly knew it was hopeless.

'What should I do?' she asked Billy and Dan when they got home. 'How can I make her see that I don't want to be running about for her and everyone else.'

'I dunno,' said Billy.

'I'd like to go out to work,' said Milly. 'To be able to meet other people.'

'You given up the idea to try and find Auntie Doris?' asked Dan.

Milly shook her head. 'I will one day.'

★ ★ ★

It was the beginning of February. Milly, who had been to the butcher's, was laughing with Jack at the organ grinder and the monkey that he kept on a lead. The creature sat on the man's shoulder rattling a tin for money. Looking up, she suddenly saw her father walking towards her.

'I'd better go,' she said quickly, and ran off.

When she reached home she stood in the kitchen, terrified, waiting for her father to appear. For a while after Helen had died he'd seemed to be more reasonable, but just lately he found fault with everything anybody did. Many times Billy or Dan had felt the back of his hand or his leather belt.

'You all right?' asked her mother as Milly stood trembling, looking at the door.

'No. Dad saw me talking to Jack, and by the look on his face he's gonna give me a belting.'

'He won't do that, not for just talking to someone.'

'I think he will. Help me, Mum. Don't let him hit me again.'

'What can I do?'

'Tell him I ain't a little kid. I can talk to who I like.'

'You know he's worried about you going off with someone, don't you?'

'Look at me.' Tearfully Milly pulled at her ragged frock. It was too small for her and bursting at the seams. 'Who would have me?'

'You're a lovely girl with lovely ways, and he's frightened of losing you.'

'He's got a funny way of showing it.'

Suddenly the door burst open. 'I thought I told you not ter see that kid again.'

'He's the butcher's boy. I have to if we want meat.'

'Don't you talk ter me like that. I told yer before, that's not all he wants. I could see the way he was eyeing you up and down. I've said before, yer nothing but a trollop.' Slowly he undid his leather belt. 'I'll give yer a lesson yer won't fergit in a hurry.'

'No, please. Please, Dad. I'm sorry.'

'You will be.'

'Mum, say something.'

'Get out, Ivy. Now.'

'Mum. Please.'

Her mother picked up the two youngest, and with the others following they quickly left the room.

'Now, young lady . . . '

★　★　★

31

Milly was sitting on a wooden box when Billy and Dan came into the outhouse. As soon as she saw them she burst into tears.

'Mil, what is it? What's happened?' asked Dan.

'He gave me a belting,' she sobbed.

'Why? What yer done?' asked Billy.

'He saw me talking to Jack.'

'Is that all?' said Dan.

Milly nodded.

'That bloke's a bloody monster. I fought after Helen died he was getting better, but this . . . D'yer know, I've said it before but I will swing fer him one day.'

'Please, Billy, don't let him hear you talk like that or else you'll get a pasting.'

'Can I do anyfink ter help?' asked Dan.

'Just find out where Auntie Doris lives. I'm gonna run away.'

'I don't know where to start. We ain't ever had any letters from her, have we?'

'Mum must know,' said Billy. 'I'll tell yer what, why don't I search her room and see if I can find a letter or somefink?'

'But she don't go out,' said Milly.

'I know, but you could keep her busy out here or with yer sewing.'

'And I can keep watch,' said Dan.

'Just as long as yer keep all the kids out the way. Yer know what Pammy's like, got her nose inter everyfink,' said Billy.

Milly brushed the tears from her cheeks and gave them a weak smile. 'Thanks. But don't get into any trouble.'

'We won't,' said Billy.

32

'This could be the only time you'll get, Mil,' said Dan. 'And you must take the moment.'

She hugged them both. 'If I get away, I'll never forget you.'

'I should 'ope not,' said Dan with a grin.

5

It was very late on Sunday night when Milly decided to leave the house in Winter Street for good. Billy and Dan stood in the outhouse with her.

'Go out through the alley, we'll block the hole after yer; that way yer don't have ter close the front door,' said Billy. 'Dan will go with yer to the end while I tell anybody who wants ter use the bog that he's in there.'

'Thanks. I'll never forget what you've done.'

'Wish I could 'ave found that address,' said Billy.

'Still, at least we know Auntie Doris lived in Southwark.'

'It was only a very old envelope. And it might not 'ave even bin from 'er.'

'Who else would write to Mum?'

'Dunno.'

'At least I've got somewhere to head for.' Milly somehow knew she would find their aunt.

'Why don't you leave it till it's light, Mil?' asked Dan. He sounded very concerned.

'No, I'd rather go now. That way I can get a long way away before he wakes up.'

'I don't like the idea of you walking the streets alone,' said Dan. 'Let me and Billy come with you.'

'I'll be fine. Don't worry. It's better this way. If Pammy wakes up and sees we've all gone, she'll make a fuss. You know what she's like.'

'What yer gonner do if you can't find Auntie Doris?' asked Dan.

'I'm sure I will.'

Milly had been very grateful when Billy had gone into their parents' room and told her he'd seen an envelope in a box at the bottom of the cupboard with a Southwark postmark. He couldn't read the letter inside, as Milly was calling that their mother was coming back in from hanging out the washing. She wondered if it was from Auntie Doris. If it was, then all these years her mother had lied to her about knowing where her sister lived. Milly had been very upset and felt that she had been betrayed.

'Good luck then. Hope you find her. Now go on with yer.' Billy hurriedly kissed her cheek and eased her towards the back door.

Dan swallowed hard. 'Come on, 'fore he walks in.'

At the end of the alley, Milly held Dan tight. When would she see her brothers again?

'Try and keep in touch.'

'I will.' She kissed him and he quickly turned and walked away. She stood watching his back. He didn't turn round. This was it. She was alone. She had saved a few pence from her sewing and she knew how to get to Southwark, but what would happen when she arrived? Where would she go?

★   ★   ★

It was very dark as Milly got close to Southwark Park. The hissing from the gas lamps was the only sound, and the park looked very dark and frightening. She carefully pushed open the gate. The noise from the hinges seemed very loud, and she stood very still with her heart pounding, expecting someone to shout at her. Looking all around her, she made her way towards the bandstand. Every little noise startled her, and the bending, creaking trees took on weird shapes in the wind. It was very cold. On the way here she had passed some lovely houses, but which one did her aunt work in? She was on her own now. She could never go back home; her father would kill her.

She went up the steps to the bandstand. At least this bit was under cover if it rained in the night. She curled up on a seat, putting her cloth bag holding her worldly goods, her other pair of drawers and a pair of stockings, under her head. She was so cold and all alone. She would miss Billy and Dan and she would never see Jack again. And what about her mother?

'Please, Mum, forgive me,' she said out loud. 'I do love you.'

Tears began to fall. She felt so unhappy. She pulled her thin coat round her. What had she done?

* * *

'Stop, Walton.'

Milly sat up. It was light. Had she been asleep all this time in a park bandstand? She looked up. A young girl who appeared to be about the same age as her was looking at her from a wheelchair.

36

She was dressed in the most beautiful blue velvet coat Milly had ever seen and was wearing a large tartan tam-o'-shanter hat. Her brown ringlets hung down to her shoulders and a thick warm blanket covered her legs. Milly would have loved that blanket round her. A tall, thin-faced woman was pushing the wheelchair and they had stopped in front of Milly.

'Hello,' said the girl. 'Are you all right?'

'Yes thank you.' Milly hurriedly dabbed her eyes.

'Well you don't look it, does she, Walton?'

Walton fussed with the blanket. A pair of well-polished brown boots stuck out from underneath. 'Come on, Miss Jane, we must get you home. It's very cold this morning.'

'Have you been sleeping here all night?' asked the girl.

Milly nodded.

'All alone?'

Milly looked down at her own shabby clothes and nodded again. She wished this girl would go away.

'What's your name?' asked Jane, ignoring the woman, who was holding the handles of the wheelchair.

'What d'you want to know for?'

'I'm curious.'

'Well it ain't none of your business, so go away and leave me alone.' Milly gathered up her bag and began to walk away.

'Please. Just a moment.'

Milly stopped. 'What d'yer want?'

'I might be able to help you.'

'How? You don't know nothing about me.'

'I know you must be on your own and could have run away from home.'

Milly stood and looked at her.

'I'm right, aren't I?'

Milly nodded and her tears began to fall. She was cold and so alone and unhappy. 'Leave me be.'

'Please, Miss Jane, don't be so inquisitive.' The woman turned to Milly. 'I'm so very sorry. Sometimes she forgets her manners.'

Milly dabbed at her eyes with a grubby piece of rag.

'Please. Let me help you. What's your name?'

'Milly.'

'Milly,' repeated Jane. 'That's a very pretty name.'

'Thank you.'

'Where do you live?'

'Not round here.'

'So what are you doing sleeping in the park?'

'Please, Miss Jane.'

'Have you run away?'

'Miss Jane, we are going home.' Walton tried to turn the wheelchair.

'No,' the girl said defiantly. She held on to the wheels of her chair and Walton had to stop.

'You have run away, haven't you? How exciting.'

Milly began to cry again. She was cold and hungry.

'Now look what you've done. You are a very wicked girl.'

Jane looked distressed. 'I'm so sorry. Please

forgive me. I didn't mean to upset you.'

Milly looked at this girl. She must come from a good home, but why was she in a wheelchair?

'That's all right,' she mumbled.

'You look very cold. You can come home with us. Cook will give you some breakfast.'

'I can't do that.'

'Why not?'

'I'm looking for me aunt.'

'Where does she live?'

'I don't know. Round Southwark somewhere.'

'We live in Southwark Park Road and my cook knows everyone. What's her name?'

'Auntie Doris.'

'What's her surname?'

Suddenly Milly felt very silly. She didn't know her mother's maiden name, or if Aunt Doris had married. 'I don't know,' she said softly.

'How can you expect to find someone if you don't know their name or where they live?'

Milly hung her head.

'That settles it. You must come with us.'

'I can't.'

'So where else can you go?'

'I don't know.'

'Right, Walton, let's go home. And you, Milly, will come with us.'

As they walked along, Jane was talking and laughing. She seemed to be a very happy girl.

'How old are you, Milly?' she asked.

'Fourteen,' Milly replied.

'How exciting. Did you have a big party on your birthday? I shall be fourteen on the twenty-third of February and I shall have a party and you must come to that. I always have a party but I don't have any friends; they are all Mama's friends' daughters. What school do you go to?'

'I don't go to school.'

'Your family haven't sent you out to work, have they?'

'No.'

'Miss Jane, I insist that you stop questioning this poor girl. You're embarrassing her.'

'I'm so sorry. It's just that I don't have any friends my own age and I'm very excited at meeting you and I want to know all about you. I like you, Milly. Will you be my friend?'

'I can't'

'Why not?'

'I must find me aunt.'

'Oh.' Jane sat back in her chair.

Milly felt sorry for this girl, who seemed to have everything but no friends. 'I really shouldn't be here.'

'Why not?' said Jane.

'Your mother will be cross with you for picking up someone like me.'

'Mama's not like that. She does a lot of charity work and often looks after strays. Sorry. I didn't mean . . . '

'That's all right.' For the first time Milly smiled. She liked this girl, and why shouldn't she go home with her and have some breakfast? After all, she was starving, and perhaps the cook would be able to help her find Auntie Doris.

★   ★   ★

40

Milly was shocked when Walton turned and walked up a long path leading to a large house that stood alone. It had windows on both sides of pillars that held a porch, and there were steps up to a thick-looking wooden door. Walton pushed the wheelchair round the back of the house and Milly followed

'Miss Jane, you're back,' said a jolly-looking woman. 'All right, Walton, I'll take her.' She grabbed the chair's handles and pushed Jane up a slope and into a bright, warm kitchen. 'What on earth made you go out so early?' she asked.

'We went to feed the swans.'

'You could have gone later.'

'I know, but Mama wants me here to meet my new tutor.'

'Oh yes. Miss Dance.'

Milly stood back.

'Betty, I want you to meet my new friend. Betty, this is Milly.'

'And where did Miss Jane find you, young lady?'

'Betty,' said Jane excitedly, 'she was sleeping in the park, all on her own.'

'Were you now?'

Milly nodded.

'She's looking for her aunt and we thought you might be able to help. Perhaps some of the traders might know of her. But first could you find her something to eat?'

Betty's hair was hidden under her mob cap, which wobbled every time she spoke. Milly stared at it, fascinated.

'Miss Jane. You know you should stop bringing

waifs and strays into the house.'

'But Milly's nice. She's not like that boy Philip.' Jane turned to Milly. 'I found him in the park and brought him back, and do you know, I thought he would be my friend, but instead he took some money and silver. Mama was furious.' She took off her hat. Her hair was tied back with a large floppy white bow.

The kitchen door opened and in walked a very smart-looking woman. Her brown hair, greying at the sides, was piled up on top of her head. She was wearing a long dark blue frock and her tiny waist was held in with a wide leather belt. She looked very regal. 'Jane, I told you to be back before ten. Miss Dance is waiting to meet you.' She looked at Milly. 'And who are you?'

'I'm sorry, Mrs Green. Jane insisted on bringing the young lady home.'

'Don't worry, Walton. We haven't time for this at the moment.' She turned to Milly. 'I'll talk to you later.' With that she pushed Jane out of the room, with Walton following.

Betty looked at Milly and said, 'Who's this aunt of yours, then?'

Milly could feel the heat from the large stove. On top of it stood a black kettle, its lid bobbing gently up and down.

'You'd better take yer coat off and sit down. I expect you'd like a cuppa.'

'Yes please.' Milly sat on one of the chairs that matched the long deal table in the centre of this large bright room. All the chairs were the same.

'So, tell me about yourself and this aunt.'

When the tea was put in front of Milly, she

42

clasped her cold hands round the delicate china cup and told Betty about Doris. She was very careful what she said, as she didn't want them to send her back home.

'So you don't know where she lives or what her surname is?'

Milly slowly shook her head.

'Well that ain't a lot to go on, is it?'

'I know. Please don't send me back home.'

Betty looked at the sad face. Somehow she knew that this girl must have suffered to make her run away. 'What about your mum and dad?'

'Me dad sometimes gets annoyed with me. Me mum's frightened of him and just does what he says. Me little sister died a while ago.'

'So your mum's on her own, then?'

'No. I've got six other brothers and sisters.'

Betty didn't comment on that. She could see that this child had been put upon. Her life must have been a misery and her clothes were shabby and worn. 'Mrs Green will be in in a mo. She's just seeing to Jane's new teacher.'

Milly's face lit up. 'Jane seems ever so nice. Why is she in a wheelchair?'

'She can't walk.'

'What happened?'

'She — '

The kitchen door opened and Mrs Green came in. 'Now, what's all this about?'

Once again Milly went through what she had told Betty.

'Well, Jane certainly seems to be taken with you.' Mrs Green smiled. 'And she can be very persuasive. So until you find your aunt, you can stay here for a few days and keep Jane company. She needs to be with someone of her own age. First of all I expect you would like a bath, and then I'll find you something to wear.' She began to walk away but stopped at the door. 'I don't suppose you have any clothes of your own?'

Milly shook her head and clutched at her bag. She wasn't going to show this woman her rags.

'I'm sure Betty can find you some jobs to do while Jane has her lessons and her afternoon nap. I'll bring in a few things of Jane's you can wear.'

'Thank you, Mrs Green, for letting me stay, just till I find me aunt,' she said hurriedly. She didn't want her to think that she would be here for ever.

'Well that's settled then,' said Mrs Green, and she left the kitchen.

Betty smiled. 'Welcome to the household.'

Milly couldn't believe her luck. Her she was in this big house and she had a friend. She was so happy she wanted to cry.

Betty was watching her closely. She was right. This child had had a terrible life. 'Come on, I'll show you where the bathroom is.'

A bathroom! Milly hadn't known that houses had bathrooms. She had always brought the tin bath from off the big hook in the yard and they all took turns on a Friday night in the same water, just adding more hot as it went cold. Her breath was almost taken away when Betty opened the door. She couldn't believe her eyes. This beautiful room had a big deep white bath and a washbasin and a lavvy. And all this inside the house.

'I'll just run the bath for you.' Betty turned a

tap on a large cylinder over the bath. It made a lot of frightening noise as hot water spurted out, and Milly jumped back. 'I'll put some of Miss Jane's lavender water in it, and if I was you I'd wash me hair as well. When you've finished, just pull the plug out and clean round the bath. I'll show you how to do it properly later.' Betty swished the water about, adding cold from the tap on the side of the bath. 'There ain't many houses that's got this,' she said proudly, straightening up.

Milly just stood looking wide-eyed. She had never seen anything like this before. These people must be very rich.

'I'll just pop along to the store cupboard and get you some of Miss Jane's clothes she's grown out of. They should fit you,' Betty added, eyeing the skinny girl.

Milly was still gazing all around her when Betty came back, placing a pile of clothes on a chair. 'There's a clean towel.'

'Thank you.'

When Betty had left, Milly picked up the towel and held it to her cheek. It was all fluffy and smelled of flowers, not like the thin, smelly scraps of cloth they had at home. Slowly she took off her clothes, though she left her vest on as she felt very scared and vulnerable. She looked at the door and then put one foot in the bath, before lowering herself carefully into the lovely-smelling water. She lay back and began to cry. What would Dan and Billy think if they could see her? Please God, she prayed don't let me wake up from this wonderful dream and find meself back in the park.

6

It was a while before Milly plucked up enough courage to take her vest off. What if someone came in? She hadn't locked the door. Were there any men in this house? What were these people like? Her imagination started to go wild. She'd heard about the white slave market in China-town. Did they send Jane out to find young girls? That woman Walton said she had picked up people before. Milly suddenly felt very vulner-able sitting in a bath of water without any clothes on.

After a while she rubbed the delicious-smelling soap all over her. It was lovely. The water was beginning to get cold, so she stepped carefully out of the bath and wrapped herself in one of the large fluffy towels. As she rubbed her hair dry, she still couldn't believe how soft it was. Home seemed a lifetime away. Would she ever see her family again? She looked at the grubby bathwater and tentatively pulled at the plug, as Betty had told her to do. When it popped out of the hole, she was terrified the water would gush out all over the floor. She stood watching it disappear. Where did it go? She got down on the floor and looked under the bath. There were a lot of pipes, so it must run away through those. She smiled and gazed around the room. It was so clean and bright. Then she inspected the clothes that Betty had placed on the chair. There was a vest, a chemise, cotton drawers and stockings, a white blouse and a dark blue overdress. She had never seen such fine clothes. When she put them on, she felt like a princess.

'Everything all right?'

Milly jumped when, after a polite knock, the door suddenly opened.

'Sorry. I didn't mean to startle you,' said Mrs Green. 'Is everything all right?' she asked again, walking into the room and looking around. 'Betty will show you how to clean the bath properly.'

Milly felt guilty about the black tidemark round the bath. It hadn't been there when she'd got in. 'Sorry.'

'Don't worry about that now. Do you like the clothes? Jane has outgrown them.'

Milly smiled broadly. 'Thank you. Why are you being so nice and kind to me and don't chuck me out?'

Mrs Green smiled. 'Don't look so worried. You see, my daughter hasn't any friends of her own age, and as long as she's happy, that's all I worry about. Now, are you pleased with those clothes? They seem to fit you just fine.'

'I ain't ever had such lovely things before. I'll give 'em back before I go.'

'It seems that Jane is really taken with you. This was her idea, so please don't let her down.'

'I won't. But I must look for me aunt.'

'Of course. Now, come along to the drawing room. Jane is waiting to see you.'

Milly was still smiling as they left the bathroom. Perhaps they didn't want girls for the white slave market after all.

Milly had followed Mrs Green along the hall, and the older woman stood to one side at the open door to let her enter the room.

'Here's Milly,' she said, adding, 'I shall be back later.'

Milly walked into a beautiful room with a very high ceiling. It almost took her breath away.

'Hello,' said Jane, who was sitting on a multicoloured tapestry sofa. Milly could only see her pretty cream-coloured slippers, as her frock and a blanket covered her legs. 'You look lovely. Come and sit next to me.' Jane patted the seat.

Very cautiously Milly sat down.

'You look very nice now, and you smell a lot better.'

'Miss Jane,' said Walton angrily.

'I'm sorry, that was very rude of me.'

Milly smiled. 'That's all right. I was a bit smelly. And thank you letting me wear your clothes.'

'You can keep them,' Jane said dismissively. 'I've grown out of them.'

'Thank you,' said Milly again. Her eyes were wide as she sank into the soft cushions on the sofa and she glanced quickly round her. She couldn't take in all the lovely things that were in this room. There was a large fireplace with a huge warm fire burning in the grate. All sorts of interesting vases stood on the mantelpiece. Lovely pictures hung on the walls, and a long window with heavy green curtains each side tied back with silk rope looked out on to a garden.

The huge clock that stood in the corner ticking loudly fascinated her; she had never seen anything like it before.

'Now. You must tell me all about yourself and why you have run away from home.'

'Miss Jane.' Walton, sitting close by in an armchair made of the same material as the sofa and doing some needle work, looked up.

'Milly doesn't mind telling me, do you? After all, she is my best friend.'

Walton just gave a sigh and returned to her sewing.

Jane giggled and took hold of Milly's hand.

'I'm looking for me aunt,' Milly said.

'Yes, I know that,' said Jane impatiently. 'But why don't you know her name or where she lives?'

Milly looked down at her hands. 'Me mum wouldn't tell me,' she said softly.

'But why? She must have had a reason.'

Walton stood up. 'Miss Jane, I must ask you to stop this at once. Your mother would be very upset if she heard you interrogating this poor young girl.'

'I just want to know all about her,' Jane said. Her big blue-grey eyes were full of sadness. 'I am sorry.'

'That's all right,' said Milly. She didn't want this girl to get in any trouble. After all, she had rescued her, and she must be worried about where she came from. She would tell her one day. That was, if she was allowed to stay.

★　★　★

As the afternoon wore on, Milly told Jane a little about herself, including the fact that she had six brothers and sisters.

'You have all those?' Jane said in amazement. Milly nodded.

'I wish I had more brothers, and a sister. I have one brother, Richard. He's older than me and goes away to school. I have a tutor who comes to teach me. Miss Dance is going to teach me now because Miss Brook left to get married. Perhaps you could come to my lessons. That would be so much fun.'

Milly noticed Walton raise an eyebrow at that.

When Betty brought tea in on a tray on wheels, Milly was fascinated. She had never seen anything like that before. Walton moved a small table from the side of the room and put it in front of Jane. Everything on the tray had the same pretty mauve flower design. She poured out the tea into delicate china cups with matching saucers. Then, after arranging one of the linen napkins on Jane's lap, she put a delicious-looking cake on a plate and placed it on the table in front of Jane.

'Thank you, Walton,' said Jane. 'Please, Milly. Help yourself. Betty is a very good cook.'

Milly had noted all that Jane had done. First she took a napkin and laid it on her lap, then she watched how Jane put sugar in her tea and stirred it very gently. Milly did the same. Then she took a cake and placed it on a plate. She watched Jane when she took up a funny-looking fork that only had three prongs and began to cut her cake up and eat it. She did the same with her own cake. It was delicious. She was very nervous, and when she picked up her cup and saucer, the cup rattled. This was a whole new world for her and she loved it. What would Billy and Dan say if they could see her? And what about her father? Who would get beaten when he found she'd gone? She shuddered.

'Are you all right?' asked Jane. 'Are you cold?'

'No. Thank you. I'm all right. I was just thinking about me brothers, Billy and Dan.'

'Tell me about them.'

'Billy is two years younger then me, he'll be twelve soon, and Dan is younger than Billy, he's eleven. Then there's Pammy and Iris . . . and Rosie and Bert.'

Jane laughed. 'How do you manage to remember all their names?'

'They're me brothers and sisters.'

'It must be lovely to have so many people around laughing and playing games together.'

Milly didn't tell her life wasn't like that.

★ ★ ★

That evening Milly sat in the kitchen with Betty while Jane, Walton and Mrs Green were having their meal. Betty had told her that Mr Green was away and that young Richard was at school.

'Don't he come home for his tea?' asked Milly.

Betty smiled. 'No. It's at boarding school. He's very clever,' she said as she filled Milly's plate. 'Now, the Missus expects you to do a few jobs round the place.'

'What should I do?' This food was the best Milly had ever had, and she was stuffing her face as fast as she could.

'Slow down a bit, girl. Nobody ain't gonna take it away from you.'

'Sorry, but it's so lovely.'

'Thank you. Now, to answer your question. I'm in charge of running things here but we have a woman, Elsie, who comes in in the mornings to do the grates and fill the coal scuttles. She does the washing as well, and you can help her with that to start with. We'll see how long Jane puts up with you, then we can go from there.'

Milly let her spoon clatter on to the plate. 'Does she bring home a lot of friends?'

'They come and go. You ain't the first. Her mother lets her have all her own way. The last one was a thief, so don't let me catch you pinching anything, otherwise you'll be out on yer ear before you can say boo to a goose.'

Milly felt sad. 'I like Jane.'

'You have to call her Miss Jane.'

'It's such a shame she's in a wheelchair. What's wrong with her?'

'She was born like that. She can't use her legs.'

'Why?'

'I dunno.' Betty looked a bit cross. 'And don't you go asking her.'

'I won't.'

'Now, clear this table and start the washing-up. They'll ring when they've finished. I'll collect the crocks and you can wash them up as well, and be careful, we don't want any breakages.'

'And you look after this big house all on your own?'

'When the master and young Richard is away I do. But I have more help when they come back.'

'Where's Mr Green?'

'Nosy little cow, ain't yer?'

'Sorry.' Milly busied herself with clearing the table. That was the best meal she had ever had in her life, and she knew she had to watch her Ps and Qs if she wanted to stay for a few more days. She looked over at Betty who had settled herself down in the wooden rocking chair next to the fire and closed her eyes. She seemed a nice, friendly woman, and Milly hoped that she liked her. How old was Betty? she wondered. And why did she live here? Did she have any family, and if so, where did they live?

Milly was busy washing up and daydreaming when the sound of a bell made her jump. There were bells on a board on the wall, and each bell had the name of a room under it. Betty stood up, straightened her overall and hurriedly left the kitchen. She returned a short while later with a trolley piled high with dirty plates.

'You start on these while I take 'em their coffee.' With that she was off again.

Milly knew she could be very happy working here and she would do her best to please everybody. At this moment she wasn't sure if she still wanted to find her aunt. If she behaved herself and worked hard, perhaps she would be allowed to stay here for ever. But deep down she knew this was just a dream. Things like that didn't happen to girls like her.

7

Over the next few days Milly quickly began to fit in with Betty and Jane's routine, and she was more than anxious to please. Elsie, who came to do the fires, was a very quiet, smiling young woman. Betty had told Milly that Elsie had four children and a husband who was very poorly. In the morning Elsie would come up to the room that Milly had been given and wake her. Milly's room was in the attic, with a low sloping ceiling that had a window set in it, and although it was very cold, she had a bed with clean white sheets, a pillow, a warm blanket and a lovely multicoloured bedspread, and to her this was heaven. At night when she went up to bed Betty gave her a stone ginger beer bottle filled with hot water to put her feet on. Milly had never known such luxury. There was a small table in the corner of the room for her knick-knacks, not that she had any, just the brush and comb that Jane had given her. The bed was against the wall and she could stand on it and look out of the sloping window. The garden below had grass and what looked like a lot of dead trees, though Betty had told her that come spring it would look a picture. But would she be here in the spring to see it? Milly wondered She was so happy, and she often had to pinch herself to make sure this wasn't all a wonderful dream.

After Milly had helped Elsie to clean out the

fireplaces, light the fires and fill the coal scuttles, Walton, Elsie, Betty and herself would sit in the kitchen and have their breakfast, then Walton would take Jane for her walk before Miss Dance came and it was time for Jane's lessons. Miss Dance seemed to be a nice young lady, but Jane told Milly that she was very strict.

'I do wish Mama would let you come and have lessons with me.'

Milly just smiled. She never replied, as she didn't want to get in the way.

After Jane had had her afternoon rest and walk, Milly always had tea with her and Walton. Milly learnt that Walton was a nurse who washed and dressed Jane and generally looked after her. During afternoon tea the girls would sit on the sofa laughing and talking while Walton read or did some sewing.

'I am so happy you are here,' said Jane.

'And I'm happy I'm here.'

Jane wanted to know all about the things Milly had seen, and Milly told her about the suffragette march.

'I've seen pictures of them. Richard said all the boys at school thought they were very silly women wanting the vote.'

'They looked so nice in their white frocks and hats with their white, green and mauve sashes.'

'But some of them have been very naughty, chaining themselves to railings and breaking windows. I believe a few of them have even gone to prison. People don't like that sort of thing.' Jane shuddered. 'I couldn't do things like that.'

Milly thought she had better get off this

conversation, as she approved of women speaking up for themselves.

'I do envy you,' said Jane, 'you must have led such an exciting life.'

Milly didn't tell her about the bad times.

When the family went for their evening meal, Milly sat with Betty in the kitchen.

'You've settled in very well, young lady,' said Betty as she dished up another delicious supper.

Milly wanted to ask if she could stay a bit longer but decided against that just yet.

'Now what about this aunt of yours? I've asked all the traders and they don't know a Doris. You sure she works round here?'

'Me brother Billy found a letter and he said the postmark was Southwark.'

'There's a lot of big houses round this way, or she might have just posted it here.'

'S'pose so.'

'Don't look so down. I'm sure we'll find her one day.'

At this moment Milly wasn't so sure she wanted to.

*   *   *

A week later Milly was busy helping to prepare the vegetables for the evening meal, when Mrs Green came in. She quickly stood up.

'Sit down, Milly.'

Milly felt her legs turn to jelly. She looked at Betty, who glanced quickly away.

Mrs Green smiled and sat at the table. 'Don't look so worried. I just wanted to enquire if you've heard anything about your aunt.'

'No. I'm sorry. Betty's asked all the men who call but they ain't heard of a Doris.'

'What are you going to do?'

Milly looked down at her hands. 'I dunno. Do you want me to go?'

'Good heavens, no. I've never seen Jane so happy. No, what I've come to ask is whether you would like to stay here till you have news of your aunt. I'm sure Betty is keeping you busy.'

Betty smiled. 'I can always find her jobs to do.'

'And is Milly good at what she does?'

'I've got no complaints, and Elsie said she is very willing.'

'That's all I wanted to hear. Milly, as you know, it's Jane's birthday next week, and we shall be having a lot of young ladies here. Now, I shall want you to take their coats and put them into Jane's room.

'Betty, when we've got over the birthday, we must discuss Easter. Richard will be here, of course, so there will be extra work. And Milly, Jane will have more free time, so I hope you'll be able to keep her amused. Do you think you could manage to take her out sometimes, just round the outside of the house and in the garden? She needs some fresh air every day. Walton will go to her family for a few days and she will teach you how to control the wheelchair before she goes.'

Although she was disappointed at not joining Jane's birthday party, Milly wanted to jump up and throw her arms round this lady. This was the best news she could have heard. She was going to be here for Easter and spend more time with Jane. She couldn't believe her luck, and she hoped she'd never find Auntie Doris.

* * *

The day of the party arrived, and Jane looked lovely in her new dress and hair ribbon.

'I wish you could come in to the party,' said Jane. 'I told Mama that you're not a servant, you're my friend, but she was worried that you might feel a little intimidated by her friends' daughters.'

In many ways Mrs Green was right. When Milly took the young ladies' coats, they looked her up and down and she knew they were laughing at her as they walked into the drawing room.

When she got into the kitchen she said to Betty, 'They look like a right lot of stuck-up cows.'

'Milly, kindly watch your language.'

Milly blushed and looked at her feet. 'I'm sorry, but they do.'

Although Betty wanted to agree with her, she knew that wouldn't do. She'd heard some of the things these so-called young ladies said when she'd gone into the room to take the tea trolley away.

* * *

The week before Easter, Richard came home. He was tall and had a mop of unruly thick fair hair and eyes the same colour as his sister's.

Milly opened the door when he first arrived, and looking at her he enquired, 'Who are you?'

Milly curtsied and he burst out laughing.

'Richard, don't be so horrid,' said Jane, coming from the drawing room. 'I'll tell Mama that you laughed at Milly.'

'I'm sorry. It's just that nobody has ever curtsied to me before.'

'They might do if you are going to be in Parliament, so perhaps you should start to get used to it.'

Milly stood almost open-mouthed.

'Richard, this is Milly, my very best friend.'

'And what park bench did she find you on?'

Whenever Milly was embarrassed she would look down at her feet.

Jane moved her wheelchair closer, almost as if she was going to run into him. 'Now say you're sorry.'

'Sorry, Milly.'

'That's all right,' she said softly.

'Well?' he asked.

'If you must know, Milly ran away from home and I brought her here. She helps Betty and Elsie. Is there anything else you wish to know?' Jane spoke with a very determined look on her face and the bow in her hair wobbled with every word.

'No, that will do for now. Just as long as you are happy, little sis.'

She gave her brother one of her beaming smiles. 'I am very happy.'

'Good. We'll talk later, Milly.' With that he

picked up his bag and went upstairs to his room.

'Please don't worry about Richard, he always thinks he knows best.'

'That's what brothers should do. Look after their little sisters.'

Jane held out her hand and took hold of Milly's. 'You are such a joy to have around.' She smiled. 'I think it is a little naughty of me, but in some ways I hope you never find your aunt. I want you to stay here for ever.'

'And I would like to stay as well, but your mum might not want me around for long.'

'As long as I'm happy, that is all that Mama worries about.'

★ ★ ★

Whenever Richard took Jane round the garden, Milly went with them. She was very shy in his company and she wasn't sure if she liked him. He always seemed to be teasing her, asking her the names of flowers that he knew she had never seen before. One day, when Jane said she wanted to go to the park, Milly said she didn't want to go with them.

'Why not?' asked Jane.

'It's too cold.'

'Well go and get that scruffy coat of yours,' said Richard. 'Not that it will keep you very warm.'

Milly was on the verge of tears.

'Richard, how could you be so horrid?' yelled Jane.

Milly had tried to clean her coat up when she

went outside with them, but she knew Richard looked down at her, and up till now they had never left the garden.

Mrs Green came to see what the trouble was.

'It's Richard, he's being horrid to Milly. Mama, could you get my blue velvet coat for Milly?'

Milly stood with her mouth open. 'No, no, I can't wear that.'

'Why not?' asked Jane.

Mrs Green looked bewildered. 'Will someone please tell me what is going on?'

Richard was beginning to look very sheepish.

'Richard will keep teasing Milly. Tell him to stop it, Mama.'

'What have you been saying?'

'He was being very rude about Milly's coat.'

'Richard, how could you?'

'I'm sorry, Milly.'

Milly only looked at her feet. She knew she didn't fit in. He was like those rotten girls at Jane's birthday party. 'That's all right,' she said softly.

8

At last spring had arrived, and Milly marvelled at the garden, which was full of brightly coloured flowers. At Easter, Richard had laughed when she'd told him she'd never even seen some of them before, so she was determined to find out their names. Jane was willing to help her friend and went to great lengths to point out various flowers and tell her what they were called. She also gave her a dictionary, and between them they would sit and write the names down properly. The following morning after Jane had finished school, Milly would ask Miss Dance if she had got them right.

This particular afternoon they were on their usual wander round the garden when Jane asked, 'Why do you write the names down?'

'I want to remember them. Besides, Miss Dance said it's always good to do some writing every day.'

'Miss Dance is very pleased with the way you are so eager to learn, you know.'

Milly smiled. 'I've got a lot of years to make up, and I enjoy trying to learn about things. I shall never be able to thank you enough for what you've done for me.'

'And what about what you've done for me? My life was very boring stuck in this chair till you came along.'

Jane had told Milly that the reason she

couldn't walk was because when she was born, she was pulled from her mother by the legs. Nobody realised her bones had been damaged until she first tried to walk, but by then it was too late. She would be in a wheelchair for the rest of her life. Her mother and father had never forgiven themselves, and that was why they granted her every wish.

* * *

One afternoon in June, Milly was having tea with Mrs Green, Jane and Walton when Mrs Green said, 'Milly, Jane and Miss Dance have asked me if I would mind you sharing lessons with my daughter.'

Milly almost dropped the plate she was holding.

Jane's eyes were shining. 'What do you say?'

'I don't know what to say.'

'Please say yes,' said Jane.

'Yes. I would love to, but why?'

Mrs Green was smiling. 'Well, Miss Dance thinks you are clever, and it would help Jane. We know you can read a little.'

'Yes, me mum taught me.' Milly was very proud of that fact.

'We know that you pick things up very quickly, and Miss Dance is most impressed with the way you ask her questions. She also thinks it would be good for Jane to have some competition.'

'But what about me,' Milly quickly corrected herself, 'my chores?'

'As you know, the lessons are only for a few

hours in the mornings, so you will be able to help Betty after that. And we do have Betty's full permission.'

Jane clapped her hands. 'It will be such fun.'

'Now I don't want you two playing about. I've told Miss Dance to keep me informed of your progress, and yours, young lady.' She wagged her finger at her daughter.

Milly was so thrilled she wanted to dance round the room. She was going to get an education. She was living in this lovely house with wonderful people; could life get any better? Or would it all go wrong? She didn't want to think about that.

When she took the tea trolley into the kitchen she said excitedly, 'I'm gonna have lessons with Miss Jane.'

'I know.'

Milly grabbed Betty and spun her round. 'Thank you. Thank you. Thank you.'

'Steady on. You'll have me come all over funny. Besides, what have you got to thank me for? What have I done?'

'If you'd said I couldn't go cos you wanted me here with you, well, I would have been . . . what's that long word that Miss Jane says? Devilstated!'

Betty laughed. 'You mean devastated, and from the little you've told me about your life, you deserve a break. After all, you're a good girl.'

Milly sat down at the table. 'I promise I'll do everything I can to help you.'

'More to the point, you make sure you learn all you can. It will help you in years to come if you have a good education and can speak well.'

'I'll do me very best.'

'That's good. Now, let's make a start on this washing-up.'

As Milly filled the sink with water, her heart was pounding. She couldn't believe she was going to be taught to read and write and to speak properly just like Miss Jane. As Betty said, it would help her get somewhere in life. Not that she ever wanted to leave here, but you never know what might happen in the future.

★   ★   ★

Everybody except Milly was getting excited at Richard coming home for the long summer holiday. She was very wary of him and his ways.

'Well you certainly seem to have grown,' he said, looking her up and down when she opened the door for him.

She felt embarrassed, as she had recently developed breasts, and she was sure that was what he was looking at.

'And as for your speech, you seem to have lost some of that dreadful twang.'

'Thank you kindly,' she said, taking his coat.

'So the lessons are coming along well then?'

'Yes thank you, sir.'

'I'll have to give you a test later. Now where's that sister and mother of mine?'

'They are in the drawing room.'

'Thought they would have been at the door welcoming me.'

'They wasn't sure it was you. They're expecting another visitor.'

65

'Anyone I know?'

'A Miss Robbins and her mother.'

'Oh no.'

'Don't you like her?'

'She's quite nice, I suppose, but it's not that.' He laughed. 'I think they're trying to get me married off.'

Milly smiled. 'I'm sure you would have something to say about that.'

'Yes, I would. If and when I marry, it will be to the woman of my choice,' he said over his shoulder as he disappeared into the drawing room.

As he closed the door, laughter and greetings erupted. Although Milly was cautious about Richard, he was obviously loved by his mother and sister, and it was nice to hear them all laughing together. She went up the stairs to put Richard's coat and bag in his bedroom and thought about her own family, as she often did. They'd never laughed together like that.

Miss Robbins and her mother arrived half an hour later. Milly didn't join them for tea when they had visitors. As she wheeled in the trolley, Richard was watching her and Miss Robbins was watching him. She was a very pretty young lady with dark hair and big blue eyes that followed his every move. Milly could see that she was really taken with him, and she smiled to herself as she left the room. Did she know what he thought of her?

'That Miss Robbins is certainly a lovely young woman,' she said to Betty when she got back into the kitchen.

'Yes. I think the missus would like to see her and Richard married one day.'

'But he's what, only sixteen?'

'The gentry like to make sure their lot marry into the right set. I can tell you, that would be some wedding'

'Richard will have something to say about it.'

'I'm sure he will.'

'When does he finish school?'

'Don't rightly know. I think he's going on to some university or something.'

'Lucky him.'

'You like your lessons, don't you?'

Milly smiled and nodded. 'There's so much to learn. I shall always be grateful to Jane for finding me on that park bench.'

'Not nearly as much as she is for finding you. I've never seen her look so happy. You're like a real tonic for her.'

Later, when the bell went for Milly to return to the drawing room to take the tea things away, Miss Robbins and her mother were ready to leave.

'Milly, could you bring the coats, please.'

Milly left the room and did as she was asked.

At the door, kisses were exchanged and Jane, who normally wheeled herself, said, 'Milly, could you help me?'

Milly suppressed a smile as she pushed her friend back into the drawing room; she knew Jane wanted to talk to her.

Richard was standing looking out of the window. 'So, Milly, what do you think of Catherine Robbins?' he asked.

'She is very pretty, and I loved those elegant clips she had in her hair.'

He laughed.

'I wish you wouldn't laugh at Milly,' said Jane. 'You'll give her an inferiority complex.'

'I don't mean to be rude, but she's always the very soul of discretion.' He sat down. 'Now tell me, do you know the meaning of those words?'

Milly looked at Richard unblinkingly. Although he could be very funny and laughed a lot, he could also be very hurtful. 'Discretion means tact and inferiority complex means to make me feel small,' she said, choosing her words carefully.

Jane clapped her hands. 'Good for you.'

Richard jumped up and, to Milly's surprise, kissed Milly's cheek. 'You certainly seem to have learned a lot in a very short while.'

'Miss Dance is really amazed at how quick she is.' Jane held out her hand for Milly. 'You are the best thing that's happened to me.'

Milly took Jane's hand. 'Would you like to go outside for a while?'

'Why not? I love the warm sun.'

When they were in the garden, Jane said, 'Don't let Richard upset you. He can be very hurtful at times.'

'Don't forget, my father was hurtful with more than just words.'

'I know.'

Milly had told Jane all about her family and how she would love to see her brothers again.

'Perhaps you will one day,' Jane had said.

* * *

'Milly,' said Richard when they were in the drawing room after they had returned from their walk. 'I'm very sorry if I have offended you.'

'That's all right.'

Jane looked at them both and smiled.

'Now you are so clever and almost part of the family, I will have to teach you to play cards,' said Richard.

Milly knew that when the family were all together, they enjoyed their card games.

'I wouldn't if I was you,' said Jane to her brother. 'You know how quickly she can pick things up. She'll have the shirt off your back before you go back to school.'

Richard laughed. 'That's something I will have to see.'

Milly stood and looked at him. She couldn't believe that he thought of her as almost part of the family, and for the first time she saw him differently from the boy who always made fun of her. He was very handsome. When he laughed, his grey-blue eyes lit up, and he had a funny way of pushing his thick fair hair back from off his forehead. She stopped herself crossly. She was just a common cockney girl who he enjoyed laughing at. How could she even think of him like this?

★   ★   ★

When it was time for Richard to go back to school, he called Milly to his room. 'I have a present for you.'

'For me?'

'Hold out your hand, and close your eyes.'

'No.'

'What?'

'The last time I did that, you put a slimy frog in my hand.'

He laughed. 'Yes, I remember, and you ran off screaming your head off and I got well and truly chastised by Mama and Jane and Betty. I did say I was sorry.'

'Yes, you did.'

'I can assure you this is not a frog. Now hold out your hand.'

Reluctantly Milly did as she was told, and he placed a small package in her hand.

'Open it.'

Slowly she unwrapped the package. It was a hair clasp just like the one Miss Robbins had been wearing. She looked up at Richard, for he was head and shoulders taller than her. 'Thank you. This is beautiful. But why?'

'Well, you admired Miss Robbins' clips, and I thought I'd better make it up with you. After all, you are so good for my sister, and despite the way I play about, I love Jane very much and like to see her happy. And I am very fond of you.'

Milly could feel herself blushing. 'You didn't have to do this.'

'Yes I did. Now help me downstairs with my bags.'

She took the bag from off the bed and on a mad impulse went and kissed his cheek. 'Sorry. I shouldn't have done that.'

He smiled. 'I don't mind one bit.'

70

She felt such a fool. 'Please. Don't tell Jane or your mother.'

'No. It will be our secret.'

★ ★ ★

As he climbed into the carriage, he turned and waved at her.

She felt her heart skip. This was silly. How could she be fond of someone like Richard? The handsome man who would go a long way? She looked at the hair clasp in her hand and knew that she would treasure it for ever.

9

In November, when it was Milly's fifteenth birthday, everybody made such a fuss of her. Betty had made her a cake and Jane had bought her a tam-o'-shanter hat just like the one she'd been wearing when they first met. She knew that Milly had admired it since that day. Milly was overwhelmed by everybody's kindness. Miss Dance gave her a book of poems, from Walton she had a scarf, and Mrs Green's present was a rich ruby-coloured skirt. Milly stood with tears running down her cheeks as they sang 'Happy Birthday' to her.

'I've never had birthday presents before, or a cake. You are all so kind.'

'It's no more than you deserve,' said Mrs Green. 'You have brought a lot of joy to my daughter and this household.'

Jane was smiling fit to bust. 'You wait till it's my birthday.'

'We've got Christmas before that,' said Betty.

'I know. I can't wait. And Daddy will be home then. You'll love him, Milly. He is so nice and kind.'

When Milly had asked Jane where her father was, she had told her that he was an ambassador who worked in Germany and only came home at Christmas. She said that he was someone very important.

A few weeks later the preparations for Christmas began in earnest.

'When Richard gets home he will decorate the drawing and dining rooms with holly and ivy. You must help him, Milly. It will be good fun.'

Milly was also beginning to get excited. She had never known an atmosphere like this, and couldn't wait for Mr Green and Richard to arrive.

All week Mrs Green kept popping into the kitchen asking if everything was under control. Betty seemed to be shouting at all the tradesmen, telling them that all the meat had better be perfect, as well as the dairy products and the vegetables.

For days everybody was in a fluster. Richard was the first to arrive, and Milly gave him a big smile.

'Everything all right then, Milly?' he asked when she opened the door to him.

'Yes thank you.'

'Good. We'll talk later.'

Milly's heart gave a little flutter.

Mr Green was due to arrive at the weekend. Milly was very nervous about meeting him for the first time, but Jane and Betty tried to reassure her that he was very nice. At the back of her mind was the thought of her own father, but nobody could be like him, not here.

Milly went into the drawing room to stoke up the fire. 'What time is your father arriving?' she asked Jane, who was sitting in front of the window watching and waiting.

'He should be here soon. I am so excited. I wish he came home more often, though he always brings me lots of exciting presents. I know that you will love him almost as much as I do when you see him.'

This was such a happy household. Even Richard was being nice to her, and Milly had told Jane about the hair slide he'd given her.

'Well he has been pretty horrible to you.'

Milly didn't have an answer.

'You must wear it at Christmas.'

'I think I will.'

Later that afternoon, a scream from the drawing room sent Milly and Betty to see what was the matter.

'He's here!' shouted Jane. 'Daddy's here.'

Milly felt almost as excited as Jane, who was trying to turn her chair around but in her hurry kept bumping into the furniture.

'Here, let me,' said Milly, who was now good at controlling the chair.

Milly pushed her into the hall just as Mrs Green opened the front door.

'I heard Jane tell everyone you were here.'

Mr Green held his wife tight and then bent down and hugged Jane. 'How are you, my little lamb?'

Milly wanted to cry. She had never seen such love and happiness.

Richard, who was standing by the front door, closed it behind his father and held out his hand. 'Welcome home, Father.'

Mr Green clasped his son's hand with both of

his own. 'And how are you, my boy? Still working hard?'

'Yes, sir.'

'Good. That's what I like to hear.' Mr Green was a tall, well-set man with thick greying hair and a moustache; he had a slightly tanned face. Taking the handles of the wheelchair he effortlessly pushed it into the drawing room as Milly hurried along to the kitchen.

As soon as the excitement died down, Betty was going to give Milly the sign and she was to help with the afternoon tea.

'What a welcome,' said Milly.

'It's always like that when he comes home. He's such a nice man and will talk to us later. Now just lay up the trolley, and don't let your finger dip in the sponge.'

Milly laughed. 'As if I would! Besides, you always save a bit for us.'

Betty laughed too. 'Go on with you. You're getting to be a right cheeky little madam.'

Milly suddenly looked serious. 'I'm sorry, Betty. As my mum would say, you mustn't get too big for your boots.' She thought about her own family and knew they had nothing at Christmas.

Betty noted her distress. 'Come on, love. I was only having a laugh. D'you know, it's a right tonic having you around.'

Milly's sad face lit with a smile. 'Thank you.'

'Right, you can come with me and hand out the plates and cake.'

'Thank you.' She went and hugged Betty.

'What was that for?'

'Just that I'm so lucky and I can't believe this is happening to me.'

Betty looked fondly at Milly for a moment. 'Come on, push that trolley. It's a good thing the everyday rooms in this house are downstairs.'

★ ★ ★

On Christmas night as Milly lay in her bed, she reflected on the past two days. Tears ran down her face. Never in her life had she experienced anything like it. But what about her own family? Did her mother wonder where she had gone? Was she well? It was then that she was filled with guilt. She knew that Christmas Day at home would have been just like any other. No presents for the children or lovely food. If only she dared try to get in touch with Dan and Billy, but that would surely put an end to her wonderful life. She knew she was being selfish, and that upset her.

Her joy had started on Christmas Eve when she and Betty went with the family to Midnight Mass. Milly had never been in such a lovely church. The family sat in the front and Milly and Betty sat at the back. She was staring at everything that was happening all around her. The sermon and the carols thrilled her; everything about her was so new, and it was such a beautiful sound when the choir's voices rose all around her that she wanted to cry. She was bubbling with joy when she got back and the family invited them into the drawing room for a drink. Milly was given ginger beer, but to drink out of crystal glasses was in itself such a privilege. When she went to bed that night she was full of apprehension and excitement and knew it would be hard to sleep, but it seemed that all too soon Elsie was standing over her.

'Come on, love, merry Christmas, it's time to rise and shine.'

Last night the family had wished her a merry Christmas; nobody had ever said that to her before.

The two of them had got on quickly and quietly with their chores, then gone into the kitchen for breakfast.

'Merry Christmas,' said Betty when they entered the warm, cosy kitchen. 'Sit yourselves down and I'll dish up. Then Milly, get yourself cleaned up and take the breakfast things in to the dining room. I daresay Miss Jane will be ringing for some help before long.'

'Mrs Green always sees to her when Walton is away,' said Milly, buttering her toast.

'I know that, but then she'll be wanting her breakfast and to see what presents she's got. That will give the missus time to get herself ready for church.'

Milly was always amazed at how lovely and regal Mrs Green looked, even in the mornings. 'I'd love to go to church again.'

'Wouldn't we all. Now get a move on. We've got a lot to do this morning,' said Betty, bustling round the table. 'Elsie can't stop as she's got to get home to her family, but Annie that's been helping out with the washing and ironing is coming in to give us a hand.'

Betty brought out of the larder the huge Christmas pudding she had made weeks ago. Milly had been fascinated and had helped in stirring it. Betty had told her to stir one way three times then plop the spoon in the middle and make a wish. Milly didn't have anything to wish for for herself, as her life was complete, so she wished for her mum to keep well. Betty wrapped the pudding in a cloth and set it to simmer gently in a large pot that hung over the fire. Also in the larder was a beautiful cake that she had made. She was such a good cook.

The milkman was banging on the back door. 'Merry Christmas, Missus.'

Milly took the jug of milk.

'Here's the cream you ordered.'

'Merry Christmas,' said Betty, handing the milkman an envelope.

He touched his hat. 'Thanks,' he said, and walked away whistling.

Milly thought of the creamery near her home. She'd hated that area; it was under the railway arches and was always dark and gloomy even on a bright day. When the trains rattled overhead the noise was frightening, and the smoke from them filled the air. She began to think of home. She would love to see her brothers again, her mother too, if only she could arrange to meet them, but she knew that would never be.

'Come on, young lady, stop daydreaing,' said Betty, bringing her back. 'Go and take your overall off and put your clean frock on and start taking the breakfast things in.'

Milly felt so happy as she pushed the laden

trolley into the dining room. For the past few days she had been helping Richard to collect holly and ivy from the garden to decorate this room and the hall. There had been much laughter as Richard teased her and chased her with the prickly holly leaves. She was beside herself with joy as they hung the garlands from the ornate mantelpiece; even the majestic grandfather clock that stood in the corner of the drawing room as well as vases and heavy picture frames were draped.

Jane was getting so excited as she pushed her chair round the room giving them their orders. She followed them into the hall and watched as they decorated that as well.

'I love Christmas. What about you, Milly?'

'Christmas didn't mean a lot in our house.'

'What a shame. Does this room look like the pictures in the book I showed you?' she asked. Milly and Jane had pored over a picture book last week admiring all the ways to decorate a room.

'Yes, it does.'

$\star$ $\star$ $\star$

'Good morning, Milly,' said Mr Green as she pushed open the dining-room door. He was sitting at the head of the table.

'Good morning, sir.' After placing the heavy silver dishes and the tea things on the sideboard, Milly poured him out a cup of tea.

'Looking forward to today?' he asked.

'Yes, sir.'

79

'Is Elsie still around?'

'I think so.'

'Could you go and ask her to come in here?'

'Yes, sir.' Milly did a little bob and scurried from the room.

'Mr Green wants to see you in the dining room,' she said as she burst into the kitchen.

Elsie took off her hat and left the room.

'What's she done?' a very worried Milly asked Betty.

'Nothing. I expect he just wants to wish her a merry Christmas.'

'Oh, that's all right then.'

When Elsie returned, she was beaming. 'Guess what? He gave me half a crown. A whole half a crown. I haven't ever had that much before. He's such a nice man.'

'Yes he is,' said Betty. 'Now you take yourself off home and give those kids and that husband of yours a good Christmas.'

'I will. And thank you, Betty, for the cake and all the bits fer our dinner.' Elsie went and kissed Betty's cheek.

Milly swallowed hard. She had never heard Elsie say so many words all at once before.

After the Greens had finished their breakfast and before they went to church, Jane came into the kitchen. She looked lovely; she was wearing a white frock Milly hadn't seen before and a huge white bow on the top of her ringlets. The ribbons of her bows always matched her frocks.

'Do you like it?' she asked, straightening her dress over her knees.

'It's lovely,' said Milly.

'Daddy brought it home with him. He's so clever at knowing my size. This is for you, Betty.' She handed Betty a small parcel. 'And this is for you, Milly.'

'Thank you. Yours is still up in my room,' said Milly.

'Good, that means I can have it later. I love Christmas. Go on, open it. I want to see if you like it.'

'I know I will,' said Milly, trying hard not to tear the pretty paper too much. She wanted to keep it for ever. 'Oh. This is lovely.' She held up a pinafore. It was white with frilly sleeves. On impulse she went and kissed Jane's cheek. 'Thank you. Thank you.'

'You can wear it tonight.'

'I will.' Milly's eyes were shining.

'And what about your present, Betty?'

'It's lovely, Miss Jane.' Betty quickly leafed through the cookbook and placed it on the table.

Mrs Green came into the kitchen. 'Come on, Jane, everybody is waiting.' She smiled at Milly and Betty. 'I will talk to you both when we get back.'

'Yes, Mrs Green,' they said together.

Milly started to do the washing-up. 'Did you like your present?'

Betty smiled. 'Jane knows I like a good cookbook. I'm always looking for something to surprise 'em with.'

'Is it always like this at Christmas?' Milly asked.

'What d'you mean?'

'Well, all this food.'

'Yes. The master likes his food and makes sure

everybody enjoys themselves. I daresay we shall be invited in to tea this afternoon. Then tonight a few of their friends will come in. You'll answer the door and take their coats and I'll help you hand out the bits I've cooked for tonight.'

'Where do I put the coats?'

'You can put them in Miss Jane's room. And Milly . . . '

'Yes, Betty.' Milly was worried. What was Betty going to say?

'Why don't you wear that pretty pinny?'

Milly face burst into smiles. 'I'm always worried when you say my name like that; I'm frightened that I've done something wrong.'

Betty laughed. 'Milly, you are a godsend and no mistake. Miss Jane finding you was the best thing that happened to this house.'

Milly had wanted to cry with joy. She had never known people could be as nice as this.

★ ★ ★

That afternoon when they went into tea with the family, Milly and Betty were given small tie pouches by Mr Green.

It wasn't till they got back into the kitchen that Milly saw that her pouch contained a shilling, and Betty had been given five shillings.

'What you going to do with that?' asked Betty.

'Don't know.' Milly wanted to say she would like to give it to her brothers, but she didn't know when or even if she would ever see them again. 'What are you going to do with yours?' she asked Betty.

Betty grinned. 'I'm going to buy meself a hat that I've had me eye on for while.'

'When did you see that?'

'Back in the summer.'

'They might have sold it by now.'

'Then I'll just have to get a different one.'

'When will you wear it?'

'You never know. I do go to church sometimes, even if it is only once a year, and that's always an excuse to dress up.'

Milly smiled. 'You looked really nice last night.'

'Thank you.'

★ ★ ★

Now Milly turned over and looked up at the stars twinkling in the black sky. She glanced at the lovely pinny that hung over her chair, and thought about the shilling that Mr Green had given her for her Christmas box. If only she could see her brothers to give it to them, but she knew that wasn't to be.

10

It was January 1910, and everybody was looking forward to a new year. Jane was very excited about her forthcoming birthday.

'I've told Mama that I only want a small party, like you had,' she said to Milly. 'I'm not going to have any of Mama's friends; they are such bores and always go on about the parties and balls they've been to, and the ball gowns they wore, knowing that I can't go anywhere. They make me very angry.'

Milly felt very sorry for Jane, who could have almost anything that money could buy, except to do things like other people. 'I'm sure we'll enjoy ourselves,' she said, hoping to ease the situation.

'I wish Daddy and Richard could be here; that would be the best present ever.'

'I'm sure they've left something very nice for you.'

A smile lifted Jane's pretty face. 'I expect they have.'

Milly had used her shilling Christmas box to buy Jane some delicate lace hankies with the letter J embroidered in the corner. They were laid out in a pretty box that had a scene of a thatched cottage on it. When the big day finally arrived in February and the household were having the birthday tea, she gave Jane her present.

Jane was thrilled. 'I've never had my own

hankies,' she said excitedly. 'Look, Betty. Isn't Milly such a thoughtful, clever girl?'

Betty nodded. Jane didn't know that Milly had been racking her brain for weeks to think of something Jane hadn't got, and it was between them that she had come up with this idea.

At the end of the day Mrs Green came into the kitchen and thanked Betty and Milly, telling them that today had been a great success.

* * *

Milly couldn't believe that she had been living here for a year. She was discussing it with Betty.

'You were such a poor shy little thing when you first arrived,' said Betty. 'And so skinny.'

'I know. And d'you know what thrilled me the most when I first got here — after all the lovely food you gave me, of course? It was the bath indoors.'

Betty laughed. 'And I remember you didn't even know how to clean it properly,' she said.

'But you soon taught me. Who would have thought that a year on I'd still be here?'

'I've always wanted to ask. Did Auntie Doris ever exist?'

'As far as I was concerned she did.'

'Funny your mum never told you anything about her.'

'I think there must have been some sort of trouble between them, but I don't suppose I shall ever find out if there was.'

'Sometimes it's best to let sleeping dogs lie.'

The next highlight on the Greens' calendar was Richard coming home at Easter.

'I wish he didn't have to go away to school,' said Jane.

Milly was thinking the same thing. She was really looking forward to him being here.

All over the holiday there were days out, and on fine days they had picnics in the local park. There was always plenty of laughter, and it seemed to Milly that Richard was near her at every opportunity.

'D'you know,' said Jane one day when they were alone, 'I think our Richard is rather taken with you.'

Milly laughed. 'Don't be silly. He's just being polite and making up for all the times he was horrid to me.'

'Yes, he was horrid. But now . . . '

'Jane, don't let your mother hear you talk like this. Remember she has ideas about him marrying Catherine.'

'I know. But does he want to marry her?'

Milly just shrugged and walked away. Although she thought the world of Jane, she didn't want to reveal the true feelings she had for her brother.

★ ★ ★

In May the nation was in mourning. The King had died. Although Jane was sad about it, she was very excited that her father was coming home for the funeral.

'Your father will only be here for a few days,' her mother told her. 'He has to represent his department.'

'Will you be going to the funeral with him, Mama?'

'Yes. But first I have to go into town to get myself a black outfit.'

Milly was in the kitchen discussing the situation with Betty.

'Always knew he had a high-up job,' said Betty. 'But to be invited to the King's funeral, well.'

'How long will Mr Green be here for?'

'Just a day or two, so the missus said.'

'That's a shame. Jane would like him to stay longer.'

The day after the funeral they all pored over the newspapers, hoping to see Mr and Mrs Green among the mourners.

'I think the new King and Queen Mary are very regal,' said Jane.

'She's always so very upright,' said Betty.

Milly laughed. 'Perhaps you have to be like that to keep the crown on.'

'Milly, I love your sense of humour,' said Jane.

Much to Jane's disappointment, Mr Green did indeed stay only two days, and she was very upset when he left.

Milly had remarked to Betty on how elegant Mrs Green looked in black.

'Let's hope it's years before she has to wear it again.'

It wasn't long before the summer was on them once again and Richard was coming home.

Elsie and Milly were busy getting his room ready; he was due home today for the long summer holiday. Milly was very excited at the thought of seeing him again. As she pulled on the clean sheets, the thought of him lying in this bed gave her feelings she had never had before.

How could she even think of him that way? she asked herself severely. After all, she was no more than a servant in this household, even if she was Jane's best friend; just a cockney girl from Rotherhithe.

When she opened the door to him she wanted to hold him and kiss him, but she knew that could never be.

'It's lovely to see you again, Richard,' she said coyly.

'And it's lovely to see you, Milly. I see you're wearing your hair clip.'

She smiled as she touched the clip. She knew it looked good in her dark hair, but she didn't want him to know that this was the prettiest thing she had ever had and that every night she looked at it lovingly.

'Am I in time for tea?' he asked.

'Of course. It's laid up in the garden. Jane likes to sit out there on fine days.'

'Thanks. Will you be joining us?'

'I think so.' Milly's heart was racing. Why was Richard having this effect on her? 'I'll take your bag up to your room.'

'Thank you.'

Their fingers touched as he handed her his bag, and excitement filled her.

In his room Milly put the bag on the bed. She longed to put his clothes away. That way she would feel very close to him, touching his personal things.

'Milly,' called Jane when she went back into the garden. 'As it's such a beautiful evening, Richard said he would take me to the park. Would you like to come with us?'

'I'd love to. I'll have to ask Betty if that's all right with her.' She was so thrilled; she was going for a walk with Jane and Richard.

★   ★   ★

They were all chatting away merrily as they made their way round the park. It was a warm evening and children were laughing and paddling in the pond.

'I'd love to put my feet in the water,' said Jane, looking longingly at the children splashing each other.

'Perhaps I could lift you and you could let the water trickle over your toes, like I used to years ago,' said Richard. 'How wonderful would that be?'

Milly looked horrified. 'You can't do that. Say you drop her, or worse still, what if someone pushes you?'

'You can keep them at bay.'

'Well I don't think it's such a good idea.'

Richard looked at her. 'This was something we

89

used to do before Walton came on the scene.'

'Oh come on, Milly. Only us three will ever know.' Jane was flushed with excitement.

'What if your mother finds out? Besides, we've nothing to dry you on.'

'Do you know, young Milly, I never took you as a spoilsport,' said Richard.

Milly was torn. She loved Jane and wanted her to be happy, but what if something happened to her? 'I've got my scarf,' she said with a smile.

She discreetly took off her friend's shoes and stockings while Richard took off his own shoes and socks. Then she held the chair while Richard lifted Jane like a baby and gently lowered her feet into the water. Jane's face was a picture, and she squealed with delight. Milly's heart was full of joy for her.

'Cor, she's a bit big to need a carry,' said a little girl who was standing watching them.

'Susan, come 'ere. I'm sorry, miss,' said a woman as she dragged the girl away. 'Can't yer see she can't walk?' she said to the child.

'That's all right,' said Jane, laughing with joy.

'I'll have to put you back, sis, you're getting too heavy.'

He placed Jane back in her chair and Milly began drying her feet.

'Thank you. That was one of the best times I've had for a long while.' Jane gripped Milly's hand. 'This is our secret.'

Milly smiled. Despite her worries, it was lovely to see Jane so happy, and Milly thought this was the most wonderful evening she had ever spent. Tenderly she watched Richard put his shoes and socks back. They were together like a family.

'Did you live near here?' asked Jane as they started to leave the park.

That question suddenly put Milly ill at ease. What if Jane wanted to see her old home?

'Is this where you came from?' asked Richard in a puzzled voice.

'This is where I found Milly,' said Jane. 'In this park.'

'It's not really near here, it's more the docks way.' She hoped that sounded convincing enough. Then another thought struck her. What if Billy or Dan were around? They would come up to her and ask her how she was getting on. She didn't want them to see her nice clothes, and Jane would want to know all about them. Suddenly all the joy of the evening vanished.

'Are you all right?' asked Richard.

'Yes thank you.'

'You've gone very pale. Let's sit for a while.'

They were sitting on a bench and Jane was facing them.

'If you like, perhaps we could go to the top of your road and try to see your brothers. I know you want to see them again,' said Jane.

'I don't think that would be a very good idea.'

'Why?' asked Richard.

As far as Milly knew, Jane had told him nothing about her family and the reason she had left home.

'Milly, you are a mystery. We know nothing about you.'

Milly looked at Jane.

'I do,' she said.

'Why did you run away?'

'It's a long story.'

Jane put her hand out to Milly. 'I'm so sorry. I didn't mean to stir up old memories. But you know me, I talk before I think. Now come on, how about we all have an ice?'

Richard looked at Milly. What had this young girl been through? He knew about men who beat women and did terrible things to them. Had Milly been violated in that way?

As they walked towards the man on a bike who was selling ice creams, the mood became very sombre.

Richard looked at Milly. She was growing into a very beautiful young lady, but why was she so upset about her past? He knew that it was very run-down near the docks and there were a lot of thieves and layabouts there. This was something he would have to ask her about one of these days. After all, Jane had found her sleeping on a park bench in the winter. Something terrible must have happened to her to make her run away, but whatever it was, it would never stop him from feeling the way he did towards her.

11

It was a long hot summer, and many evenings Richard, Jane and Milly would go to the park. After that first evening Milly decided to take a towel along to dry Jane's feet, but it took a lot of persuading before she would have a paddle herself. It did look very tempting, but she was reluctant to remove her shoes and stockings in front of Richard. After plenty of coaxing from Jane and Richard, though, she gave in, and once she had overcome her shyness she enjoyed it almost as much as Jane did.

During the afternoon they would sit in the garden and talk. They were growing up and the conversations were very intense, and Milly was learning so much. They talked of many things and would read the papers together, and Richard was always eager to answer any questions Milly had about world affairs. She found him easy to talk to; he didn't appear to regard her as a waif or someone to be laughed at any longer. He was very clever and seemed to enjoy her company, and would often come into the kitchen to find out if she was busy. Sometimes he'd sit and watch her preparing the veg, and all the while they would laugh and talk together. When it was time for Jane to have her rest, they would sit and talk about their future.

'What do you want to do with your life eventually, Milly?'

'I don't know. I haven't really thought about it. I just take one day at a time.' Truth was, she was frightened of her future; all she knew was that she didn't want to leave here.

'You know father has now decided that I should go into the army?'

'Yes, but why? There isn't any fighting now.'

'You never know when one of these upstarts might decide they want something another country has, and we have to be ready for that. Also, look at when the King has visitors. Look at all the pomp and ceremony we have then. On those occasions he needs soldiers to line the Mall, and I hope to be one of them.'

'My brother Dan said he wanted to join the army. Billy wants to join the navy and see the world,' Milly said, then added wistfully, 'We all had wild dreams back then. It seems I was the lucky one.'

'Do you ever want to go and see your family?'

'Sometimes.'

'You know I would always go with you?'

'No. I couldn't.' The thought of Richard seeing her home and her father filled her with horror. Was he still as angry and aggressive? Was it Pammy that was suffering now?

As Richard looked at her, he could see what a hard life she must have had, and sensing that she didn't want to talk about it, he decided to change the subject. 'Who knows, perhaps when I'm an officer, your brother might be in my regiment.'

'If he is, you will look after him, won't you?'

'For you, anything.'

She blushed and looked away.

'You don't wanna get too fond of him, me dear,' said Betty one afternoon when Milly came in laughing, her eyes shining.

'I can't help it. He's so nice to me.'

'That's his way. Remember he's going in the army when he leaves school, and then he could be sent away like his father.'

'I know.' Milly was painfully aware that she was getting very fond of Richard, but she knew that was hopeless. What would he say if he knew how she felt? As her mother would have said to her, 'Don't you start getting above your station, young lady.'

★ ★ ★

As he lay on his bed, Richard often thought about Milly. She was so different from the girls his mother was always bringing to the house when he was home. She was honest and full of laughter. He knew he could get very fond of her if things were different. Although the family liked her, he knew that she would never be accepted as one of them. What was her background? Jane would never break her promise to Milly and tell him. Perhaps when he was away he could write to her. Sometimes it was better to put your feelings down on paper. That was it. When he went away he would write to her. He'd ask Jane to pass on the letters, as he knew his mother wouldn't approve of him writing to Milly.

★ ★ ★

The summer was almost over and Richard had gone back to school.

All through the autumn Milly worked hard at her lessons, and one day Miss Dance suggested she did an exam to gain a certificate.

'I can't do that,' Milly said.

'Why not?' asked Jane. 'You are very clever and I think you should.'

'I agree with Miss Jane. Milly, you should take this opportunity.'

'What if I fail?'

'Then we shall know your weaknesses and work on them.'

'But . . . '

'There's no but about it, you must take it.' Jane smiled at Milly. 'Besides, Richard would be so proud of you if you passed.'

Milly looked at Jane. Did she know how she felt about her brother? He had written a few letters to her, but they were always in with Jane's and not sealed, so Jane knew exactly what he had written and they were always very formal.

'Please.' Jane held out her hand to Milly. 'You are my very best friend and you could go far with a good education. Who knows how long you will want to stay here with me?'

Milly went to speak, but Jane shook her head.

'None of us knows what will happen in the future, so you must take the moment.'

Milly bent her head. What did Jane mean? Did she know of something that might happen one day? Had the family been talking about sending her away? Milly quickly dismissed that thought; she knew Mr and Mrs Green would do anything for Jane. She also knew her friend was right. This was a wonderful opportunity and she should take it. 'All right, I'll do it.'

Miss Dance clapped her hands and her face was wreathed in smiles. 'I shall be so proud to help you on your way.'

Jane was smiling too. 'And so will I.'

'Thank you.' Milly knew that she would work hard and pass.

12

Once again winter was on them, and Milly was very excited when Betty told her that she was going to make the Christmas pudding again. She remembered last year and how she'd helped Betty put all the ingredients into the large bowl, stirring it all the time. Then when it was well mixed, it was ready to be transferred to another bowl and gently lowered into the pan of boiling water to simmer for eight hours. For Milly, Christmas had begun. She couldn't believe that she had been living here for almost two years. She had worked very hard to change; she no longer had a cockney accent and she was also a lot wiser. So many times she thought about home and felt guilty, and she knew that one day she would have to go and face her family. Would Richard really be willing to go with her? Christmas meant that he would be home. She hugged herself and wished it were his arms round her. As she busied herself with her chores, she hoped that he would want her to help gather the holly and ivy and decorate the rooms again.

Mr Green was also due home, and the whole household buzzed with excitement and anticipation.

'I love it when we are all together. Are you looking forward to coming to Midnight Mass next week?' asked Jane.

'Yes, I am,' said Milly. 'At least I'll be able to

read all the words this time. Betty has bought a new hat and can't wait to wear it.' But it was the thought of Richard being home that thrilled her more than anything else. She treasured the letters she'd had from him, reading over and over again about all that was happening to him and how pleased he was that she was going to take the exams.

At last the great day came when Mr Green arrived. When Milly opened the door she thought he looked a little different. He'd lost a lot of weight and his skin was very white. She noticed that Mrs Green looked shocked as she followed him into the drawing room and quickly closed the door behind her.

Milly took his bags up to his room and hurried down to Betty.

'You wait till you see him. He's so thin and pale. Has he been ill?'

'Don't know. Mrs G ain't ever said.'

'Perhaps he's never told her.'

'Could be. Mind you, you never know what kind of terrible disease he could pick up in those foreign parts. Don't hold with all this travelling about meself.'

'But that's his job. He's some sort of ambassador, so Jane told me. I don't think she really knows what he does, though he must be quite high up. After all he did go to the King's funeral. All she knows is that he works in an office in Germany.'

'Does he speak German then?'

Milly shrugged. 'Don't know.'

The bell rang for tea and Milly pushed the trolley into the drawing room.

'Hello, Milly,' said Mr Green. 'I've been looking forward to a nice cup of English tea.'

'Welcome home, sir.'

'Thank you, and it's good to be home.'

'Do you want me to pour?' Milly asked Mrs Green.

'No thank you. I'll do it.'

Milly looked at Jane, who had a worried look on her face. Milly gave a little bob and left. For all her being part of the family, she still felt slightly intimidated when Mr Green was around.

'You could cut the atmosphere with a knife in there. Something's wrong, I can feel it,' she said when she got back into the kitchen.

'Don't be so dramatic,' said Betty. 'I expect he's just tired.'

'Could be. But he wasn't like this last year.'

'Perhaps he's got a cold.'

Milly spent the rest of the afternoon deep in thought. What if Mr Green was ill, and that was what Jane had meant when she said she should take the moment. Was he coming back home for good, and would things be very different if he did? And what if he was ill and —

'You're very quiet,' said Betty, interrupting her thoughts. 'You all right?'

'I was just thinking about Mr Green.'

'I shouldn't worry about him too much. He'll be fine after a few days of my cooking.'

But Milly was concerned. What would happen to her if things changed? She knew she was being selfish and just thinking about herself, but she loved her life here, and she was always afraid that one day it could all end.

The following day Richard arrived, and Milly was over the moon when he held her hand and kissed her cheek.

'Lovely to see you, Milly. And later I want to know everything that has happened and all about these exams you're going to take. Family in the drawing room?'

Milly could only nod as she opened the door for him.

When she got back into the kitchen she said to Betty, 'Whatever is wrong with Mr G, Richard doesn't know anything about it.'

'I told you it's nothing to worry about.'

★ ★ ★

Mr Green wasn't at breakfast the following morning, and Mrs Green came into the kitchen and told Milly to do a tray with something light. 'Perhaps just an egg and some toast. I'll take it up to my husband, as he's feeling a little under the weather.'

'See, what did I tell you?' said Betty after Mrs Green had left. 'He'll be right as rain in no time.'

'I hope so.'

Walton had taken Jane out, and as lessons had finished for the term, Milly didn't get to see Jane on her own.

At teatime, when Milly pushed the trolley into the drawing room, the family were sitting around and it was very quiet, not like last year, when everyone was talking at once.

101

Once again Milly voiced her fears to Betty.

'Well Mrs G ain't said nothing to me, and I think you're worrying unnecessarily.'

'I hope so.' Milly was wondering how she could manage to see Jane on her own. It was always very difficult when the family were together, but they did usually include her when they had tea, or sometimes during the evenings when they played cards or just sat and talked. She loved those evenings, but these last few days that hadn't happened.

★　★　★

Tomorrow would be Christmas Eve and nobody had talked about going to Midnight Mass. For the past two days Mr Green hadn't been down to breakfast, although he was always around later.

That afternoon Milly was building up the dining-room fire when Richard walked in. He carefully closed the door behind him and Milly stood up.

'You must be wondering what's wrong.'

Milly nodded. 'Is your father ill?'

Richard looked worried. 'Yes.'

Milly took a sharp intake of breath and put her hand to her mouth.

Richard smiled. 'Don't worry, it's not life-threatening. He's just very under the weather. It seems he's had a lot of bad days at the office. The government in Germany are having endless meetings and he's been having sleepless nights. He'll be fine by tomorrow. He

102

just needed to rest and to be away from all the stress that goes with the job.' Richard took Milly's hand. 'Let's sit down.' He pulled out a chair and they sat at the table.

'He's not going to lose his job, is he?'

Richard smiled. 'No, but you mustn't worry about us. Now I want to hear all about you.'

They sat for a while and talked. Milly found him so easy to talk to. He wanted to know all about the exams she was taking, and whether she needed any help.

'Jane thinks you are going to sail through.'

'I hope so. I don't want to let her or Miss Dance down.'

He leant forward and ran his thumb along her brow. 'Don't frown. Do you know, you are very pretty.'

She blushed. She wanted to grab his hand and kiss it. 'Thank you,' she whispered. If only she could tell him how she felt, but she knew that could never be.

'Now, this afternoon we are going to decorate the hall, drawing room and this room. Will you help me cut down the holly and the ivy? Of course Jane will be supervising as usual.'

Milly smiled broadly. 'Yes please.' Suddenly all the gloom that had surrounded her these past few days had disappeared. This was how she wanted things to be, everybody making plans.

'Jane said she's sorry she hasn't been able to talk to you, but she has been very worried about Father. Now that he appears to be a little better, she said you must have tea with us this afternoon after we've finished.'

'I would like that.'

'Then tomorrow night we shall all be going to Midnight Mass.'

Milly didn't wait to be asked as she blurted out, 'Betty's got a new hat.'

'And what about you, have you got a new hat?'

'No.'

'That's a pity. Now go and see if Betty needs you this afternoon, then come back with your hat and coat on and we'll start cutting what we need. By the way, I'm pleased you had a nice birthday.'

'Yes, I did, and thank you for my card.'

'That's all right. I shouldn't say this, but Jane threatens me if I forget anyone's birthday. Including Betty's and now yours.'

Milly was a little sad at that remark; she'd thought he'd remembered it because he cared about her. She left him sitting at the table. She knew she loved him, but what good would it do?

* * *

Richard watched Milly leave the room. He hadn't needed to be reminded of her birthday, but he'd had to say something. He knew that he had feelings for her, but he couldn't make them known. She was so honest and trustworthy. What would happen to her in the future? Could she stay here for ever? Would Jane get tired of her? She could take Walton's place when the nurse retired, but when would that be? Could they ever be together? he wondered.

13

'What d'you think?' Betty asked Milly, as she looked at herself this way and that in front of the large hall mirror, which had been decorated with holly and ivy.

'It looks lovely, and that navy colour really suits you.'

Betty was still fiddling with the veil on her new hat when Jane came out of her room. 'Betty, you look lovely, doesn't she, Milly?'

Milly was beaming as she nodded. 'I've just told her that. And so do you.'

'Always have to have new ribbons for Christmas. It's one of the things I can wear proudly, and I make sure my hair is one of my best features.' When Jane laughed, her large pink bow bobbed up and down.

'You have very pretty hair,' said Milly. 'Not like my straight locks.'

'To get these ringlets I go through a lot of agony at night when Walton or Mother put all the rags in.' She touched her hair. 'As long as it looks fine, that's all I worry about.'

Milly, wearing the tam-o'-shanter that Jane had bought her last Christmas, looked around. She felt a lot happier now that whatever was wrong with Mr Green seemed to have passed and once again things were back to normal.

As they made their way to the church, despite the cold everyone was laughing and talking at once. In the church, the singing lifted Milly's heart, and everyone was still singing on the walk home. When Richard took hold of her hand, she felt a thrill rush through her. She wanted this night to last for ever.

When they arrived at the house, Mr Green said, 'Betty and Milly, you must join us for a drink.'

'Thank you, sir,' they said together.

It wasn't long before Betty said, 'Now, begging your pardon, but I must be off to bed. Milly, remember we have a very busy day tomorrow.'

'I think you mean today,' said Richard. He had a flushed face and Milly had noted that he had been drinking since they arrived back at the house.

Betty laughed. Her eyes were sparkling. 'So I do. Come on, Milly. Good night, sir and madam, and thank you.' She gave a slight bow and left the room.

Milly quickly said her good nights and followed.

She was just getting into bed when there was a tap on her door.

'Milly. Can I talk to you?' It was Richard.

'What do you want?'

'Let me in.' His voice was a hushed whisper.

'I can't.' Milly sat on the bed, too frightened to move. She knew the door wasn't locked; she had never had any need to. Besides Elsie had to come and wake her in the mornings.

'Please.'

'No, go away. What will your mother and father say?'

'They don't need to know.'

'I think you've had a bit too much to drink.'

'This is the only way I can get up the courage to tell you how I feel about you.'

'I'm very flattered, Richard, but please go away.' Although Milly was taken aback, she was thrilled that he wanted to tell her how he felt. She wanted to throw open the door and invite him in, but she knew that would be wrong. She was terrified someone would hear him and come to see what was going on. She always lived in dread of having to leave here. What would she do? Where could she go?

'Please, Milly, let me in. I only want to talk.'

She jumped off the bed, half hoping he would open the door and she would be in his arms, but that couldn't be. 'Please, Richard, go away.' She said it very half-heartedly.

He didn't reply. She strained her ears for a sound, but none came. Perhaps he had gone away. She slowly opened the door. He was lying on the floor just outside. What should she do? She shut the door quickly. Should she try and wake him up? But what if he turned and pushed her back into the bedroom? She knew she wouldn't be able to resist him. Fear ran through her. She couldn't call for anyone to help her. Betty wouldn't climb all these stairs, and that only left Mr and Mrs Green. Shivering, she took her coat from the hook behind the door and sat on the bed, contemplating what to do. It was very cold in the attic; perhaps that would wake him and he'd go back to his room.

Milly put the chair under the handle of the

door and got into bed. She lay wide awake, listening for the slightest sound. Despite her worry, she smiled to herself. He liked her. He'd come all the way up here to tell her that he liked her. But what good would that do? They came from different worlds. Then another thought went through her mind: had he come up here for another reason? She knew all about what men did to women. Was that what he wanted? She also knew that men could be very different when they'd had a few drinks. What if she had invited him in? Would she finish up with a baby? She shuddered. Although she loved him, she knew she had to keep him at bay for both their sakes.

★ ★ ★

Milly woke with a start. Elsie was knocking on her door and calling her name. Jumping out of bed, she moved the chair away.

'What yer doing putting the chair behind the door?'

Milly quickly dressed herself in her work clothes. 'It's nothing.'

' 'Ere, that Mister Richard ain't been after yer, has he?'

Milly looked at Elsie. It wasn't like her to talk about the family.

'I've seen the way he looks at yer. Yer wanna be careful of the likes of him. Think they can have who they like just cos they've got a few bob.'

Milly was shocked.

'Right, best foot forward. Oh, by the way, merry Christmas.'

'Merry Christmas to you, Elsie,' said Milly as she followed her down the narrow staircase.

'Everything all right?' asked Betty when they walked into the kitchen.

'Yes thanks,' said Milly. 'Merry Christmas.'

'And the same to you. Now get on with the grates, then your breakfasts will be ready. Did you sleep all right?' asked Betty.

Milly looked at her with surprise. She'd never asked her that before. Did she know something? Had she heard Richard?

All the while she was on her hands and knees in front of the fireplaces, she was terrified Richard would come in and make some comment. But the start of the morning passed without any problems.

Mr Green called them into the dining room just before the family sat down to breakfast and gave them small purses with money in. They thanked him and left the room to prepare the light lunch and the evening meal. Milly couldn't look at Richard, although she could see that he was smiling like everyone else in the room.

'I will give you both your presents when we get back from church,' said Jane.

'Thank you,' said Betty and Milly together.

When they were in the kitchen, Milly asked Betty, 'Do you think Jane will like the scarf I've got her?'

'I think she'll be over the moon. You know how she likes pretty things.'

'I hope so.'

'You're very quiet this morning, you all right?'

Milly nodded. How could she tell Betty about

last night? And was she reading too much into it? She knew she would have to talk to Richard at some time.

'Just as long as you ain't coming down with something,' said Betty, interrupting her thoughts.

Milly had placed the food for lunch on the dining-room table before the family returned from church. When the front door burst open, she could hear everyone laughing, and she felt a little easier.

Jane went to her room and returned to the kitchen with two beautifully wrapped parcels. 'This is for you, Betty. And this is for you, Milly.' Her eyes were shining. 'I hope you like it. Mama said I should wait till this afternoon when she will be giving you hers, but you know me, I can't wait.'

Milly sat at the table and carefully opened her present. It was a book of short stories. 'Oh Jane, this is wonderful. Thank you. Thank you so much.' She kissed her friend's cheek.

'Miss Dance got it for me. She knows how you love reading and thought that some of the questions might be about authors.'

Milly clasped the book to her. She was so happy. This was the best present she had ever had.

Betty was busy admiring her gloves.

'I hope they fit,' said Jane.

'They are lovely. Thank you, Miss Jane.'

Mrs Green came into the kitchen and smiled. 'I see my daughter couldn't wait. You must come into the drawing room when we've finished lunch. Do the gloves fit, Betty?'

110

'Yes thank you.'

'Jane, my present for you is in my room,' said Milly.

'Jane will have to be patient.' Her mother took hold of the handles of her chair and pushed her towards the door. 'Lunch first, miss. Then the rest of the presents.'

'Mama always likes to make things last.' Jane waved as she left the room.

Milly danced round the kitchen, clutching her book. 'I am so lucky,' she said, going up to Betty and plonking a loud kiss on her cheek.

Betty laughed. This young girl deserved all the happiness she could get, and if anybody ever found out where Auntie Doris was, Betty knew she would keep that information to herself.

⋆ ⋆ ⋆

Milly and Betty had to sit down when they were given their presents from Mrs Green. Betty was given a scarf the same beige colour as her gloves and Milly's present was another book. This one was a history book.

'Thank you,' said Milly, who was close to tears she was so happy.

'We all know how you love to read,' said Richard.

'Yes, I do.' Milly was waiting for him to give her a present but he didn't. Was he angry with her for not letting him into her room last night?

Jane sat with her scarf round her neck. She was fingering the fringe. 'I love this. Thank you, Milly.'

111

'I thought you might.'

'Now let's have tea,' said Mr Green. 'Do you know, that's what I miss the most when I'm away, a lovely cup of tea. Cheers.' He raised his cup and laughed.

Milly was pleased to see that everything was now back to normal.

Betty laughed. 'Begging your pardon, but this always seems wrong, you waiting on us.'

'I only do it once a year,' said Mrs Green.

Richard handed Milly one of the bone-china plates, and as he did so he looked into her eyes and his hand touched hers. She felt a thrill run up her arm. Whatever was going through his mind last night, she could never be angry with him.

★ ★ ★

On Christmas evening Betty and Milly were in with the family, enjoying playing games. Milly could feel Richard's eyes on her every time she moved.

'Didn't you get Milly a present?' Jane asked him.

Milly blushed.

'I thought you liked her.'

Milly wanted Jane to stop.

'Sorry, Milly. Never had time.'

'That's all right. I don't expect one.'

'I'll get you something for Easter when I'm home again.'

'You don't have to get me presents.'

Everybody's eyes were on her; she was so

112

embarrassed she wanted to run away. 'I'll just take these plates to the kitchen,' she said.

'No, leave 'em,' said Betty. 'I'll do it.'

Milly looked pleadingly at Betty.

'I'll help you,' said Richard.

Milly wanted the ground to open up. Why was he doing this to her?

Once they were in the kitchen she turned on him. 'What's wrong with you? Why are you behaving like this?'

'I'm sorry about last night. I drank too much and I wanted to give you your Christmas present.'

'But you said — '

'I know what I said. I didn't want the family to see what I've bought you.' He put his hand into his jacket pocket and pulled out a small velvet box.

Milly stared at it. 'I can't accept this.'

'You don't know what it is.'

'I can see that it's very expensive.'

'Quickly, put it in your pocket. I can hear Jane coming.'

Jane pushed open the kitchen door. 'Now what are you two up to?'

'Nothing,' said Richard. 'I was just helping Milly.'

'Why? You've never helped anyone before.'

'I wanted her to hurry up so we can play cards.'

Milly said nothing. Did Jane suspect?

'Betty said to leave the washing-up. It can be done in the morning. Now come on, both of you. Let's get back to the family.' Jane turned her chair round and they followed her.

Milly fingered the case nestling in the pocket of her pinny. What was it? She would have loved to open it there and then, but she knew it must be something very special for Richard to give it to her when they were alone.

At last it was time for everyone to go to bed. Milly kissed Jane and said good night to the family.

14

It wasn't till she was safely in her bedroom that Milly could bring herself to open the present Richard had given her. She sat on the bed and carefully undid the clasp on the velvet box, then quickly put her hand to her mouth. The box was lined with red silk, and in its folds was a beautiful gold bracelet. She sat looking at it. It was the most wonderful thing she had ever seen. What must it have cost? She couldn't bring herself to take it out of the box. It had to go back. What had he been thinking of? She was nothing more than somebody who worked in his parents' house and was a friend of his sister. She couldn't accept such a beautiful gift.

That night as she lay in bed, her thoughts were full of the bracelet and Richard. What on earth had made him buy her such an expensive gift? Was it really this that had made him come to her room last night? Had he wanted to give it to her when they were alone? Had she been too harsh? But what would Jane and his parents say if they saw it? If she kept it, when would she be able to wear it? All these thoughts were going round and round in her mind. She knew she wouldn't be able to sleep.

She was woken by Elsie shaking her.

'Don't know what's the matter with you these last couple o' mornings. Normally you're up and dressed 'fore I gets all the way up here.'

Milly quickly glanced around the room. She was pleased that she'd put the box under her pillow.

'Must have been all the excitement of yesterday.'

Quickly dressing herself, she caught up with Elsie on the stairs. 'Did you have a nice Christmas, Elsie?' she asked to ease the situation.

'Yes thanks. Could have done with staying at home this morning, though. Me husband don't look too good.'

'I'm sorry to hear that. Look, I'll have a word with Betty and ask her if you can go home. I can see to the grates and coal. No one will be up for a while yet.'

'I can't let you do that.'

'Come on. Let's talk to Betty.'

Betty said she didn't mind just as long as Milly was happy about it. With that, Elsie left.

Milly was on her hands and knees in front of the fireplace when she heard the drawing-room door click shut. She turned and was surprised to see Richard standing there.

'You're up early,' she said, as lightly as she could.

'I had to see you on your own.'

Milly stood up and ran her hands down the front of her apron. 'And I want to see you.'

A smile lit up his face and he went to step forward, but Milly backed away and put up her hand. 'Why did you give me such an expensive present?'

'Don't you like it. I can change it if — '

'It's the most beautiful thing I have ever seen.'

'I think so as well.'

'But why did you give it to me?'

'I am very, very fond of you. And I want it to be a keepsake. It will be our secret, and who knows, in years to come you can wear it with pride when we walk out together.'

For a moment Milly was speechless, but she quickly recovered. 'I think your parents would have something to say about us walking out together. I expect they have someone already planned for you. Richard, I am very flattered and I do like you.'

'I've never met anyone like you. Remember, I am off to the military school soon, so please keep the bracelet. Don't tell Jane, and who knows, perhaps one day . . . '

He left Milly standing bewildered in front of the fireplace. What should she do? She was thrilled that Richard liked her and was talking about their future together, but fond of him as she was, she knew it could never be. They came from different worlds.

'You look bothered. Anything wrong? Is it too much doing the grates and that on your own?' asked Betty when Milly came into the kitchen for her breakfast.

She gave Betty a smile. 'No, I've managed. Just as long as Elsie doesn't think I'm pinching her job.'

'She won't think that. She's got a lot on her plate, has that one. So what is it, then?'

'I'm just concerned about these exams Miss Dance is going to set for me.'

'According to her, you should sail through them.'

'I hope so,' Milly said, buttering her toast. 'I do want to get a certificate. Never had anything like that before.'

'Nor me,' said Betty.

* * *

In January things settled down. Mr Green went back to Germany and Richard went to the army school. Mrs Green had told them that her husband was worried about the situation in Germany, and that was why he was so down. It seemed he had been to many meetings and some had gone on all through the night.

'Just as long as the Kaiser doesn't start something,' said Mrs Green.

Neither Milly nor Betty understood what she meant, and they quickly dismissed it.

After all, what went on in Germany was nothing to do with them.

* * *

This year Jane's birthday was another very low-key affair. She said she didn't want a lot of silly girls and their mothers here.

'But think of all the presents you'll miss,' said Milly when Jane told her.

'I don't care, you're my best present, and they think I shouldn't invite you when they're here.'

Milly went and hugged her. 'Thank you. That's the nicest thing anyone has ever said to me.'

118

Milly settled down to her everyday chores, and the day came for her to sit her exams. Miss Dance said they were the same as some of the schools set their pupils. Milly was very nervous, and when she finished she said that she hoped she had given the correct answers.

'Don't worry about it,' said Jane as they were sitting having tea. 'You've probably sailed through them.'

'I hope so. I don't want to let you or Miss Dance down.'

'You'll never do that.'

One afternoon after it had been snowing, Jane, who had been looking out of the window, said she wanted Milly to take her into the garden. Walton forbade it, saying it was too dangerous for a wheelchair.

'What if you were tipped out? The chair is very heavy and Milly couldn't manage to put it upright again.'

The sun was shining and it did look very beautiful.

'It looks just like a picture postcard,' said Milly.

'Do you know, I've never touched snow,' said Jane.

Milly went and spoke to Mrs Green, then ran to the kitchen. 'Betty, can I have a bowl?'

'Now what do you want a bowl for?'

'Some snow.'

'What?'

'Jane's never touched snow, and I thought I'd bring some in for her. Mrs Green said it would be all right.'

Betty laughed. 'You certainly come up with some funny ideas.'

A few minutes later, Milly was outside, scooping up snow. She made a snowball and threw it down the garden.

Jane was watching from the window, and clapped her hands with delight. 'What's she doing, Mama?'

'Wait and see.'

Milly came into the room with the bowl, and after making sure that Jane's knees were well covered with a towel, she placed it on her lap. 'It's very cold. Put your hand in and feel.'

Jane did as she was told. 'It's all lovely and soft. And look, it soon melts.' Laughing, she held up her wet hands.

Milly looked at Mrs Green. 'I'll get another towel.'

Mrs Green could only nod. She had never seen her daughter look so happy. This girl was certainly a ray of sunshine in Jane's life. Who would have thought a simple thing like this could bring so much joy? But what if Milly's family ever came looking for her? She knew very little about this girl or where she came from; Jane must know something, as the two girls were very close, but she hadn't told her. She watched Milly laughing and drying Jane's hands. She always seemed to be happy and smiling, but what if one day she left them and went back home? That would break her daughter's heart.

* * *

Winter gave way to spring, and Betty and Milly were very worried about Elsie. Her husband's health had got worse, so she was working less and less.

'She's such a poor little thing,' said Betty. 'I've asked Mrs Green if you can take some bits round to her.'

'Of course. I'll ask Mrs Green if I can take Jane with me. She'll like an outing, just as long as Walton don't mind.'

'That's a good idea.'

Jane was thrilled when Milly told her, and that afternoon they went off with Jane holding a basket of goodies on her lap.

Elsie was very surprised when she opened the door to them. 'Milly. Miss Jane.' She looked flustered. 'Fancy you coming to see me.'

'Betty's done you up a basket,' said Jane, holding it out.

'That's very kind of her, and of you for bringing it to me.'

Two little tots came up to Elsie and held on to her skirt.

'Why is that lady sitting in that chair with wheels?' asked the older of the two.

Elsie looked embarrassed. 'I'm sorry.'

'Don't worry about it. I'm used to it.'

Elsie began to look agitated and pushed the children away. 'I'd ask you in, but I can't get your chair through the door.'

'No, that's all right,' said Jane quickly.

'How's your husband?' asked Milly.

'Not too good. Don't know when I can get back.'

'Betty said for you not to worry about it.'

121

'Thank you.'

Milly turned Jane's chair round. 'We'll be off now.'

'Bye,' said Elsie, clutching the basket. 'And thank you.'

'That was a nice outing,' Jane said.

Milly was thinking how hard things must be for Elsie and her family. She could understand her not wanting them to go into her house. Milly's mother would have died if anyone had wanted to go into their house.

Jane was still talking, and Milly listened.

'It makes a nice change for me to go somewhere different. We'll have to go out again, now that Mama trusts you pushing me about.'

'That'll be good. Just as long as Walton doesn't mind. Right now, hold on, off we go.'

Jane was laughing as Milly pushed her a lot faster than Walton would have done.

* * *

Walton had begun to look tired and worried.

'Don't know what's wrong with her,' said Jane to Milly one afternoon when they were alone.

'Perhaps things aren't very good at home.'

'Could be. Don't know much about her home life. I suppose she must have one.'

'Where does she live?'

Jane shrugged. 'Don't know. Must be quite near, though she doesn't say a lot.'

'Perhaps she has a secret,' said Milly.

'Could be a lover, and . . . ' She beckoned for Milly to come closer. 'Perhaps he keeps her up all night, you know!'

'Miss Jane, you are very naughty,' said Milly, laughing.

'I need something to talk about. Every day is the same and so boring. We must go out together again.'

'I'll see what your mother has to say about it.'

★　★　★

Milly had been pushing Jane round the garden.

'Come on, time to go back,' said Jane.

'It's not like you to want to go in on such a lovely day. You look a bit flushed. Are you all right?'

'I'm fine. I just want my tea.'

'Right. Hold on.'

The girls were still giggling when they went into the drawing room. Miss Dance walked in after them.

'Miss Dance,' said Milly, looking surprised. 'Is everything all right?'

'Yes thank you.'

'We don't usually see you here in the afternoon.' Milly began to pour the tea. 'Would you like a cup?'

'Yes please. This is a special afternoon.'

Milly looked at Jane, who was sitting on the sofa grinning. Even Mrs Green and Walton were smiling. Then Betty came in and joined them.

Milly looked bewildered. 'What is it?' She didn't know why, but the thought that quickly went through her mind was that they had found Aunt Doris.

'Millicent Ash, it gives me great pleasure to hand you your certificate. You have passed your exams.'

Everybody clapped and said congratulations as Milly stood looking bewildered. She now had a real certificate to tell everyone how clever she was. 'Thank you. This is lovely,' she said, gazing at the paper. 'I shall keep it for ever.'

'I'll get the cake,' said Betty.

'A cake?' repeated Milly.

'Yes, I've made a special one.'

'Well this does call for a celebration,' said Jane. 'After all, I can't believe that the scruffy cockney girl I found in the park could turn out not only to be very clever, but a beautiful swan.'

Milly blushed. 'Thank you.' She clutched her certificate and held back the tears of joy. She realised how lucky she was. Jane had rescued her from the park and given her an education. She could now go out into the world and be someone. She went to Jane and held her tight. 'Thank you so much for everything. I shall be in your debt for ever.'

Jane held her friend close.

'You'll have to write and tell Richard,' she said.

'I don't suppose he'll be interested.'

'I think he will.'

Milly was thrilled that Jane had suggested she write to him.

For Jane too this was a wonderful day. If only they could go shopping, say, or to a restaurant — really celebrate.

Summer, when it arrived, was hot and sultry. One June afternoon Jane was looking through the window and seemed very unhappy.

'I'm sick of sitting in this chair,' she shouted at Walton, who was doing some sewing.

'I'm so sorry, Miss Jane.'

'I want go to the park and watch the children running around.'

'Just let me finish this first, then we'll go.'

'No. I want to go now. Get Milly to take me.'

'You know that's not possible.'

'I want Milly. Get her in here now.' Jane was shouting.

Walton rang the bell.

Milly was in the kitchen, preparing the afternoon tea trolley.

'Now what does she want?' said Betty, glancing up. Her face was red and she looked very hot and bothered.

'She was in a bad mood at lessons this morning,' said Milly.

'Must be the heat getting her down. Poor girl, stuck in that chair all the time.'

'I'll go and see what she wants.' As Mrs Green was out, they both knew it was Jane who was ringing.

Milly pushed open the drawing-room door.

'About time too.'

Milly was taken back. It wasn't like Jane to speak to her like that. 'Is something wrong?' she asked.

'I want to go to the park, but Walton here is

too busy, so you can take me.'

Walton looked bewildered. 'I've asked her to wait just a moment.'

Milly looked surprised. 'Jane, you know I can't do that.'

'Why not?'

'I'm only allowed to push you round the garden and just a short way round the roads. Besides, it's almost teatime.'

Jane began to cry.

'Miss Jane,' said Walton, going to her. 'What ever is wrong?'

'This damn chair. I hate it. I hate it.' She banged the arms. 'I want to be like other girls. I want to run and dance.' Her sobs were sad to hear.

Milly stood bewildered. She had never seen her friend so upset. 'Look, let me take you into the garden and we can have our tea under the tree. Would that be all right, Walton?'

'I think that is a very good idea, Milly.'

Once they were outside, Milly bent down and said, 'Now come on, this isn't like you. Dry those tears.'

'I'm sorry. It's just that I feel so helpless sitting here on such a lovely day. I want to run and be with other people.'

'I know that. Perhaps we could try and think of some games you can play. Did you ever play games with Richard?'

'We'd play hide and seek when we were little.'

'Well we can play that.'

'No, I don't want to. It's childish. Besides, there's not many places you can hide a wheel-chair.'

126

'That's true.'

'What games did you play with your brothers and sisters?'

'Never had time to play games. We were all too busy doing our chores and trying to earn some money.'

'You must think I'm very selfish.'

'No, I don't. I think you're a very nice person and I like you very much. Now I'd better go and get the tea trolley. It's a good thing we have these ramps to get you in and out.'

'Milly.'

'Yes.'

'Come here.'

Milly did as she was told, and Jane took hold of her face with both hands and kissed her cheek.

Milly stood up and put her hand up to her face. 'What was that for?' she asked softly.

'For being my friend.'

She stood for a while looking at Jane, then turned and hurried away before the tears fell. First Richard and now Jane. She felt so happy here; nobody had ever been this nice to her before. But at the back of her mind was always the fear that something might happen to put an end to her comfortable life.

15

There was great excitement in the Green household when the telegram arrived informing them that Mr Green would be coming home for the Coronation.

'It will only be for a few days,' said Mrs Green.

'Will you be going with him?' asked Betty.

'Yes. I'm really looking forward to it. It should be a very grand affair. I shall need new outfits and we will be staying at a hotel for two nights.'

'Will you get to see the King and Queen?' asked Betty.

'I think so.'

'It must be very exciting for you,' said Milly.

'Yes, it is. Milly, I want you to help Walton with Jane while I'm away.'

'Of course I will.'

'Mr Green will only be coming here for two days, then he has to go back to Germany.' She gave them a beaming smile and left the kitchen.

'It's going to be such a sight,' said Milly. 'Jane was saying how much she would love to go.'

'It's such a shame, poor girl, she misses out on so many things.'

'I know.'

When Jane and Milly had been discussing the forthcoming event, Jane had said that her father was going to bring her back a souvenir. Then she got very angry. 'I wish I was going instead of being stuck in this bloody chair.'

Milly was taken by surprise. She had never heard Jane swear before and she looked around quickly. Fortunately Walton and Mrs Green had just left the room.

'Jane. For goodness' sake don't let your mother hear you swear. She'll think I've been teaching you.'

'No she wouldn't; you can't do any wrong in my mother's eyes.'

'Come on, cheer up.'

'I want to be there.'

'I know you do. Look, why don't we get Walton to take you round the shops? They must look really lovely with all the decorations.'

Jane half smiled. 'I suppose that will have to do. That's what I love about you, you always come up with something new to do.'

Milly knew that if it was up to her, somehow she would try to make Jane's life a little more interesting.

★ ★ ★

After Mr Green went back to Germany, everything in the household drifted along pleasantly. Richard was happy at the military school and occasionally enclosed a letter for Milly in with Jane's. They were always very light-hearted, telling her about his fellow students and what they all got up to in their spare time.

The summer was full of sunshine, and many people were complaining about the heat. Milly and Jane, though, were looking forward to when Richard came home for the holiday.

The two girls were now sixteen and their friendship was very special to both of them. More and more Milly was taking Jane out for short walks. Those afternoons were always full of laughter as the girls giggled and played about like children. Sometimes Jane complained that she wanted to go to the park, but despite the trust Mrs Green had in Milly, that was only allowed when they were with Walton.

'Milly is taking me out today,' Jane said to Walton one afternoon.

'If you say so, Miss Jane.'

Milly looked at Walton, who appeared to be very down.

As they were getting ready to go outside, she said to Jane, 'Do you think Walton is worried about losing her job?'

'She shouldn't be. Who else could put me in the bath or massage my legs and bottom and the many other unpleasant things she does for me?'

'I don't know.'

'I wish my legs would work properly, then I wouldn't have to have Walton around.'

Milly could see Jane was getting distressed, and that always upset her. She hated to see her friend like that. 'I'll have a word with her when we get back and put her mind at rest.'

'All right, if you must.' Jane was obviously put out. 'After all, she should be pleased that she doesn't have to push me around the whole time and listen to all my silly comments.'

Milly laughed. 'I can see you're getting cross, because when you're annoyed your head wobbles, and then that starts your bow wobbling as well.'

Jane laughed. 'Does it? Push me to the mirror so that I can see.'

Milly did so, and the two of them were laughing at themselves in the hall mirror when Mrs Green came along.

'What's going on here?' she asked.

'Milly was saying that when I get cross, my bow wobbles.' Jane moved her head about.

'Yes, it does,' said her mother. 'Now why are you cross?'

'Just wish I could go somewhere exciting.'

Mrs Green looked sad. 'I wish we could find some way of taking you to somewhere exciting.'

Jane looked down. 'I'm sorry. I know you do all you can for me.'

Mrs Green bent down and hugged her daughter. 'Perhaps one day. Who knows.' She stood up. 'So where are you off to today?'

'Not too far,' said Milly quickly.

'That's good. Remember, Betty has done a nice tea and Mrs Robbins and Catherine will be here for tea.'

Jane screwed up her nose. 'She's such a bore.'

'Don't be unkind, Jane. Now, be off with you both.' Mrs Green stood at the door and watched Milly skilfully manoeuvre the chair down the ramp. It upset her when Jane was down; she always felt that she was to blame for her daughter's condition. Thank goodness for Milly; she was such a tonic for Jane. But increasingly she had fears about Milly's future. Now that she was better educated, would she leave them one day?

Mrs Green wandered back into the drawing room. Walton was sitting at the writing desk. 'Are you happy, Walton?' she asked.

'Begging your pardon, Mrs Green, but I am worried about my position here.'

'Why?'

'Well, Milly seems to be taking over Miss Jane more and more.'

'I don't think you have any worries about that. Milly can't do the things you do for my daughter. Besides, who knows, one of these days she might decide to leave us, then where would we be?'

'Nothing was ever found out about her aunt, then?'

'No, and I know that Betty has tried. But please don't worry. All the time my daughter needs helps, you have a position here.'

'Thank you.' Walton let a smile lift her tired face. 'That makes me feel a lot better.' She hadn't told anyone that she too had been trying to find this elusive aunt. Did she really exist?

Walton settled down to her tapestry and Mrs Green picked up her book, but the older woman was also beginning to worry about the effect Milly was having on her family. She was a wonderful companion to Jane, there was no doubt about that; it was Richard who worried her lately. Over the years she had seen the way he looked at Milly. He always seemed to be near her and touching her hand whenever he thought no one was looking. She knew that he sent her letters, as Jane had told her when she'd seen her passing one to Milly, but what were they about? Were they sealed? She knew Jane would be very cross if she asked her. It was a good thing Richard was away at school, but what about when he was in the army? He would be a man then and could do just as he pleased. Could Milly become an officer's wife? She shuddered at the thought. Although she liked the girl, the thought of her being part of the family filled her with horror. She had never bothered her husband with her fears. He had enough problems on his plate and would dismiss them as simply her imagination. The whole world seemed to be in turmoil, everyone wanting something that belonged to someone else. She went back to her book and tried to concentrate on what she was reading, but her thoughts were still on Milly.

★ ★ ★

Milly was pushing Jane along the pavement and they were singing together. Jane began laughing. 'What say we go to the park one afternoon?'

'You know I'm not allowed to take you that far.'

'I know. But who would tell?'

'No one, I suppose.'

'Well then. We'll go next week.'

Milly was worried. She didn't want to get into trouble. What if Mrs Green found out? Could she lose her job?

'Don't look so worried,' Jane said, smiling. 'If Mama said anything, then I would say it was my fault, I made you.'

'Yes, but I'm the one pushing you.'

'Don't be such a spoilsport.'

'Oh, all right then.'

Jane laughed. 'See. I always get my own way.'

'Yes, you do. Now come on, let's get back. Miss Robbins and her mother will have arrived by now and will be wanting their tea.'

'Let them wait.'

* * *

When they arrived back home, the visitors were already in the drawing room.

'Milly, you are very late and we are waiting to start tea,' said Mrs Green. She looked a little cross.

'I'm sorry.'

'That is my fault, Mama. It is such a lovely day that we took our time and I was admiring some of the gardens round here. The flowers are so lovely.'

Mrs Green pushed her daughter into the drawing room.

'Jane, darling, how well you look,' said Mrs Robbins in a loud, strident voice.

'I'll see to the tea,' said Milly quickly.

'Where you been?' asked Betty as Milly made her way into the kitchen.

She quickly took off her coat and hat and donned her apron.

'The missus was getting in a bit of a state. You should have been back before this.'

'I know. But you know Jane, she didn't want to hurry back.'

'If you're gonna take her out more often,

you'll have to be in charge and not let her have things all her own way.'

'I know,' mumbled Milly. 'Shall I push the trolley in?'

'Yes, go on with you.' As Milly left the kitchen, Betty was worried. Jane was able to twist Milly round her little finger. She had done a lot for Milly and the girl would always be grateful, but she had to be careful. They were both growing up and one of these days Milly might want to leave, and what would Jane do about that?

The kitchen door opened and Milly came back in. 'That Mrs Robbins looked down her nose when I walked in, and as I left I heard her say to Mrs Green, 'Well, I certainly wouldn't let a servant of mine do what she likes.' Bloody cheek. I ain't no servant of hers.'

'Milly!'

'Sorry, Betty. But that sort make me angry. Just because they have money, they think they can do and say what they like.'

'And that's when you go back to your old way of speaking.'

'Yes, I know. I'll have to be more careful when I get cross.'

'Yes, you will. Now, those potatoes want peeling.'

Milly sat at the table and picked up the knife. Perhaps she was beginning to take things for granted; after all, she was still just a servant, a common girl picked up from off the streets. She would have to be more careful in future and not get so cocky; after all, all this could disappear overnight.

135

When the bell rang, she went into the drawing room.

'Milly, could you bring Mrs Robbins' wrap.'

As Milly collected the wrap from the hall, the thought that went through her mind was: I'd like to wrap this round her neck, but she smiled sweetly and handed it to the woman.

There was no thank you.

She opened the front door and mother and daughter left.

As soon as the door was shut, Jane turned on her mother. 'I do wish you wouldn't let that woman talk about Milly like that. She's not a servant, she's a friend.'

'Yes, I know, dear. But I didn't want to say too much, because as you know, I'm hoping that Catherine will become a very good friend of Richard's.' Mrs Green turned and looked deliberately at Milly as she said that.

Milly felt uncomfortable. Did Mrs Green know how Richard felt about her? Had anything been said?

'I think Richard would have something to say about that,' said Jane.

'Maybe. But when he's in the army and requires a suitable partner to take to dinners and balls, it will have to be someone who is of the same standing as himself.'

Jane looked at Milly. 'I think Richard will make up his own mind.'

'I just want to be sure.' Mrs Green smiled.

When Milly left the room, she felt uneasy. Had she outstayed her welcome here? Would Mrs Green like to see her go? What would Jane say

136

about it if she were to leave? Milly felt very unhappy that night, and for a long while she sat looking at her bracelet. What would Richard say if she went away? Should she tell him her true feelings?

16

The following day they were outside when Jane said, 'Let's go to the park.'

'Do you want me to get the sack?'

'You can't get the sack. I won't let anybody send you away.'

Milly smiled at the back of Jane's head.

'So it's the park, or else I'll tell my mother that you hit me and tipped me out of my chair.'

'What? Jane, how could you?'

'Well I have to get my own way somehow.'

'You, Miss Jane, are very naughty.'

'I know.' She laughed. 'Don't be angry. After all, it's the only pleasure I get. Come on, let's go.'

Reluctantly Milly did as Jane asked. As they wandered round, Milly was aware of the time, but as they passed the paddling pool, Jane said, 'I want to paddle.'

'What? Why are you behaving like this?'

Jane looked up at Milly, her big blue-grey eyes shining with mischief. She batted her eyelids. 'All I said was I would like to have a paddle like I did when Richard was here.'

'And look at all the fuss it created when your mother found out.'

'Yes, well that was Richard's fault, he shouldn't have said anything. Come on. Please.'

'How do you think I'm going to be able to lift you out and hold you?'

'You can. After all, you're a strong girl.'

'And you're a big lump.'

'I'm not that big.'

'I know.'

'Well then?'

'No, I can't. What if I dropped you?'

'That would be very funny.'

Milly was getting angry. 'I don't think so.'

'You could push my chair to the edge of the water and let me dangle my feet.'

'I can do no such thing.'

'Yes you can.'

'We are going back.'

Jane began laughing. 'You look so funny when you're angry. You should wear a bow, then it would wobble like mine.'

'Don't be silly.'

'Oh Milly, don't get upset. I only want to do what other people do.'

'I know that and I'm very sorry. But I do have to look after you.'

Everywhere women were sitting on benches fanning themselves. Jane settled back in her chair and Milly arranged her parasol to keep the sun off her head and the thin cover over her knees. Then she turned the wheelchair round and they made their way home.

They were both very quiet, lost in their own thoughts. Milly was thinking that perhaps she could bring a towel with them next time, and push Jane's wheelchair to the edge. After all, it was only a gentle slope down to the water.

Jane was thinking how she would love to be like other people. Perhaps she could get Walton to help her try to walk, now she was stronger. She smiled to herself. She knew that if she kept on to Milly, she would let her paddle. Next time she would bring a towel, as she dared not go home with wet feet.

★ ★ ★

A week later, Milly was able to take Jane to the park again.

Although it was a warm afternoon, there weren't many people around. Milly sat on a bench and watched the sunlight sparkle on the pond.

'Please, Milly, let me dangle my feet in the lovely cool water,' pleaded Jane.

'No.'

'I've brought a towel with me. Look.' She produced it from under her cover.

'I can't. I'm worried that something terrible might happen.'

'What could possibly happen?'

Milly was trying desperately to find an excuse. 'Somebody might see you and tell your mother.'

'Who knows my mother round here?'

'You never know.'

'Please, let me, nobody will know. Besides, it isn't that deep. You see children running in and out all the time.

Milly looked around. 'It's not very ladylike to take your stockings off in public.'

Jane laughed. 'I'm no lady, and anyway, you did it very discreetly when Richard was here.'

'I know. And you will have to wait till Richard comes home next week.'

'It might rain then. Besides, I can do all sorts under my blanket. Come on, it won't hurt. Please.'

Milly looked at her friend. She would do anything to make Jane happy, and it did look very inviting. 'Oh all right then.' She took off Jane's shoes and stockings and gently pushed her to the edge. The water lapped gently over the wheels, and Jane could feel it round her feet.

'This is lovely.' She was smiling.

'Right. That's enough.' Milly pulled the wheelchair back and proceeded to dry Jane's feet and put her shoes and stockings back on.

'Thank you. That was wonderful.'

'I was a bundle of nerves in case someone saw us.'

'But they didn't. Thank you, Milly. You are a true friend.'

Although Milly was happy to see Jane so contented, she was still very anxious.

'Don't worry, this will be our little secret.'

'But I *am* worried. I would hate to be sent away from you.'

Jane put out her hand. 'You need never worry about that. Nobody will send you away, not while I'm around.'

*   *   *

'You all right?' asked Betty when Milly came in from having tea with Walton, Mrs Green and Jane.

'Yes, I'm fine,' she said, putting the dishes in the sink.

'You don't look it. Did something happen while you was out?'

'No,' said Milly sharply.

'That answer tells me that something did. Mind you, Jane seemed in a good mood when you got home.'

Milly continued washing the dishes.

'Did you see someone you know? Was it one of your family?'

Milly looked up. 'No.' She had eventually told Betty where she came from and why she didn't want to find Auntie Doris.

Betty was busy stirring some flour into a mixing bowl. 'Well it must have been something.'

'Betty . . . ' Milly began wiping her hands.

'Come on, tell me. What is it?'

Milly told her about letting Jane dangle her feet.

'What!'

'I know it was wrong, but what could I do? She looked so happy when she had her feet in the water.'

'You should have turned the chair round and come straight back home. What was you doing in the park anyway?'

Milly looked very guilty. 'Please don't tell Mrs Green, but we've been there before.'

'What!' Betty said again. 'You are supposed to be in charge.'

'I know, but you should have seen her face. She said she wanted to be like other people. Besides, it's so hot.'

'I know that, don't I? This kitchen's like an oven. Everybody's talking about this heatwave.'

Betty mopped her brow with the bottom of her apron.

'I know I shouldn't, but I feel so sorry for her.'

'I can see you had a problem. Poor girl, it is a shame. But you know the Missus, she worships that girl, and if anything happened to her, well, I dread to think of the consequences.'

'Don't say things like that. I wish Richard was here, then it would be out of my hands.'

Betty was thinking that if Richard was here, Milly could have another problem.

* * *

Milly's dilemma was solved when Richard came home. He took Jane to the park whenever she wanted, and she was able to dangle her feet. The laughter that accompanied the three of them was a joy to hear. Both Richard and Milly joined in and paddled, and didn't care who saw them, and at every opportunity Richard held Milly's hand. She loved every minute of her days and didn't want them to end. She loved him, and in her wildest moments she thought that if he attempted to come up to her room, she would welcome him with open arms and worry about the consequences afterwards. She was worried, though, that she might show her feelings when others were around. Jane thought it was lovely that they were so happy together. Richard had told his sister not to mention it to the family.

'If you do, you know Ma would send Milly away, and you don't want that, do you?'

Jane shook her head. 'My lips are sealed,' she

143

said, smiling at them.

At the end of August, Milly was very sad when it was time for Richard to go back to college. He had told her that he loved her, and as much as he wanted to come to her room, he knew it wouldn't be very wise.

Although Milly admired his strength, she was disappointed, and deep down she knew nothing could ever come of this relationship. He would meet someone of his own class one day.

* * *

It was still very warm at the beginning of September, and Milly continued to take Jane to the park and let her have her little paddle. Although she always felt very guilty, it pleased her to see her friend so happy, and they laughed and ate ice creams and were almost like children again. But she knew that if Mrs Green found out what they did, that would be the end of their trips, and could be the end of her life with the family.

This particular day, she told Jane she was only going to push her round the houses, but Jane insisted that she wanted to go to the park.

'I love going there, and I've got a towel with me,' she said almost as soon as they left the house.

'Oh no. We're not going through that again, are we? Why can't you just be happy that I'm taking you out?'

'It's because I want to be naughty and enjoy being disobedient; after all, I'm not a child. Besides, it's hot today and I'm sure you would like a paddle too.'

Jane could be very persuasive, and Milly had to admit that it was warm, and the water would look very cool and appealing. So against all her common sense, she found herself heading for the park.

'Please, Milly. Push me to the water's edge.' Jane mopped her flushed face with her handkerchief. 'You can come in as well; that way you can hang on to my chair and then I can go in a bit deeper. Please.'

'I will do no such thing.'

'You are such a spoilsport. It does look inviting, doesn't it? And I am so hot I think I might faint.'

'Please, Jane, don't keep on.' Milly sat on the bench; she too was feeling the heat. Pushing the heavy chair always made her hot, and the sparkling water looked wonderful.

'Come on, Milly. Please.'

Jane's pleading got through to Milly. She knew her friend must be very uncomfortable in her chair, and the parasol they always carried hardly kept the sun off her. 'All right then. But for goodness' sake don't let your mother know.'

Jane was laughing as Milly sat on a bench and discreetly took off her shoes and stockings. Then putting the blanket over her friend's legs, she did the same for Jane.

The water lapped gently over their feet, and Milly had to admit it felt wonderful.

They were laughing and splashing, and after a while Milly said, 'That's enough, we have to go back now.'

She took hold of the wheelchair's handles, but

Jane put her hands on the wheels and stopped her from moving it.

'I don't want to go.'

'Jane. Let go.'

'No. I told you, I don't want to go.'

'Please, Jane, stop it. People are looking at you.'

'I don't care.'

'Well I do.'

'You should do as I ask.'

'Jane, please be reasonable.' Milly was beginning to panic. 'Your mother will wonder where we are.'

'I told you, I'm not going home just yet, so let go.' With that she pushed herself forward. As she did so, Milly slipped and sat down hard in the water, looking on in horror as the chair rolled down the slope and into the deeper water, where it tipped over.

'Jane!' screamed Milly. She got to her feet and paddled after her, but her long skirt quickly became waterlogged, making it difficult for her to move fast.

One or two people looked up and came towards the water.

'What happened?' asked a woman who was standing on the edge.

'Help me. My friend's under the chair.' Milly was desperately trying to right the chair, but it was very heavy. She pulled at the blanket, which was weighed down with water, and tried to drag Jane free. Jane was struggling, but Milly couldn't move her, as her feet were wedged under the chair. Frantically she tried to lift Jane's head

146

above the water, but the sodden blanket was holding it down. 'Help me!' she was screaming. She was filled with horror. She looked helplessly at the people who were watching the scene. 'Help me!' she screamed again. 'For God's sake someone help me.'

Milly felt she had been struggling in the water for hours when a man waded in and after a struggle helped her to right the chair.

'Oh my God,' he said, taking the blanket off Jane's face. 'I fink she's gone.'

'No!' screamed Milly. 'She can't have.' She began shaking her friend, but there was no response. She stood in the water looking at the beautiful ringlets hanging straight and straggly over Jane's lovely face. Gently she pushed the hair away and kissed her friend's wet cheeks. As she held the lifeless body, she could see her friend's soggy bow bobbing about on the water.

'Miss, where d'yer live? Miss? Miss?' The man was shaking Milly's arm.

Milly knelt down and held Jane close. She rocked her backwards and forwards, chanting, 'Jane. Talk to me, Jane. Please talk to me.'

The man tried to pull her away as people began to crowd round them, but she held on.

'I saw yer. What was yer doing pushing her in the water like that? You ought ter have more sense. Silly moo,' said someone.

'Leave it out, Maud, can't yer see the poor little cow's in shock?'

'Better go for the cops,' said a woman holding on to a pram that contained a screaming baby. 'Shut up, you,' she yelled at the pram, rocking it hard back and forth.

'Fink somebody's gorn for the park keeper,' said another woman.

'Poor little cow. What was wrong with 'er, love? What was she doing in that chair?'

All this was going on around Milly, but she didn't really hear anything; her thoughts were full of her friend. Why had she let her go in the water? It was all her fault for agreeing to it, and now she had killed her. She continued to hold Jane and rock her backwards and forwards as tears ran down her face. People were all around her asking questions, but she wasn't listening. Her thoughts were concerned only with Jane. She'd loved this girl and now, as she held her close, she knew she had lost her best and only friend.

17

'You wicked girl!' Walton was shaking Milly and screaming at her. 'I hope they send you to prison.'

'It was an accident,' sobbed Milly.

'But you were supposed to be looking after her. What were you thinking of taking her to the park?' Walton was visibly shaking herself.

'She wanted to go. I'm so sorry. I tried so hard to help her, I really did. You know I would never hurt Jane. You know that, don't you, Betty?' Milly asked Betty, who had just come into the kitchen.

Walton was still holding on to Milly and shaking her with every word, making her teeth rattle. 'It's no good you being sorry. You should be ashamed of yourself. All that this family have done for you, and you have killed their daughter. They trusted you.'

Milly was sobbing so much she couldn't hear everything Walton was saying, but one word was clear.

'You know you could go to prison for murder!'

'Murder? I didn't murder Jane.'

'You did in the eyes of the law.'

Betty looked at Milly. She was a sorry sight. Her eyes were red and sore and her face blotchy. Betty nervously smoothed down the front of her apron and said, 'I've given the missus a hot drink, and the doctor's with her and is going to give her a sedative. The police have sent telegrams to Mr Green and Mr Richard. Hopefully Mr Richard will be here tonight.' She sat down at the table. 'I can't believe this has happened. Whatever made you do it?'

'I've told her that she could go to prison for this; she could even hang.' Walton had suddenly grown in stature and confidence.

At that statement Milly felt her knees buckle, and she slid to the floor.

★ ★ ★

'Milly. Milly.' Betty was gently patting her cheek. 'Come on, there's a love, wake up.'

Milly opened her eyes, looked around her and quickly closed them again. She didn't want to remember what had happened. She hoped it had been a bad dream, a nightmare.

'Drink this,' said Betty, holding a cup to her lips. 'It won't hurt you, it's a drop of brandy. Medicinal.'

Milly took a sip, and coughed as the fiery liquid took her breath away.

'That's better.'

'Has Walton gone?'

'Yes.'

Milly grabbed Betty's arm. 'I didn't mean for it to happen.'

'I know you didn't.'

'What am I going to do?' She clung on to Betty's hand. 'Could they hang me?' She gave a long, deep sob. 'You know that I wouldn't hurt Jane for anything. She was my best friend. I loved her.'

'Of course I do.'

150

'But will the police believe me?'

'I hope so.'

'What shall I do? I can't face Mr or Mrs Green or Richard ever again.'

'I don't know, love. I really don't.' But in Betty's mind she knew that Milly had to get away from here. The Greens were very influential people, and Milly could finish up in prison. She didn't deserve that.

Milly knew that her life here had ended. Her wonderful world had crashed all around her. But the worst thing of all was that Jane, her beloved friend, had gone, and it was all her fault. She knew Walton was right, she shouldn't have taken her to the park, but it had happened, and Milly would give anything to turn the clock back. But that was impossible. 'I'm going up to my room. I'll be down in a little while,' she said as she stood up.

'All right, love. Try not to bump into Walton, she's very upset.'

Although her legs were a little wobbly, she gave Betty a faint smile. 'I'll try.'

*   *   *

Sitting on her bed, Milly was frightened. What Walton had said worried her. Could she go to prison? Surely if the police thought she had done something wrong they would have taken her to the police station and questioned her there. Perhaps they were coming back. After all, when they'd brought her home she'd been wearing wet clothes. Betty had dried her off and given her

151

clean ones. She had answered their many questions and they'd seemed satisfied, but what if they came back and arrested her? She lay back and closed her eyes, hoping this nightmare would go away, but it didn't. She could still see Jane's pale face and hear her gargling noises as she struggled to get free of the blanket. Why didn't I take the blanket away before we went into the water? she asked herself in despair. It wasn't that deep, but the wheelchair was very heavy and I couldn't turn it over. And poor Jane was trapped underneath. Tears ran down her face. What could she do? Her mind was in turmoil. What would Richard say? She knew she couldn't stay here, but where could she go? She stared up at the ceiling, trying to think.

After a while she realised that she had to leave right away, before the police came back. She began packing some of her clothes. She felt guilty about taking them, as the family had given them to her. It felt like stealing, but she knew she had to have a few things if she was to start a new life. Carefully she put them in a cloth bag, then looked around the room, tears running down her face. She was having to leave this wonderful place, but poor darling Jane would never come back here, and it was all her fault.

Milly made her way silently downstairs. She didn't want to bump into anyone. She knew that Mrs Green was in her room and Betty was in the kitchen, so she had to go out of the front door. It was Walton who worried her most. She had never seen the woman so angry, but then she would be. She had loved Jane almost as much as Milly had.

Milly closed the front door behind her and ran down the path without looking back. Out in the streets, she avoided walking anywhere near the park. She was worried that someone might recognise her. Could she be had up for murder? Her mind was in turmoil and she was wandering aimlessly, unaware of where she was going. She wasn't thinking of anything except Jane and what had happened. She knew she would never see or speak to her friend again. She felt so guilty and sad. Suddenly she realised she was just a few streets away from her old home. She stopped. Did she want to go back there? Did she want them to see her again? Would they want to see her? She would love to see her mother, but could she face the wrath of her father?

She turned in to Winter Street and stood looking at the houses. Peeling paint and shabby curtains gave the place a sad, neglected look. The stench of horse pee and manure mixed with the smell of tar that always came up on a hot day. Snotty-nosed kids ran around, some without shoes and all wearing dirty, torn clothes. She felt very out of place and overdressed in her nice hat and coat. She couldn't stay here, and turned to go.

'Milly, Milly Ash?'

A voice behind her caused her to suddenly stop. Somebody had recognised her.

''Ere, ain't you our Milly?' asked a young girl pushing a dilapidated old pram. Milly recognised the pram.

'What the bloody 'ell are you doing round 'ere?' said the girl aggressively.

'Pammy?' said Milly, shocked at her younger sister's sorry-looking state. Her frock was too tight and her hair was dirty, long and matted.

'That's me.' She looked Milly up and down. 'And be the looks of fings yer fell on yer feet. So what yer doing round 'ere?'

Milly didn't answer. She looked in the pram. The baby inside had sores round its mouth and running eyes.

'I asked yer a question.'

'I don't know.'

'Yer up the spout and yer boyfriend chucked yer out?'

'No.' Milly couldn't believe how Pammy had grown in confidence. 'Whose baby is this?' she asked, hoping to change the subject.

'This is yer new brother, Fred,' said Pammy, pulling a threadbare blanket round the baby, who began grizzling.

Milly wanted to retch as the smell from the pram hit her. 'Mum had another one? How is she?'

'Dead.'

'What?'

'She's dead.'

'Oh no.' Milly couldn't believe she was hearing about another death so soon, and this was her own mother. How much more grief could she take? Was she being punished in some way for leaving home and bettering herself? Guilt filled her. She should have been here. She should never have left home, then perhaps both Jane and her mother would still be alive. 'How long ago?' she asked tentatively.

154

'Six months ago, when she had this one.' It was all said so matter-of-factly; there didn't seem to be any sorrow in Pammy's voice.

'Is Dad all right?'

'Yer. You coming back home then?'

'I don't know.'

'I could do with some money, and by the look of things you must 'ave a few bob.'

'I don't have a lot of money.' Milly opened her cloth bag.

Pammy grabbed it and looked inside. 'Looks like some decent stuff in 'ere that could bring a few bob in the pawn shop.'

Milly snatched the bag back. 'I don't think so.'

'I don't fink so,' mimicked Pammy. 'You don't 'alf talk posh. Where yer bin?'

'It's a long story.'

'So what yer doing round 'ere then. Yer coming back home?'

'I don't think I'll be very welcome.'

'I dunno. Yer could be. As I said, looks like yer got some posh clobber.' Pammy was eyeing Milly up and down.

Milly looked at her sister. She had grown in height and stature. She was confident and appeared to be in charge. 'Are Billy and Dan still around?'

'No, they scarpered just after you did, so that left me to look after Mum and the kids.'

'I'm so sorry, Pammy.'

'So you should be.'

The heavy burden of guilt was weighing Milly down, and she knew she had no choice but to go home. It was the last thing she wanted to do, but

155

this was her sister, and she had the world on her young shoulders. 'All right. I'll come home and try and help out.'

'I could do with some help.'

'Don't think Dad will be very pleased.'

'Dunno.'

Milly felt very overdressed as they walked down Winter Street. The kids in the street stopped playing and looked at them.

'Who's yer posh mate then, Pammy?' asked a boy who was sucking a sweet then passing it on to the others.

'Me long-lorst sister.'

'Cor, she looks a bit of all right.'

Milly winced. How would she fit in here again, and how would her father react to seeing her? She was stronger now and knew it was her duty; she had to help in any way she could. It was going to be hard, and what was worse, she would be without her mum or Billy and Dan to help her.

18

Milly pushed open the front door. She had forgotten how dark and smelly this house was. As she went into the kitchen she wanted to cry. She was so unhappy, everything had gone so wrong. The smell of dried pee filled her nostrils and she brushed away the flies that were buzzing around the two children sitting on the bare floorboards squabbling.

'Pack it in, you two,' said Pammy, giving the one sitting nearest to her a clip round the ear.

'Ow. That 'urt.'

'It was meant to.'

Milly wanted to turn and run away. This wasn't what she wanted out of life.

'This 'ere is Milly, she's yer sister,' Pammy told them. 'You remember 'er, she's the one wot run away.'

'Hello,' Milly said. 'My, how you've all grown since I saw you last. You must be . . . ' she hesitated. It was four years since she'd seen them. 'Bertie?'

''Ere!' The boy that Milly thought was Bertie stood up. 'Don't she talk funny? And I ain't Bertie,' he said, mimicking her. 'Me name's Bert.'

'I'm very sorry.'

At that, the girl who Milly guessed was Iris screamed with laughter.

Pammy was also laughing. 'I ain't 'eard 'em

laugh like that fer years.'

Milly was still standing in the untidy room, wondering what was going to happen to her. Would she finish up like them? Could she end up talking like them again? Even though she felt full of guilt, she didn't want to stay. Suddenly the door burst open and a young girl stood looking at her.

'Rosie, this is — ' But Pammy got no further before she was interrupted.

'I know, it's Milly. 'Allo Milly.' Rosie ran to her and held her waist tightly. 'I always said yer'd come back.'

Milly held back the tears. 'Hello, Rosie. How are you?'

'All right.' She looked at Pammy. 'Billy and Dan said you'd come back one day. You gonna stay?'

'I don't know.'

'I want you to stay. Please.'

Milly bent down to hug the girl; she was so thin she was afraid she would break her in two. It was then that her mind was made up for her. 'All right. I'll stay,' she whispered.

'That's good. Mum always said you'd come back. I miss Mum. Where yer bin?'

'It's a very long story.'

'Right,' said Pammy. 'You lot get this place cleared up. Yer dad will be home soon and he'll want 'is tea.'

Milly could see that Pammy was in charge.

'What we got?' asked Bert.

'Bread and cheese and some apples.'

Bert stood up, looking very proud. 'I pinched

158

'em off a stall down the market.'

Pammy smiled at him. 'He's a good lad, keeps us in fire wood and gets a lot of food.' She ruffled his unruly hair.

Rosie began putting newspaper on the table.

'Has Dad got work now?' Milly asked Pammy.

'Yeah, he tries to get a bit of labouring down the docks.'

Bert began rummaging through Milly's bag.

'Stop that. What do you think you're doing?' Milly grabbed the bag from him.

'Just looking ter see what we can pawn.'

'Well just you keep your nose out of my belongings.'

'Look, Mil. If yer gonna stay you'll muck in with the rest of us. And that means getting rid of some of those posh clothes.'

'If Dad lets me stay, I'll need my posh clothes as you call them to get a decent job. I can't go out to work looking scruffy.'

'She's got a point,' said Pammy to Bert.

'S'pose so.'

'So what can yer do?'

'Well, I can read, write and add up, so there should be something round here I can do.' She wasn't going to tell them that she had a certificate to prove all this. She didn't want to give away too much.

The front door slammed and Milly stiffened as the kitchen door opened. Her father stood staring at her, and everybody else was looking at her as well.

It wasn't till he'd taken off his coat and cap and hung them behind the door that he spoke.

'Wot you doing 'ere?'

Milly swallowed hard. 'I've come back home.'

'Have yer now? Well yer can just sling yer bloody hook ter where yer come from. We ain't feeding another mouth.' He settled down in his battered armchair. 'We don't want yer 'ere. Pammy love, what's fer tea?'

'It's only bread and cheese, Dad, and a bit of apple.'

Milly remembered how he would shout and lash out at such a paltry meal when her mother was alive.

'Dad, let Milly stay. She can go out to work and bring in a bit more.'

He began undoing his laces and very slowly removed his heavy working boots. When he'd finished, he sat back. 'So what yer doing back 'ere, then? Got yerself up the duff and yer boyfriend chucked yer out?'

Why did both Pammy and her father think she was having a baby? 'I don't have a boyfriend and I'm not expecting.'

'So what yer after?'

'Nothing.'

'Yer must 'ave a reason fer coming back.'

Milly was trying to think fast. What could she say? 'I missed Mum.'

'Well she's dead, so what's ter keep yer?'

'Nothing, I suppose.'

'Well wherever yer bin, you know how ter talk posh.'

'I got a job in service. They were well-off people.'

''Ere,' said Bert. 'Did yer pinch somefink and

they chased yer out?'

Milly didn't answer. They could think that if they wanted to. 'Would you like me to go and get something more for tea? Is there anything you would like?'

'Some pie and mash would go down well,' said Pammy.

'Cor, we ain't 'ad pie and mash before, but when I pass the shop the smell always makes me mouth water,' said Bert. 'Tried ter pinch a pie once, but the bloke caught me and gave me a clip round the ear.' He grinned.

Milly smiled. 'Pie and mash it is. Have you got enough milk for the baby?'

'No.'

'I'll get some.' Milly held out her hand. 'Would you like to come with me, Rosie?'

'Can I?'

'Of course. I'd better take a plate for the mash.'

Milly took a chipped plate from off the dresser, picked up her bag and left the house hand in hand with Rosie. She felt so out of place as they made their way to the market, but Rosie was skipping along happily, chattering on about how Dan and Billy had left after a big row with their dad. 'D'yer know, Billy wanted to keep on bashing 'im. Dad was on the floor, but Dan said it wouldn't be right. I'm glad they didn't, cos then Dad would 'ave hit us.'

'Does he still hit you?'

'Yer, but not Pammy. She's his favourite.'

'Well she does have a big job looking after the rest of you.'

161

'I know. I miss Mum.'

Milly swallowed hard. She knew she should have been here for her mother. Now she was here for this little girl. She looked down, and Rosie gave her such a beaming smile that Milly found it hard to keep the tears back.

'What yer crying for, Milly?'

'Nothing. It's just so nice to see you all again, especially you.'

Rosie smiled, and her big brown eyes twinkled, lighting up her face.

How could she even think of leaving? Her thoughts went to Jane and all the good times they'd shared, but that was all over. What would the family say if they knew the real reason she had come back?

★ ★ ★

It was like a feeding frenzy when Milly put the pies and mash on the table.

Pammy was wearing their mother's wrap-round overall, which was much too long for her, and looked as if she was well and truly in charge. She slapped their hands as they went to grab the food. 'Pack it in, you lot. I'll dish it out proper like.' She carefully put a pie and some mash on each of the plates. She smiled at her father. ''Ere, Dad.' His plate had the largest amount on.

'Cor, Milly, we ain't ever 'ad a treat like this before,' said Bert, ramming as much as he could into his mouth.

'Be careful, you might choke,' she said,

162

watching in amazement as the food disappeared. She could remember the times when she was hungry and would have given anything to have a meal like this.

After a short while, every scrap had disappeared.

Her father belched and went and sat in his chair, and Milly helped Pammy and Rosie take the dirty crocks into the scullery.

The place was a tip. Their mother had always kept it clean and tidy, but the line of dead blue-bottles on the windowsill made Milly shudder.

'I know,' said Pammy. 'It could do with a clean-up, but I ain't got time, what with looking after Fred. 'E's only quiet when I'm pushing 'im round the streets, and this lot ain't much 'elp. Rosie's always daydreaming.'

Rosie looked at Milly. 'Well I do 'ave ter go out and try and get food, and I do a job for old Bella on the market.'

'I remember Bella. She's still around then?'

Rosie nodded and wiped her nose on her sleeve.

'What do you do for Bella, Rosie?'

'Sort the buttons she gits from old clothes.'

Milly looked sadly at the two girls.

She wanted to have a wee, but was dreading the thought of going to the lav. 'Is there anybody living upstairs?' she asked casually.

'Yer, an old man,' said Pammy.

'And 'e don't 'alf make the lav stink after 'e's bin in there,' said Rosie.

'Thanks for the warning.' Milly knew she had to go.

Outside, it was just as she was dreading. But this was to be her home now, so she knew she had better make the most of it. So many people had gone from her life: Jane, her mother, even Billy and Dan had left home. Would she ever see them again?

19

Pammy was busy getting everyone ready for bed, and Milly went about helping her. As she plumped up the old mattress in the bedroom, the smell of dried pee was almost overpowering. She dragged it into the middle of the room.

'You can kip in 'ere with Bert, Iris and Rosie.'

Milly shuddered at the thought of lying on that. 'What about you and the baby?'

'We're in Dad's room.'

'Why can't you sleep in here with the others?'

'Cos Dad likes Freddie in with him. And Freddie needs feeding in the night so I 'ave ter do it. Sides, it's nice being in a proper bed.'

'I would have thought that Dad would have preferred to be on his own.'

'Well he don't, and you know what 'e was like with Helen.'

'He's been like that with all the babies, then as soon as they start to toddle he don't want to know.'

'Fink that was because there was always annuver on the way.'

'I would rather be on my own in the kitchen if you don't mind.'

'Please yerself. There ain't any bedding ter spare, but it's warm in there. You'll have ter kip on the chair and make do with yer coat.'

'That's all right.' Milly wanted to be on her own. Tomorrow she would go and look for a job.

If she was going to stay here, she needed to be out all day.

In the night it was very quiet in the house and Milly sat thinking about the Greens and Betty. How she wished she could turn the clock back to when Jane was still alive and they were laughing together, but then she would see Jane struggling under that blanket, a picture that would haunt her for the rest of her days. Why didn't I take the damn cover away? she asked herself over and over again. But she knew why. Jane would never let her do that in public, as she hated anyone to see her thin white legs. Although her long dresses hid her legs, her stockings always hung in wrinkles, and no matter how she tried to keep them up, they always slipped down to her ankles. Poor Jane. Milly shifted about in the chair and let her thoughts go to the good times, and how wonderful her life had been. Then there was Richard. She loved him. Could she ever love anyone else? She whispered a prayer. 'Please God, look after Jane and my mum.' She hadn't really been surprised when Pammy told her their mother had died; she had been exhausted for years. After baby Helen was born, the woman who had brought her into the world told Ivy not to have any more children as it could kill her, but women didn't tell their husbands what to do. Milly thought about her father. He was a strange person. Fancy wanting Pammy and little Freddie in with him.

★　★　★

166

Milly screamed as she tried to pull the blanket away from her face. She was drowning and fighting for breath. She sat up quickly. Where was she? Daylight was just beginning to come through the window, and as she looked around her she remembered what had happened and why she was here. She began to cry. 'Jane,' she whispered. 'Jane. What did I do to you?' She sat for a moment thinking again of all that had happened. She knew that those memories were going to haunt her for the rest of her life. She got up. Today she had to find a job.

She was in the scullery washing herself when her father walked in. She hurriedly pulled the small piece of towelling close to hide herself.

'What yer doing standing there showing yerself orf?'

'I'm having a wash.'

'Why's that? Think yer dirty just cos yer slept 'ere?'

'No. I always wash in the mornings.' Milly wished she was in that wonderful bathroom.

'Not in this house yer don't. Now get out the way and make me a cuppa.'

'I'm waiting for the kettle to boil.' Milly had remembered that the kettle was always left overnight on the low fire for tea in the mornings, but had thought it was too early for her father to be up and so had used it to wash with.

He came towards her. 'You used the water to 'ave a wash?'

'I'm sorry. I didn't think you'd be up just yet.'

'Well yer thought wrong, didn't yer? Me tea

comes first in this house, so remember that if yer gonna stay.'

Milly quickly gathered her clothes and hurried outside to the lav to get dressed. Back in the kitchen she stood in front of the mottled piece of mirror that even after all this time was still wedged up on the mantelpiece. She combed her hair and arranged her hat, then picked up her bag and left.

As she closed the door she wondered what today would bring forth. She just hoped she could get a job so that she could bring some money into this sad household.

* * *

Today being Friday, everywhere was busy with women doing their shopping. All morning Milly had been walking along the familiar streets, pushing her way through the crowds at the market, looking at the shopkeepers standing in their doorways hoping to attract customers with their wares. The market traders tried to tempt people to part with their money, the smell of rotting fruit and veg mixed with horse dung filled the air, and the stallholders shouted at kids as they tried to pinch their goods. Nothing had changed. Passing the organ grinder, who was rolling out his tinny tunes, Milly went into a couple of the shops, asking if there were any jobs, but was a shop a wise place for her to work? She pulled her brown felt hat down over her eyes. What if someone recognised her? She could finish up in prison. She decided that shop work was not for her.

After walking the streets for what seemed like hours, the smells coming from the food factories and cafés made her stomach churn with hunger. She was parched, too. After her father had come into the scullery this morning, she hadn't even stayed long enough to have a cup of tea. She went into a café and sat at a table away from the window. She looked in her purse; she knew she had to be careful with money. She had all the money she had saved while she was living with the Greens. She hadn't had anything to spend it on there, only the odd ice cream when she was out with Jane, or presents at Christmas and Jane's birthday. Those days were over now.

'You all right, love?' asked the waitress, coming over to her.

'Yes thanks.' She wiped away a tear that had trickled down her cheek. 'Can I have a cup of tea, please?

'Course.'

A few minutes later the girl was back. Putting the tea on the table she said, 'This should buck you up.'

'Thanks.' Milly gave her a smile.

The young girl went about her business and Milly sat drinking her tea very slowly. What could she do? Could she wait on tables? No, that would bring her face to face with the public. Had the accident been in the papers? She bent her head. Would the girl know of any jobs going round here? 'Excuse me, miss,' she called.

'Another cuppa?'

'No thank you. I was wondering. You don't happen to know if there are any vacancies for

169

young women round here at all?'

'Not really. What can you do?'

'Anything.'

'Well, there's the biscuit place round the corner. They always seem to be looking for people.'

A smile lifted Milly's sad face. 'Thank you. I'll go round and enquire.'

'You do talk ever so nice and they might want somebody. Some of 'em who work there come in here at lunchtime. They seem a nice bunch of girls, and there's some blokes with 'em as well, but that's all I can tell you.' She looked round when another customer called her. 'Coming,' she called and turned away.

When Milly had left home this morning, she had thought about getting a job in the shirt factory nearby, but decided against that in case someone recognised her. This factory would be different. It was further away from home, so nobody would know her. She gathered her bag to her, and thanking the girl, left and walked round the corner.

There were plenty of impressive-looking buildings around; some were very old and beautiful, with carving and fancy stonework and chimneys belching black smoke. She felt a little bit happier than she had felt for days. This could be where she would find work. She stood watching and noted people going in and out, and they weren't all workmen. Getting closer, she could see a board announcing that they wanted girls. Should she go in? After a while she pushed open the door. They could only say no, she decided.

The lady sitting behind the desk looked up as Milly walked in. 'Yes?' she asked.

'I was wondering if you have any vacancies.'

The woman leafed through a book. 'Have a seat and I'll get someone to take you round to the factory.'

Milly noted that the woman had sharp features and greying hair pulled back into a bun. As she moved over to a switchboard, Milly admired her white blouse with big leg-of-mutton sleeves, and the waist of her navy blue skirt held in with a wide belt. She looked very elegant. After putting some plugs into the board, she asked for a Mr Forest to come to the office.

'Could I have your name?' she said to Milly.

Milly froze. Should she use her real name? What if the police come looking for her? She panicked 'Millicent Rose.' It was all she could think of.

'Have you worked in a factory before?' the woman asked.

'No.'

'Do you think you'll like it?'

'I don't know.'

'Where were you before?'

'I was a nanny.'

'You speak very nice, and that makes a change.'

'Thank you.'

'Have you had some education?'

Milly was getting embarrassed with all these questions. 'Yes, I have.'

'That could be interesting.' The woman looked up as a tall man wearing brown overalls came in.

'Mr Forest, Miss Rose here would like a job.'

'Right. Come with me and we'll see what you can do.'

*   *   *

The sickly smell in the factory was almost as bad as the noise.

'You'll get used to the stench, and the racket. We'll go along to the packing room. It's not so bad in there.'

Milly followed him.

The large room they entered was quieter. The row of women standing next to a long moving table were busy packing tins of biscuits into cardboard boxes. They all looked very bored.

'Sometimes it's tins and sometimes it's packets; it depends where they have to be shipped to.'

Milly could see by his expression as Mr Forest smiled and nodded to the girls that he really loved his job.

They slowly made their way along the long table. As they passed the row of girls and women, Mr Forest acknowledged them all with a word or two.

Milly was fascinated. As soon as the cardboard boxes were full, the girls expertly folded the tops down. Young men took the boxes away and piled them up, and empty ones were put in their place.

'What did you do before?' Mr Forest asked Milly.

'I was a nanny.'

'Can see you're well dressed. What made you leave?'

'The family was moving abroad and the little girl was getting too old for a nanny.' Milly was surprised at how easy it was to lie.

'Do you live near here?'

'Yes.'

'That's good. Come back to the office with me and I'll get Miss Toms to take down your particulars.'

'Thank you. Have I got a job?'

'Can't see why not.'

'Where will I be working?' She was hoping it would be in the quiet packing place.

'Not up ter me.'

Miss Toms smiled when they walked back in. 'Well, will she do?' she asked Mr Forest.

'Only time will tell.' He turned to Milly. 'We have a good relationship with our workers. Mind you, we don't stand for any larking about.'

'Take a seat, Miss Rose, and I'll take down your particulars.' Miss Toms smiled at Mr Forest. 'That'll be all for now.'

He turned and walked away. 'Could be seeing you later then?'

Milly smiled too.

'Could you give me the name and address of your previous employer?' asked Miss Toms.

Milly was stunned. She hadn't thought about that. 'They've gone abroad,' she said hastily. She thought that Miss Toms was eyeing her very suspiciously.

'Do you think you will be happy here?' Miss Toms was busy writing.

'Yes. Yes, I'm sure I will.'

'Good. Now we expect you to be here at eight

o'clock. Can you start on Monday?'

'Yes.'

'That's good. You get five shillings a week to start with, then after a month, and if you're satisfactory, your wages will go up to seven and six. We keep a week's wages in hand and you will be on trial for a month.'

Milly went to stand up.

Miss Toms continued. 'We also expect you to look clean and smart at all times.'

'I understand.'

A slight smile lifted Miss Toms' face. 'That's all for now. You come in through the factory gates, which are round the corner.'

'Thank you.'

'We will see you on Monday.'

Outside, Milly wanted to jump for joy. She had a job; she was going to get five shillings now and then seven and six. It sounded like a fortune. She didn't have to stay in that house all day, and now that she was Milly Rose, nobody would recognise her. She couldn't believe how much her life had changed in two days.

20

As Milly walked home, her mind was turning over and over. She knew that she had to be very careful with her money, but for the first time in her life she was going out to work and getting paid. She remembered the nights she and her mother had sat sewing buttons on shirts for just a few pence. That was a lifetime away, and now her mother had gone. All the while she was living at Jane's, her own family had hardly filled her mind. She had been so selfish, and she had never even thought that she would come back and live in Winter Street again.

As she was going to start work on Monday, this weekend she would get down to trying to clean the place up. After living with the Greens, she couldn't put up with such squalor again, although it had never been this bad when her mother was alive. Pammy had enough to do looking after Freddie, who was only six months old and a very fretful child. She still didn't understand why Pammy slept in the same room as her father. A terrible thought went through her mind, but she quickly dismissed it; after all, he was her father.

Wandering round the market she thought about what she would take back for their tea. As she got near to the butcher's, it brought back memories of Jack. Did he still work there? She remembered the day she'd been hoping to go to

175

the zoo, and how her father had beaten her when he found out she was going with Jack. She choked back a sob. Well he certainly wouldn't take his belt to her ever again, now that she was a woman. Then Dan and Billy filled her mind. She wished they were still around. Did Billy join the navy, and was Dan in the army? She remembered telling Richard about Dan, and how he'd said that if Dan was ever in his regiment he would look after him, but she wouldn't want Dan to be near Richard, not now. Richard might be angry with him, and might even come looking for her.

In the butcher's, Milly looked around for Jack, but like so many other people she had known, he was no longer around.

She took home some scrag ends of meat and a few potatoes and carrots. Although the weather was still very hot, she would make them a stew.

★　★　★

As Milly pushed open the front door, she could hear laughter.

'Look wot Bert pinched terday,' said Pammy, holding up a fluffy toy.

Bert was looking very important.

'You want to be careful, Bert,' said Milly. 'You don't want the police round here after you.'

'Why, yer frightened they'd find yer and yer'd git caught?'

Milly couldn't answer that.

'Come on. What d'yer pinch from the big house yer worked in?'

'That's my business.'

'Did yer do time fer it?'

'No.' Milly began to walk away.

'See, I told yer, she's done a runner. Wot d'yer do with yer goods? I bet they finished up in a pawn shop. Yer wanna be careful of that; they trace fings, yer know.'

'You're very knowledgeable.'

'Yeah, I am, and I'm too fast and clever fer 'em. This is only a little present, the stall won't miss it.' He waggled the toy in front of Freddie.

'Don't spoil it, Mil,' said Pammy. 'It's nice when 'e brings Freddie somethink.'

Milly didn't answer.

'So,' asked Pammy, 'how did yer git on?'

'I start in the biscuit factory on Monday.'

Pammy grinned. 'So you'll be bringing in a decent wage, then?'

'I hope so. I've got to work a week in hand.'

''Ow much yer gitting?' asked Pammy.

'That's my business.'

'No it ain't, not if yer gonna feed us.'

'I've managed to get some scrag ends and a few veg. I thought I'd do a stew for today.'

'It's a bit 'ot fer that, but if that's all yer got, it'll 'ave ter do.'

Milly was hurt; she'd thought they might have been a little bit pleased. 'I've bought some cleaning stuff as well. I thought I'd have a go at cleaning this place up over the weekend.'

'Please yerself,' said Pammy. 'It's good enough fer us, but if yer fink it needs a bit of a clean then we won't stop yer, will we?' She looked at Bert, who was still playing with the toy he said he'd got for Freddie.

Milly wanted to ask Pammy how she could live in such a place, but she didn't say anything. After all, she knew she had to tread very carefully.

*　　*　　*

On Saturday morning Milly found an old piece of sacking to wrap round herself. When Pammy saw her, she asked, 'Wot yer doing?'

'I told you. I know you don't have time to clean up, so I thought I'd do it. Besides, it'll give me something to do. I don't want to dirty my clothes, so I found this.' Although the sacking was stiff and smelly, Milly wasn't going to mess up her nice clothes. She knew she had to be very careful to keep them clean.

'There's one of Mum's overalls somewhere. I'll find it for yer when I git back.'

'Thanks. Where you off to?'

'Just gonna wheel Freddie round. Might go to the docks and meet Dad ter see if 'e's got a few pence ter give us.'

Milly thought that their father might not like that; he'd rather take his earnings and give them to the pub, but she didn't comment.

*　　*　　*

Milly was on her knees scrubbing the flagstones in the scullery when a man's voice startled her.

'What yer doing down there?' A short, skinny man with a shock of white hair and whiskers came through the door.

She sat back and mopped her brow. 'Who are you?'

'I live upstairs. Who are you?'

'Milly. I live here.'

'Oh, so you're the mysterious Milly.'

'Mysterious.' She smiled. 'Never been called that before.'

'Yer mum used to talk about yer all the time.'

'Did she?'

'She told me you'd gorn ter live with some aunt.'

'Yes, I did at first.' She wasn't going to tell anyone where she'd been.

'Lovely woman yer mother was.'

'I know.'

'Sad day when she passed on.'

'I didn't know about it at the time.'

'So what brought yer back 'ere, then?'

Milly was getting tired of everybody asking questions. 'I lost my job.'

'Oh. Gotta go to the bog.' With that he left her.

She shuddered. He didn't look that clean, and she had to wash it down after him. I just hope he keeps it in the pan, she thought.

* * *

Milly cleaned the windows and was tempted to wash the scrappy piece of lace curtain, but she knew it would fall apart. Next week when she got her wages she would go and get a remnant off one of the stalls at the Blue Anchor market. She threw the pile of dead bluebottles out, then set about the kitchen.

The large dresser had fewer crocks than she remembered. She took them all down and washed every one, then cleaned the shelves and put everything back. There were some things that needed replacing, and a nice paper border would look grand. She was standing back admiring her work when her father walked in; he looked at her and went straight back out.

''E's gorn ter the pub,' said Rosie.

'I thought Pammy was going to meet him.'

'Must'a missed 'im. It's hard ter see 'em when they all come out tergether. 'E always goes ter the pub when 'e's been ter work. 'E'll come 'ome drunk, so someone will git a bashing.'

'Why?'

Rosie, who was sitting at the table, shrugged. 'Dunno. That's the way 'e is.' She went back to sifting through the buttons for Bella on the haberdashery stall. She was given a boxful and had to sort them by colour and size, then put them into paper bags. She only got a couple of pence for it, but just like before, everybody had to do something in this family.

Milly looked at the clock that had been on the mantelpiece ever since she could remember. Her mother had always told her it was a wedding present from her sister Doris. She would never find Doris now her mother had died and taken her secret with her.

The pubs were open all day, and she knew her father would run out of money and then be thrown out. Milly knew that she wouldn't be the one to get a bashing now, so she carried on with her cleaning.

On Monday morning Milly was up first. She didn't like her father walking in when she was washing. She dressed herself quickly and left.

At the factory there was a lot of laughing as the girls greeted each other.

'You look a bit lost, love, you just starting?' asked a woman who looked a bit older than Milly.

'Yes.'

'Come with us. You'll have ter see Mr Forest and he'll tell yer where you'll be working.'

Milly followed this woman, who seemed to know everybody. Once inside the building she called out, 'Mr Forest. I've got . . . ' She turned to Milly. 'What's yer name, love?'

'Milly.'

'I've got Milly here.'

Mr Forest strode towards them smiling. 'Good to see you're on time. Thanks, Sally,' he said to Milly's companion. 'Now, come with me and we'll see how you get on in the biscuit room. You have to watch as the biscuits come along and make sure they are all perfect. If they're not, pick them out.'

Milly panicked. 'What if I miss one?'

'You're not alone. What you miss, someone further down the line will spot.'

All morning Milly watched the hundreds of biscuits that passed her. She was getting quite quick at spotting the wrong ones, but her eyes felt as if they would never close again.

When the hooter went for lunch and the

machines stopped, she stood looking bewildered.

'Come on, love. It's lunchtime,' said the young woman who was working just along from her. 'Did yer bring a sandwich?'

Milly shook her head.

'Well you just remember termorrer. It's a long day ter go without a bite ter eat.'

'I will.' Milly sat on the wall next to the girl, who was about her own age.

'Here, have one of mine.'

'I couldn't.'

'Come on, don't be daft. Me name's Rita, but I don't like it when people call me Reet.'

'I'll remember that.' Milly smiled as she took the doorstep Rita offered her. 'Thank you.'

'I like the way you talk. I'm always trying to talk nice. I think it helps you to meet the right people. Mind you, you have a bit of a job round my way meeting anyone nice.'

'Where do you live?'

'Belina Road.'

'I know that, it's near to where I live in Winter Street. I was always frightened walking round there with all the trains overhead.'

'I know. Those arches are a bit low.' Rita smiled. 'Perhaps we can walk home together?'

'I'd like that,' said Milly. She was pleased to find someone to talk to.

When the hooter went for them to start work, Rita said, 'I'll meet you outside when we finish.'

Milly nodded.

★ ★ ★

182

At the end of the day Milly walked home with Rita. She had been on her feet all day and her eyes ached. This was so different to anything she had done before. Tears began to slide down her cheeks. She was living in a house she didn't like, with her father constantly watching her, and now she was doing a job she wasn't happy with. But what else could she do? This was her life now, and she knew she had to accept it.

21

For Milly time moved very slowly as the days rolled into weeks. Next week it would be her seventeenth birthday. She hadn't told anybody; she knew the family didn't even think about Christmas, and birthdays were just forgotten.

Despite everything, she was reasonably happy. She was still sleeping in the kitchen, but had managed to buy herself a small feather mattress, which was taken during the day into the children's bedroom. She also got a cardboard box to put her clothes in, as she was fed up with the girls at work asking her what she carried about in her cloth bag. One of them joked that she must have the Crown Jewels in there the way she guarded it. She always told them she had to get shopping for some of the neighbours, but she was sure that they didn't believe her. On the whole she kept herself to herself, and the only person she really talked to was Rita, who worked next to her.

Every morning before she left home, Milly would carefully check her precious clothes, then tie the box with a ribbon. She threatened Bert with his life if he looked inside and took any of her belongings and pawned them. Her money and her prize possession, her bracelet, was with her at all times. Although she'd felt guilty at taking the bracelet when she left the Greens, she'd thought it was best that Richard didn't

184

have to answer any awkward questions. Most evenings when she was in bed she would hold it and think of him. She would never forget him, and deep down she knew that she would love him for ever, although it would be a fruitless love. She didn't care, though; she knew she had to have a dream of some sort.

The house was now cleaner and the family were better fed, and now and again they even had a treat of broken biscuits that Milly got very cheap from the factory.

In a funny way Milly had made friends with old Bill who lived upstairs. He was a pot man at the Rose and Crown pub up the road, and on Saturday afternoons after he'd finished his shift he would often come down and talk to her while she cleaned. He told her about his life and family and how they had fallen on hard times. His wife had left him and taken his six kids back to her mother's in Essex. He asked her why she'd left her job and come back home, and she always told the same story about the family going abroad, although she did wonder if he believed her when one day he said, 'Young Bert said you pinched somethink from yer boss, is that right?'

Milly didn't answer.

'I know, you don't wanna talk about it.'

'You don't want to believe everything you hear from Bert.'

'Your Bert's a bit of a toerag.' He moved closer. 'He wants ter watch it. He could end up in front of the beak before he's much older.'

'I know.'

'You do speak ever so nice. They must have

been nice people you worked for.'

'Yes, they were.' Milly was very aware of how she spoke, and was determined not to slip back into her old ways.

★ ★ ★

On Saturday afternoons after she'd been paid, Milly did the shopping on her way home from work. She always went to the market for food and the odd thing she could get at a reasonable price; she wasn't going to waste her money on luxuries. Once home, she would don her mother's wrap-round overall and get down to the cleaning. Pammy never thanked her and her father never commented; in fact he hardly spoke to her at all, which pleased Milly. There were a few more crocks on the dresser now, and better food to put on the mismatched plates. On Sundays Milly would go to church. She felt safe there, and she needed to pray for her mother and for Jane.

'What's it like in church?' asked Rosie one Sunday morning as she watched Milly getting ready.

'Very serene.'

'What's that?'

'Calm and tranquil.'

Bert laughed. 'I bet yer go there ter confess yer sins.'

'You use such lovely long words,' said Rosie.

Milly smiled at her.

'I'd like ter go ter church,' Rosie said.

'I'll take you one Sunday if you like.'

'I'd like that, but I ain't got nice clothes like you.'

Although Milly was determined to save some of her wages, as she knew that one day she would move on, she said, 'Look, when I go to the market on Saturday, I'll see if I can get you a coat.'

Rosie came up to Milly and hugged her.

*   *   *

The following Saturday Milly went to the market and bought Rosie a second-hand coat and shoes.

'Here's a present for you,' she said when she got home.

'A present for me?' Rosie's eyes were shining.

'Well if I'm going to take you to church one Sunday, you need something decent to wear.'

Rosie held up the green coat with a black velvet collar. 'Cor, Mil, this is smashing.' She quickly put it on. 'And look, it fits.'

'The sleeves are a bit long. I'll turn them up for you. What about the shoes?'

'I'll grow inter 'em. I can put some paper in them fer now.' She walked proudly round the kitchen. 'It'll be nice not ter have wet feet when it rains.'

Milly could remember the days when she had to put cardboard in her own boots to help keep her feet dry; not that it ever did, for once the cardboard got wet, it disintegrated, making a soggy, uncomfortable mess inside her boots. She sighed and watched Rosie parading around in her new coat and shoes. She held her young sister's shoulders and looked at her. 'Now, Rosie. I don't want you wearing this coat or these shoes to go street-raking. These are for when I take you out. And don't let Bert take them to the pawn shop. Understand?' Rosie nodded her head vigorously.

Looking down at the little girl's head, Milly knew that a nit comb was the next thing she had to get her.

* * *

On Sunday morning as they walked to church, Milly smiled at Rosie to see how excited she was as she skipped along. At the door the vicar gave Milly a nod, and once they were inside, Rosie's large brown eyes were full of wonder as she clutched Milly's hand very tight, looking all around her. Milly remembered the thrill she'd got the first time she went to church herself. She would be forever grateful to Jane for showing her another life; a life she'd loved but one that would never come again. She choked back a sob, and Rosie looked up at her and smiled.

When they got home, Rosie couldn't stop telling everyone about her morning, but nobody was interested.

* * *

Life for Milly was the same day after day. Her father only spoke when necessary, and she didn't go out of her way to make conversation, not after the time she had asked him why he had Pammy in with him at night. Milly still shivered when she remembered his rage.

'Dad, don't you think it's wrong to have Pammy sleeping in your bed?'

He put down his paper and looked at her. 'Wot did yer say?'

Bert was out, and Pammy had taken Freddie into the bedroom to get him to sleep. Rosie and Iris scampered to their room.

'Just you remember this is my house,' her father said, jumping up and pounding his chest with his fist. 'And wot I do in it is my business, d'yer hear? I like Pammy, she's a good kid and she looks after Freddie. She won't bugger orf like you did. So keep yer nose out, and if yer don't like it, you can always bugger orf again. We managed wivout yer before and we can do it again.'

'But it's wrong.' The anger in his eyes worried Milly, though she knew he wouldn't hit her, but this needed to be said.

He came up close to her. 'What you did when you buggered orf, I don't care, but I can tell yer, keep yer nose outa my business, ovverwise you'll feel this.' He started to undo his wide leather belt.

'Wot's going on in 'ere?' said Pammy, bursting into the kitchen. 'Yer gorn and frightened the life out o' the kids.'

'Ask 'er.' He sat in his chair and picked up the paper.

'All I said was that I don't think it's right you sleeping with him.'

'I told yer before, Mil. I like it. I like being

189

cuddled and warm in a proper bed, so mind yer own bloody business.'

Milly could see that Pammy was also very angry. One day she would tell her sister to take care, but would she listen to her? She didn't think so, but she had to try; she was concerned about Pammy and worried at what could happen to her. But for now she just had to wait.

* * *

Milly was reasonably happy at work, and for the past month had been walking home with Rita. At first she had been wary when Rita asked about where she'd worked before coming to the factory.

'I went away to work with my aunt, who was a domestic in a big house.'

'That must 'ave been interesting.'

'Yes, it was.'

'What made you leave?'

'The family went abroad.'

As time went on, Milly found that she was laughing again and enjoying Rita's company. Rita, who was the same age as Milly, told her all about her own family. Her mum stayed at home as her father did shift work; he worked the machines in a newspaper printer's. He had managed to get her older brother John in there as well. The print union was very strong and you had to have connections.

'You'll like John, he's good-looking and a real laugh.'

Milly only smiled. She didn't want any man in

her life; she was still in love with Richard. As Rita was always nicely dressed, Milly could tell that the family were quite comfortably off.

One miserable evening the rain was a fine mist and everywhere looked damp and dreary. The hissing streetlights were giving out a dull glow, and as they were walking home Milly said, 'I hate days like this. It seems to stay dark and gloomy all day.'

'I know what you mean,' said Rita. 'Say, how d'you fancy coming to the music hall with me on Saturday?'

'I'd love to. I've never been to one of those.'

'They're lovely. I went once with me mum. I'll call on you and we can go together if you like.'

Milly panicked. She didn't want Rita to see her house or meet any of the family. 'No, that's all right, I can meet you outside.'

'The one in Rotherhithe New Road starts at seven, is that all right?'

'That'll be lovely.' Milly was very excited; she had a friend and for the first time ever she was going to the music hall.

When the lights went down and the orchestra started playing, Milly sat spellbound. A man came on the stage and announced that the show was starting with jugglers on one-wheeled cycles. A woman singing followed that. Then came two men doing silly things and throwing pies at each other. Milly was laughing so much that tears ran down her cheeks. The big finish was a line of girls in short skirts kicking their legs very high in the air.

When it was all over Milly sat mesmerised.

She didn't want to leave.

'Well, what did you think?' asked Rita as they walked home.

'I thought it was wonderful. I couldn't believe it. You felt you wanted to get up there and touch them. Could we go again?'

Rita smiled as she took her arm. 'Of course. How about a bit of shopping one Saturday afternoon? We can go up West if you like and see the Christmas decorations.'

'I'd love that. But I can't afford to buy anything.'

'That's all right. Everything's much too dear anyway, but it's nice just looking in the windows at all the fancy clothes, and the displays look smashing. I love Christmas, don't you?'

'I used to when I was working away, but my family's not got a lot and in some ways I'm the only real breadwinner.'

Rita looked shocked. 'What about your dad?'

'He had an accident years ago and can't work all the time.' Milly was surprised at what she was saying. In some ways she was sticking up for her father's ways.

Milly was so happy with her new-found friend. But what if Rita ever discoverd what she had done; would she still want to be her friend?

⋆　⋆　⋆

Walking past the shops in the West End, the girls were laughing at some of the fashions and gazing in wonder at the Christmas decorations.

'Those skirts look a bit daring,' said Rita.

'Don't know if I fancy showing off me ankles like that.'

'I don't know,' said Milly. 'Could make life a lot easier if you have to run for one of these horseless carriages.'

'S'pose so.'

The noise coming from along Oxford Street sent everyone to the edge of the kerb.

The suffragettes came marching past blowing whistles, ringing bells, waving their banners and shouting, 'Votes for women!'

Milly felt a ripple of excitement. She did admire these women, who wanted to make a difference for all women.

But not everyone in the crowd agreed with them, and there were shouts of 'Go home, you silly cows, and git on with yer washing' and 'Git back ter yer kitchen and cook yer old man's dinner'.

The policemen who were walking beside the marchers looked very fed up.

'I think it's disgraceful,' said a strident voice behind Rita and Milly. 'What do women know about politics?'

To Milly's surprise Rita turned round and said very loudly, 'It would be nice if they were given half a chance.'

The bewhiskered old man looked very angry. 'Is this the sort of thing they want to breed? Slips of girls answering back to their elders.'

Milly smiled. She hadn't known her friend felt the same way she did.

The man raised his silver-topped cane.

'You hit me, and I'll scream so hard you'll

have half the police force on to you,' yelled Rita.

By now a small crowd had gathered round them.

'Let's leave it, Rita,' said Milly.

'Come on, Harvey,' said the old man's companion. 'We don't want to start any trouble.'

As the pair walked away, Rita laughed. 'See, he still does as he's told by his old woman,' she called after him.

There was a ripple of laughter in the crowd and a few women began clapping.

Milly was getting worried. She didn't want any policemen round here asking questions. 'Let's go and have a cuppa,' she said, taking her friend's arm and moving her away.

22

Milly and Rita were sitting in Lyons Corner House.

'This is the life,' said Rita as she poured the tea. 'I'd love to be a lady.'

'It sounds to me like you have a good life as it is.'

Rita grinned. 'I suppose I do.'

Milly gave her a weak smile. She had known the good times with bone-china crockery and nice cakes.

'I forgot, you used to wait on the rich, didn't you? Did they have a nice big house?'

'Yes, they did,'

'I bet you miss it.'

'Yes, I do.'

'Would have thought that they would have sent you to a friend's house to work when they went off.'

'None of their friends needed anyone.'

Rita took a cake and examined it, then said, 'Did you do something you shouldn't have? That why they let you go?'

Milly looked shocked and quickly crossed her fingers, as she was about to tell another lie. 'No, I didn't do anything. I told you, they moved abroad. Mr . . . ' She stopped herself from naming Mr Green. 'Sir worked in Germany and they moved there.'

'Pity they didn't think to take you as well.'

195

'He already had staff.'

'These cakes are smashing. Go on, take one. I think we pay for the lot, so we might as well eat 'em.'

Milly picked up a cake, and as she took a bite, she was reminded of Betty's wonderful cooking. Would she ever get over her life in that house? 'I loved the way you stood up to that old man,' she said, hoping to change the subject.

'I ain't got any time for pompous old devils like that.'

'What do you think about those women, the suffragettes?' asked Milly.

'I think it's great that they're standing up for themselves, but I don't hold with all this breaking windows and going to prison.'

'You have to admit, they are very brave.'

'Yes. Me dad likes it, as it gives the papers plenty to write about.'

Milly sat with her elbows on the table holding her cup, something she would never have done in the Greens' household, as she would have risked a telling-off from Betty. She had a dreamy look in her eyes as she remembered.

'You were far away then. Thinking about something good?'

She came back quickly to the present. 'D'you know, I wouldn't mind going to one of their meetings, just to find out what it's all about.'

'You wouldn't catch me there. Me dad would have forty fits if he thought I'd got mixed up in anything like that.'

'I don't know. I think it could be very interesting.'

'Where do they hold their meetings?'

'I don't know. We should have picked up one of those leaflets they were handing out.'

'You wouldn't really go to one, would you?'

'Well it wouldn't do any harm. Not if you just went to listen and find out what they're on about.'

'You want to be careful. You could end up in clink.'

Milly laughed. 'I only said I would go to a meeting, I didn't say I'd join them.' The last thing she wanted was to attract the attention of the police; she had far too much to hide.

As they walked home, Milly's thoughts were still on the marching suffragettes. Women should be able to have some say in matters, be it political or their lives. She had seen too many women knocked about by their husbands, and legally they couldn't do a thing about it. By the time she said goodbye to Rita, she had made up her mind: she would find out when there was a meeting nearby and go along to see for herself what this was all about.

* * *

At seven o'clock the following Wednesday evening, Milly made her way to the hall where the women were going to hold a meeting. She was very nervous as she approached. A smiling woman in a white dress with a green, white and purple sash over her shoulder held the door open for her.

'Good evening. I hope you enjoy our little

197

get-together. Is this your first time?'

Milly nodded.

'There's nothing to worry about, we're only going to tell you what we are all about. Please take a seat. The meeting starts in about a quarter of an hour's time.'

Milly noted that the hall was decked out with banners and flags and looked very colourful. She went and sat next to a young woman who was looking all around her.

'Hello,' she said. The young woman looked as nervous as Milly felt. 'Is this your first time?'

The young woman nodded. 'Have you been before?'

'No.'

'I'm a bit worried about being here. If me husband found out, he'd kill me.'

'I know what you mean, my dad's the same.'

The woman was very fidgety and moved about on her chair. 'I think I might go.'

'As you've got this far, you should wait and find out what it's all about.'

She gave Milly a faint smile.

There was a lot of shuffling, and suddenly the buzz in the hall started to recede, and then stopped as a well-dressed woman walked down to the front and up on to the stage.

'Good evening, ladies,' she said in a very well-spoken voice. She was dressed in the white dress and coloured sash of the movement. She was also wearing a very expensive-looking, beautiful large white hat.

'Good evening, Mrs Bolton,' came the reply.

Milly was entranced as Mrs Bolton explained

198

to them why she so passionately believed that women should have the vote.

'We should have the chance to say who should be in Parliament and let women have a say in looking after women. We have repeatedly tried to influence the government with petitions and the like, but it has always been useless, so now we have started to take other measures to make ourselves heard.'

Milly was shocked when she heard the details of the things that had happened to those women who had been imprisoned, and the conditions they had to put up with. Some of them were even being force-fed. Mrs Bolton then went on to say how they were opening new shops and offices up and down the country to raise funds and make themselves heard. She told them that they were looking for recruits for their cause. Milly found she was clapping with enthusiasm along with everyone else. She felt a sense of purpose and wanted to be part of it.

When the speeches were over and the women began milling around and talking amongst themselves, Milly just sat and looked around. Her companion who had been sitting next to her had left.

'Hello,' said a young woman who looked a little older than Milly. 'Haven't seen you here before.'

'No, this is my first time.'

She sat next to Milly. 'My name's Ada Roberts.'

'Milly Ash,' said Milly, holding out her hand. She didn't care that she had given her real name this time.

'Pleased to meet you, Milly. I was watching you, you seemed to enjoy the meeting.'

'Yes, I did.'

'Mrs Bolton's a wonderful speaker. We were very lucky to get her here tonight.'

'She's not part of your group, then?'

'No. We haven't anybody that important. We have only been going for a few months, so we are just finding our feet, so to speak. Would you be interested in joining us?'

'I don't think so. I couldn't go on marches, breaking windows and going to prison.'

Ada laughed. 'We don't all do that. Our job is mostly administration; it's more to do with writing the newsletter and sending it out.'

'That sounds interesting.'

Somebody was calling for Ada.

'Coming,' she replied. She turned to Milly. 'I must go, but if you are interested, come and see me in our office. I work all day.'

'I can't, I work as well.'

Ada's name was being called again.

'Try and come into the office, this is the address.' She handed Milly a leaflet.

Milly watched Ada walk away. She seemed very nice, and the office wasn't that far away. Perhaps one Saturday afternoon she'd drop in there. After all, she had nothing to lose.

*　*　*

On Monday evening Milly was telling Rita about the meeting she had been to.

'Did they all sing and bang a drum?'

'No, it was very good. A lady gave a talk and told us about those who had been to prison and some of the things they did. They must really believe they should be getting the vote.'

'I don't know what all the fuss is about. Why do they want the vote anyway?'

'It's very important to them. They seem well-educated ladies so they must really believe in it.'

'What for?'

'To make a difference for women.'

'But will it?'

'I don't know.'

'Here, they didn't tell you what they were going to get up to next time, did they?'

'No, why?'

'I could tell me dad, and he would make sure the papers were there to report it.'

Milly was taken aback.

'So, are you going again?'

'I don't know. You could come with me if you want.'

'I don't think so.'

Milly knew then that if she had any intentions of going to another meeting it would have to be alone.

'So when you going again?' asked Rita.

'I don't know. Perhaps when it gets a bit warmer.'

Rita laughed. 'I don't think those who go to prison worry about the weather.'

★ ★ ★

201

It was Saturday the twenty-third of December and very cold. Milly wandered round the stalls at the market, looking for something she could give as a treat, a little present for everyone in the family. It was very colourful and noisy, with the traders shouting out about their wares. It certainly had an air of the festive season. There were chestnuts roasting in the braziers, and the organ grinder was churning out a noise that was supposed to be a tune that his monkey danced to, much to the children's joy. Their little faces were pinched with the cold, some didn't have decent boots or gloves to keep their hands or feet warm, but they all looked very happy and clapped enthusiastically. The butcher's shop front was full of chickens and other birds, not that many round here could afford such luxuries. Milly could see some suffragettes handing out leaflets, and her thoughts turned fleetingly to Ada and the meeting that she had been to. She would leave going to see her till the new year, as she knew she had to try and make this Christmas in the Ash household the best they had ever had.

On the second-hand stall she found woolly gloves for Pammy and Bert and warm knitted scarves for Rosie and Iris. Some of the stitches had been dropped, which gave them a lacy-looking effect. She even managed to find a toy for Freddie. Even though it meant she had to spend another thruppence, she bought her father a pair of socks that had been neatly darned a couple of times. She smiled as she put her purchases in her bag. What would her father say about that? It was the thought that counted, though. A couple of chicken legs meant they were going to have a good Christmas dinner. As always, her thought went to the Christmases she'd spent with the Greens. She knew she would never get over those wonderful years, but they had gone for ever and she would never, ever forgive herself for what happened to Jane. A tear slid slowly down her cheek. If only she could turn the clock back, but she knew that could never be.

23

The new year started very cold, and Milly was pleased she slept in the kitchen, as the warmth from the fire was comforting. In the morning she scraped the ice off the inside of the scullery window, and she knew that the cistern in the lav would be frozen. At least it was reasonably warm in the factory. As she passed the news-stand and read the headlines, she could see that the suffragettes hadn't given up their quest to get votes for women. She knew that she would be going to see Ada soon, as she wanted to know more about the movement.

It was one Saturday afternoon at the end of January that she called into the suffragettes' office. She was surprised at all the posters that were displayed round the walls announcing forth-coming meetings. Ada was at the back of the room turning a handle on some noisy machine that appeared to be spilling out paper.

'Hello,' said Milly tentatively to a young woman who was sitting at a desk.

'Milly,' called Ada when she turned and saw who it was. 'You came. How wonderful. Eve, this is Milly. Milly was at the meeting when Mrs Bolton came and spoke to us.'

Eve stood up smiling. 'Pleased to meet you I'm sure.'

Milly was taken back by this reception, and by the fact that Ada had remembered her name. 'I just thought I'd come along to see what you do here.'

'Well, as I told you, we send out a newsletter, and we also cut out all the remarks and pictures from the newspapers and store them. Who knows, one day when we get the vote, this could become part of history.' Ada had an air of excitement about her. 'We also accept any donations.'

'People give you money?'

'Yes, you'd be surprised at the amount some men give us, but they always ask us never to disclose their names, as they have to appear to disapprove of us.'

'Please, take a seat, and would you like a cup of tea?' asked Eve.

'Thank you.'

'Now,' said Ada, sitting next to her. 'What do you want to know?'

'I don't know really. Why do you think it's so important that women get the vote?'

'I suppose it means that we will be able to voice our opinions in Parliament and tell men what we want, rather than men always telling us what they want us to do.'

Milly said, 'I see,' It was beginning to make a lot of sense.

'We are always looking for volunteers to help us with our work.'

'Don't you get paid?'

'Most are volunteers, although some of us do get paid.'

'How do they manage?'

Ada smiled. 'Some of them have very rich daddies.'

'I don't,' said Eve as she put Milly's tea on the desk.

'How do you get by?' asked Milly.

'I do get a wage.'

'Eve is a very good typist, and we had to pay someone to work for us full time,' said Ada. 'But we are always looking for volunteers who are willing to spend a few hours putting letters in envelopes and making tea. Could we interest you, Milly?'

'I have to work for a wage,' said Milly.

'I understand that. But we would be very grateful if you could come along for just a few hours a week.'

Milly was mulling this over. What harm would it do? It could be interesting. After all, she didn't have to go out and get herself arrested, and she would be helping the cause. Besides, it would be nice to be among these women. 'All right,' she said.

Ada beamed at her. 'Thank you. I knew you would. Thank you.'

Ada proceeded to tell Milly what she would be expected to do, and Milly said that she would come most evenings after work.

'Some evenings we won't be here, as we may have a rally to go to, but we will always tell you.'

'And some evenings I don't work, but when I'm here I'll show you what to do,' said Eve.

'I can stay now if you like,' said Milly. She was fired up with enthusiasm. She liked her new-found friends, and somehow she knew this was going to be far more interesting than the factory.

'Wonderful,' said Ada.

Milly took off her coat and began filling envelopes with the Votes For Women newsletter.

★ ★ ★

Most evenings Milly would make her way to the office, and Rita wasn't always happy about it.

'I don't know why you like going there to work for nothink.'

'I enjoy their company, and besides, it's better than being indoors with my family. I told you, if you want to go out somewhere any evening, you only have to say. After all, I am only a volunteer, and besides, I don't go if they are going on a rally or to a meeting.'

'I know, but you always say that you're doing something special when I've asked.'

'It was only that once.' Milly knew that Rita was sulking. 'Look, why don't we go to the music hall one evening?'

'I'd like that.'

'Well you tell me what night you want to go, all right?'

'Thanks, Milly.'

It wasn't only Rita who was unhappy about Milly being out most evenings and Saturday afternoons.

'I dunno why yer always out,' said Pammy. 'Who's gonna keep this place clean? I ain't got time.'

'I manage to fit it in.'

'Dad reckons yer on the game.'

'He would. I told you, I go and work in an

office for a few hours.'

'But you don't get any money for it, do yer?'

'No. I told you, it's for a good cause.' When Milly started to get home late from work, she told Pammy she was doing evening work. Pammy wanted to know if she would be getting more money and Milly told her no, that people did it for nothing. Pammy thought she was mad, but at least she didn't have to go into any details.

Even old Bill from upstairs wondered where she got to, and one afternoon when she was home, she told him.

'You wanna be careful of that lot. Got nuffink better ter do than worry the government. They should be at home looking after their menfolk.'

Milly didn't reply. These were very intelligent women and this was the sort of attitude they were trying to stop.

When she was in the office and the printing machine wasn't working, it was very quiet, and Milly enjoyed working in such a peaceful atmosphere. As she sat busy folding letters or writing envelopes, she thought about Jane and smiled. She could almost see her friend doing something like this. How Jane would have loved every moment, just as Milly was. Whatever she did, Jane and Richard were never far from her thoughts.

In April, the sinking of the *Titanic* filled the pages of the newspapers.

For days everybody was talking about it, and as Rita and Milly walked home from work one evening, Rita said, 'Me dad was saying that people are waiting outside his office for news of friends and relations. He said when they put the list up outside of survivors and those that died, some of the women's crying was awful.'

'It must be a sad time for so many people. A lot of women are coming into the office crying over lost loved ones. There are some very rich women who had relations on that ship.'

'Well that gives 'em something else to worry about, instead of going round doing all that damage.'

Milly didn't answer.

★　★　★

It was May and a lovely spring evening, Milly was in the back room busy making tea when there was an almighty crash and the glass window was shattered. She ran to the front and could see that blood was pouring from Ada's arm. Pat, another volunteer, rushed outside, but whoever had done it had run off.

'I'll get some bandages,' said Milly. She knew they had a first-aid box; these women had to be ready for anything.

'I'm all right,' said Ada.

'It looks very deep,' said Milly as she tore the sleeve of Ada's blouse away.

Suddenly Ada groaned and slumped in her chair.

Milly looked on in shock. 'Quick, get her some water,' she said to Pat.

Milly began gently tapping Ada's cheek. 'Ada. Ada.' But there wasn't any response. She looked up at Pat. 'What we going to do?'

'Dunno. There's some smelling salts in the cupboard.'

'Could you go for a doctor?'

'Where's the nearest?'

'I don't know. Go next door and ask the butcher.'

'He's closed.'

'Bang on his door till he opens it.'

'He won't like that. He don't like us.'

'I know he doesn't, but this could be a matter of life and death.' As soon as Milly said that, she felt sick. She had been through this sort of thing before, and she could see herself fighting for Jane's life. A crowd had gathered outside the window but nobody came in. 'Please, someone help us,' she called out.

'You lot get all you deserve,' shouted one man.

'You wanna fink about all the winders you've broken.'

'It keeps the glass blokes busy, though, don't it?' yelled a woman with a cackle of a laugh.

'Here comes the coppers now.'

A policeman walked in and looked at the situation. 'I think this lady had better go to the hospital,' he said.

Milly was sitting with Ada, who had come round after the smelling salts had been put under her nose. She assured Milly that she could walk to the bus.

The journey seemed long, and Milly was worried that Ada would pass out on her again. People looked at them but nobody said a word.

At the hospital, a nurse showed them into a small room.

'This is quite deep. I'll have to put some

stitches in it,' said the doctor who was examining Ada's arm. 'I hope you told the policeman how it happened.'

'I'm afraid we don't get a lot of sympathy from the police,' said Milly.

'Well that doesn't surprise me.' He gave her a smile. 'And have you been on any marches, young lady?'

Milly was taken aback. 'No. I'm in the office.'

He smiled again. 'What do you do there?'

'Help with the letters.'

'I see. Now, that should be better,' he said to Ada when he'd finished. 'I'll get the nurse to bandage you up.'

'Thank you,' said Ada.

'Made a bit of a mess of your lovely blouse,' said the nurse as she finished and stood looking at her handiwork.

'It couldn't be helped,' Ada said. She went to stand up, but was a little wobbly.

'Are you sure you'll be all right?' asked the nurse.

'Yes thank you.'

As they went outside, Milly was worried that Ada looked very pale, but she was soon her old self again as they made their way back.

'That doctor was rather nice,' she said Ada.

'I suppose he was. I never noticed,' said Milly.

'At least they've boarded up the window,' said Ada when they got back to the office. 'I hope they didn't give Pat too much trouble, although I think she can handle things.'

'Are you sure you don't want to go home?' asked Milly.

'I'll just stay for a little while to make sure everything's all right.'

Pat was in the back room. 'Thank goodness you're back,' she said when they walked in. 'The police have been here but they said they couldn't do anything about it.'

'I'm not surprised,' said Ada as she sat down. 'They think it's all we deserve.'

'The man who boarded up the window said he'd be here in the morning to put the glass in.'

'Thanks. I think we'd better close for tonight.'

'Will you be all right getting home?' asked Milly.

Ada smiled. 'Yes thank you. I'll be fine.'

As Milly walked home, she thought about the evening. She was certainly seeing life and enjoying working with Ada and Eve. How she would love to work there full time. She would give it a little while, then ask Ada if she could go on the pay roll. It was the sort of job she would really like, and the more she found out about the cause, the more she believed in it. The thought of wearing one of those lovely white frocks and a big white hat really appealed to her. She smiled to herself. That wasn't really the reason to become a suffragette.

Her thoughts went to the doctor and she began daydreaming. It would be so nice to go out with someone like that. After knowing people like the Greens, she enjoyed that sort of company. People who talked nicely and about interesting things. She missed Jane so much. She gave a silent sob. Where would her life be now if that dreadful day had never been?

24

Spring moved on to summer, and Milly was very happy with her evening job, though she wished she could spend more time with Ada, Pat and Eve and the other volunteers who came to help out. Whenever she was told about the visitors to the office — people like the Pankhursts — she felt very left out.

'We have to open these boxes and display and price all this lovely merchandise,' said Ada, bustling around the latest delivery.

'I wish I could work here full time,' said Milly when Ada was telling her about how they were getting more and more literature and goods to sell.

'As a matter of fact I have been in contact with someone and told them we need help, and I think we may be able to give you a full-time post.'

Milly threw her arms round Ada.

'We must wait a while till it goes through all the various channels, but I'm sure it will be fine.'

One evening Milly was walking home from the office deep in thought, when someone behind her said hello.

She turned and was surprised to see the doctor who had attended to Ada's arm. 'Hello,' she said.

'Been on any rallies lately?' he asked as he walked beside her. He was just like a hero in a book. Tall, dark and good-looking.

'No. Like I said, I work in the office.'

'I've just called in there and was told that you had gone.'

'I've just finished.' Milly was surprised at his remark. She wanted to ask him what he was doing round here, but didn't think that would be right. And why was he asking after her?

'I just called in to see the lady who cut her arm.'

'She's fine now.'

'Yes, I could see that. It shouldn't scar.'

'I don't think she'll be worried about that.'

'No, not when you think of what some of these women go through with this force-feeding.'

'It must be awful to have those tubes put up your nose and down your throat,' Milly agreed.

'I do admire you women.' He smiled. 'I have to, as my mother is very sympathetic to your cause.'

Milly looked surprised.

They stopped at the kerb and he took her arm and guided her across the road. Milly knew that under his brown leather gloves he had long, sensitive fingers.

'Where are you going?' he asked.

'Home,' she replied. She wanted to ask him where he was going, but that was being too forward. Instead she asked tentatively, 'Do you follow up all your patients?'

'No. Only those that have a pretty assistant.'

Milly felt herself blushing.

'My name's Tom, by the way. And you are?'

'Milly.'

'Is that short for Millicent?'

She nodded.

'Do you live far from here?'

'A little way away.'

'Could I walk with you?'

This was the last thing Milly wanted. 'Shouldn't you be at the hospital?'

'No, it's my evening off. They do let us get away sometimes. So, may I walk with you?'

Milly stopped. 'I'd rather you didn't.' Although he was tall and very good-looking and she was flattered, she wanted him to go away.

'Oh.' He looked surprised. 'Is there a reason?'

'It's just that my father doesn't like me being at the office and he wouldn't like it if I told him how I came to know you.' Milly was surprising herself with how quickly she had thought up this story.

'Would he have to know?' Tom asked.

Milly couldn't think of an answer, so she remained silent.

'I see. I would like to see you again, Milly. Could I take you out for tea one afternoon? I'm sure Miss Roberts would let you have an hour off.'

'You know Ada's surname?'

'I made a point of finding it out before I came looking for you.'

He had come looking for her. How could she tell him that she worked at the biscuit factory all day?

'Can we walk for a while now?'

Milly smiled.

'You have a lovely smile.'

'And you are very persistent.'

'Yes, I am. Now come on, let's go for a stroll round the park.'

Milly froze. The park was the last place she wanted to go. 'I'd rather have a cup of tea somewhere.'

'Why not?'

Milly found Tom easy to talk to. Over tea he told her that he was an only child and his mother was a widow. She had made sure that he had a good education and then went on to be a doctor.

'Now, you know all about me, what about you?'

'Not a lot to tell. I used to work in a big house and now I don't.'

He grinned and his face lit up. He was very handsome with his dark hair and dark eyes. 'Is that it?'

'Yes.'

'Where did you work? My mother might know of the people.'

Milly looked at him. For months she had kept her past hidden and she wasn't about to tell someone she had only known for a short while. 'They moved abroad. Besides, what do you want to know all about me for?'

'Just curious. And now you work at the suffragettes' office?'

Milly didn't answer. Although she was flattered and enjoyed being with this handsome young man, she wanted to get away from him and his questions as soon as possible. 'Look, I must go.' She stood up.

He jumped to his feet. 'Milly, please let me take you out.'

Milly looked about her. 'Please. People are looking.'

'I'm sorry, I don't wish to embarrass you.'

He followed her outside.

'Just say you'll come out next week. I can call for you at the office about seven on Thursday, that's my evening off.'

'I don't know.'

He smiled. 'I can see I'm beginning to wear you down. Now please say yes.'

'All right. Seven next Thursday.'

He quickly kissed her cheek and went off in the opposite direction.

Milly stood for a while watching him as he walked away. She touched her cheek. She had never met anyone like Tom before and she rather liked the idea of going out with him, but what if he learned about her background? She knew she was being silly, as this acquaintance would never come to anything.

★　★　★

On Thursday Milly made sure she had her best frock on when she went to work that morning.

'You look all dolled up. Where you off to?' asked Rita when they met up as they left the factory.

'I'm going to see someone.'

Rita laughed. 'I bet he ain't tall, dark and handsome.'

Milly laughed too. 'I wish.' She didn't have any intention of telling Rita about Tom.

'Where you going then?'

217

'A meeting.'

'I might have guessed. You wanna be careful you don't get caught up in one of their rallies and find yerself chained to the railings.'

'Not everybody wants to be chained to railings. Besides, I always stay well back and don't voice my opinions.' Although Milly liked Rita, she would be glad when she worked at the office full time.

As soon as she got to the office she told Ada she wouldn't be stopping this evening and the reason why.

'So you're going to go out with Dr Walsh,' said Ada.

'Is that his name?' asked Milly. 'Do you mind?'

'Of course not, my dear. He seems a very nice young man, and you say his mother has sympathy for us?'

Milly nodded.

'You just go and enjoy yourself.'

'He's meeting me here at seven.'

At eight o'clock Milly was still waiting. She had busied herself while she waited, and was making the tea when Pat came into the kitchen.

'I reckon he's been busy and can't get away,' said Pat.

'He said it was his night off.'

'I know, love, but doctors can't always do what they want to.'

Milly was disappointed. For the first time since Jane died she was just beginning to enjoy life, and the thought of going out with someone as clever and nice as Tom had thrilled her. Whenever she thought about Jane, she remembered Richard. She often looked at the lovely

218

bracelet he'd given her. She had loved him in her own way, but that was all in the past now. She knew that going out with men like Tom and Richard wasn't for the likes of her.

* * *

It wasn't till the following week that Tom found Milly at the office. Ada had told her that he had been to see her earlier in the week but she had been out with Rita.

'Milly. I'm so pleased to see you. I'm so sorry that I couldn't make it last week. We had a terrible rush on and I was called back in. Ada told me that you only come here some evenings.' It was all said in a rush.

'That's all right.'

'Look, could we go somewhere and talk?'

Milly looked at Ada.

'Go on, be off with you.'

Milly smiled. 'Thanks.'

Once again they were sitting in a café.

'So do you work during the day?'

Milly nodded.

'And where's that?'

'You know, you are very nosy.'

'It's just that you're a very pretty girl and you intrigue me.'

Milly laughed. 'What, me?'

'Yes. And I would like to know more about you.'

'I bet you say that to all your nurses.'

'No. Milly, could I take you out?'

'No.'

'Why?'

'I have my reasons.'

'Do you have a young man?'

'In a way.'

'I see. I'm very sorry to force myself on to you.'

Milly didn't reply. She didn't want to let him go, but she knew she had to. He wasn't for the likes of her. 'I'm sorry.'

'No, it should be me apologising.'

Milly stood up. 'I must go.'

Tom quickly jumped to his feet. 'Please, Milly, forgive me.'

'There's nothing to forgive.' She left the restaurant without looking back. She had tears in her eyes. Tom was a lovely person but she knew that it wasn't to be. Their lives were worlds apart.

25

All through the summer the suffragettes continued to make themselves seen and heard.

Milly was thrilled when the week after her birthday in November she was asked to work at the office full time.

She hugged Ada. 'This is the best birthday present I could have.'

Ada laughed. 'Well I've watched you over these past months and seen how willing you are and knew that you should be here full time.'

Milly knew that Rita wouldn't be that happy about it, but she had to move on. The family didn't appear to be worried; they were only concerned about money. When Milly was told she would be getting ten shillings a week she was excited, and the thought that came quickly into her head was that now she might even begin to think about moving out.

As she knew how the office was run, she had no problem in being there all day and for most of the evening.

'You know you don't have to stay every evening,' said Ada.

'I know, but I haven't got a lot to rush home for.'

Although Milly hadn't said too much about her home life, Ada had guessed she wasn't that happy.

One morning as Milly was getting ready to go to work, there had been an argument over the fact that she was wearing a new frock.

'Where's that come from?' asked Pammy.

'I bought it. I needed a new one.'

'What about us lot? Yer don't think about us, do yer?'

'Pammy, I give you nearly all my wages. If Dad got himself a proper job, that would help.'

'Yer know he can't work cos of his leg.'

'Yes. I've heard all that before.' Milly went to walk away, but Pammy grabbed her arm.

'We need yer money.'

'I know, now let go.'

Milly was angry as she walked to work. Why did they have to rely on her? How would they manage if she hadn't come back?

* * *

Once again Christmas was approaching, and Milly was wandering round the market. She was worried because Ada had said she was getting presents for Eve and Pat. Did that mean that she would have to get Ada something really nice? Once again her thoughts went to the past and things she had bought Jane and Betty. She remembered that Jane had been really thrilled with the scarf. So perhaps it could be a scarf for Ada and hankies for Eve and Pat.

There was a commotion a bit further along the market that made her look up, and to her horror she saw Bertie being dragged off by a policeman. Milly froze. Bertie was screaming that he hadn't done anything. Should she go and interfere? Should she pay for whatever he'd pinched? She quickly went behind a stall, out of sight. She still had the fear that the police could be looking for her.

She spent a while ambling round, taking in the sight and smells, and when she finished shopping she went home.

When she walked into the kitchen, Pammy was looking anxious and pacing the floor with Freddie thrown over her shoulder. She looked so pathetic that Milly felt sorry for her. What sort of life was this for a young girl? 'Everything all right?' she asked.

'No it bloody well ain't.'

'Why, what's wrong now?'

'Bert's gone and got 'imself locked up. Got caught pinching.'

'I knew he would one day. Where is he?'

'At the police station. 'E's gotta pay a ten-bob fine.'

'What?'

'You 'eard.'

'Who told you that?'

'Dad. The coppers come 'ere for 'im.'

'What happens if he doesn't pay?'

''E goes ter clink.'

'But he's only a child,'

'Don't make a bit of difference to the beak.'

Milly was trying to think. Bertie had only just been arrested. 'When did he do this?'

'A couple of weeks ago. The coppers 'ave been looking for 'im, and terday they caught 'im pinching again. The judge always sits on a Sat'day afternoon, cos a lot of villains get caught on Sat'days.'

'I see. How are we going to pay to get him back?'

'Dunno. Could spend the rest of 'is days locked up.'

'I can't see that happening.'

'Well 'ow's 'e gonna git the money? Mind you, you might 'ave it if yer didn't spend it on fancy clothes.'

Milly ignored that remark. She wasn't going to start arguing with her sister.

That night as she lay on her mattress she thought about Bert. He was only a child, despite his cocky ways. She knew she had to help, but a whole week's wages . . . it would take her weeks to save that, and how would he fare in prison for all that time? She had heard of some of the terrible things they did to the suffragettes. And how would she feel if he was in prison over Christmas? Although Christmas didn't mean much in this household, she still didn't want Bert to be away. Should she ask Ada for a loan? No, that would mean telling her about her family, and she didn't want anyone to know too much about her past.

She took her bracelet from her bag and looked at it fondly. She loved it so much; it reminded her of Richard. If only things had worked out differently. She loved him and would never forget him, but she had to be practical. This was something she'd been hoping to keep for ever, but it was only an object, and she knew then she had to pawn her prize possession and get her young brother back with his family.

On Monday morning Milly went in to the pawnbroker's. Most mornings she passed women trundling along pushing old prams that had seen better days. Babies sat on top of bundles of old clothes and bedding as they made their way to the shop with the three brass balls hanging from the wall. Looking through the glass door, Milly could see that the place was full of women pawning their husbands' suits and blankets. They were standing around chatting to one another. It was clear that this was a weekly jaunt and they all knew each other. When she pushed open the door and the bell above began ringing its dull sound, the women all stopped talking and looked at her.

'Come in, love,' said the fat man behind the counter.

Milly hesitated. She didn't want these women to know her business.

'Don't mind this lot, it's a weekly outing fer 'em.'

The women parted and Milly slowly made her way to the counter.

'Now, what can I do fer yer?'

Milly looked around.

'Don't be shy, love,' said a toothless old lady behind her. 'We know what it's like ter fall on 'ard times.'

'I'll come back tomorrow when you're not so busy.' Milly turned and started to walk away.

'Prices will be lower termorrer,' said the man.

She stopped. What should she do? She didn't

want all these women to see her lovely bracelet, but she had to think about Bert stuck in prison. 'Is there a room where I can talk to you in private?'

'Oooh, 'ark at 'er. Private indeed. 'Ere, Will, can we all see yer in private?'

'Mind yer, if we did, we might get more than a few bob fer our old man's suit,' said another.

Loud cackling laughter filled the shop.

Milly wanted to die. She'd kill Bert when she got hold of him, making her feel so humiliated.

The fat man grinned. 'Come on through ter the back. Maudie,' he yelled out, 'come and keep yer eye on this lot.'

A thin woman with her grey hair scragged back from her pale face came from the back room. She was dressed completely in black, and Milly was fascinated by the lacy black gloves she was wearing. She tugged at them and then cuffed her nose.

'And don't you lot pinch anyfink while I'm gorn,' said the man. 'Come on, love, this way.'

Reluctantly Milly followed him to a room behind the counter.

'Right, sit yerself down and show me what yer got.'

Milly took the bracelet from her handbag and handed it to him.

He took a small black eyeglass from his gaudy waistcoat pocket, and after putting in to his eye gave out a whistle. 'I don't take any knocked-orf goods. Got me reputation and the cops ter worry about.'

'It wasn't stolen, it was given to me.'

226

He grinned. 'Fer services rendered, I suppose?'

He could think what he liked; Milly wasn't going to go into details. 'What will you give me for it?'

'It's 'all marked, but I'd 'ave a job selling it if yer didn't redeem it. Not a lot of call fer lovely gold bracelets like this round here.'

Milly put out her hand to take it back, but he pulled away out of reach.

'Didn't say I wouldn't take it, though, did I?'

Milly knew he was playing with her, but what could she do? 'Just tell me how much.'

He took the eyeglass from his eye and looked at her. 'How much yer in trouble for?'

'I'm not in trouble.'

He sat back. 'Don't give me that.'

'It's my young brother.'

'I've 'eard all the excuses, love.'

'The money is for my young brother, he's the one in trouble.' Milly was beginning to get angry. 'If you're not going to give me what I want, then I shall go elsewhere.'

'How much do you want?'

Milly hesitated. 'A pound.'

'A pound? This ain't a charity, yer know.'

'Well in that case . . . ' She held out her hand.

'I'll give yer ten bob.'

'I'll take it.' She felt pleased with herself. This was just the amount she wanted.

'I fink I've just done meself.'

'If I can raise the money, I'll be back for it.'

'I've 'eard that before.'

Back in the shop, the fat man went to a drawer

under the counter and took out a ten-shilling note.

'Look at that,' said a customer. 'What she 'ave ter do ter git that, then?'

The fat man grinned and touched the side of his nose.

Milly wanted to smack his face, but she knew that wouldn't do any good, so she grabbed her money and stalked out.

★　★　★

As she walked to the office, she wondered how she was going to get the money to the police station. She didn't want to go there herself, but could she trust Pammy to deliver it? What option did she have?

'Sorry I'm late,' she said, taking off her hat. 'We had a bit of trouble at home.'

'I'm sorry to hear that,' said Ada. 'You know you don't have to stay if someone is ill.'

Milly smiled. 'No. It's nothing like that.' She wasn't going to elaborate.

'There's a batch of letters to be stamped and posted. Could you do that this morning?'

'Yes, of course.' Milly knew that that was the answer. She would post the money.

★　★　★

The following evening she had to look surprised when she walked into the kitchen to hear Bert telling everybody how someone had sent the money to pay for the goods he'd stolen.

228

'You must have a secret benefactor somewhere,' said Milly.

'Don't know wot that means, but fank Gord for 'im. Didn't like it in clink.'

'Now you might think twice about going round stealing.'

'He will fer a little while,' said Pammy. She looked at Milly. 'I wonder who sent the money.'

Milly shrugged. She certainly wasn't going to tell them.

26

In 1913 the suffragettes were truly making themselves heard. There had been many incidents and
arrests, but it was in June that they received the
greatest amount of publicity.

One afternoon Ada came rushing into the
office with tears running down her face.

Milly jumped up to comfort her. 'What is it?
What's happened? Eve, get Ada a glass of water.'

They sat Ada down and waited for the sobs to
subside.

'You remember the Epsom Derby, when Emily
Davison threw herself under the King's horse.'

There was a quick intake of breath from all
who were present.

'Yes. Why?' asked Eve.

'We believe she wanted to stop the horse. It
was a protest that went horribly wrong, and she
was taken to the hospital. I've just heard it was
too late.'

Milly sat at her desk. She suddenly felt she
should do more. Like everybody else she was
aware of the imprisonment and the hunger
strikes, but this was the first time someone had
actually died for the cause.

★　★　★

The papers were full of the death of Emily
Davison. It was the talk of the streets. On the day

of the funeral many ordinary people stood at the roadside to watch the cortege pass by and say their last goodbyes. The office had been draped in black, and although it was a very sombre affair, for Milly like countless others, the funeral was the grandest thing she had ever attended. To walk with the women and to hear the sound of the muffled drums brought tears to her eyes. The women who lined the route were crying, and even the men with bowed heads were silent. It was very emotional.

'We must get the vote now,' Ada said. 'Surely this has to be the supreme sacrifice.'

★　★　★

Towards the end of the year Milly's life took another turn. Last week had been her nineteenth birthday. Now she was well into the movement and had been on a few marches but always managed to stay out of trouble. At the rallies she was thrilled by speeches by the Pankhursts and other women, and admired their passion and dedication.

The so-called cat-and-mouse game was also in the news. When the women in prison became ill through being on hunger strike, they were given a temporary discharge and sent home to recover then arrested again. It was all very sad.

'Milly,' said Ada one morning as soon as she arrived at the office.

Milly, who was busy writing at her desk, looked up. She was always worried when Ada used that tone of voice. Had she done something wrong?

'Don't look so apprehensive.' Ada seemed excited and quickly removed her hat and coat. 'As you know, we have a tenant in the two rooms upstairs, who is leaving soon. Now, I know you are not very happy at home, and I was wondering if you would like to move into the upstairs rooms.'

Milly sat with her mouth open.

'You don't have to answer me now. Think about it and let me know.'

'What about the rent? I don't think I could afford it.'

'We have thought about that, and we, that is the movement, were wondering if you wouldn't mind sharing.'

Milly was still in shock. 'No. No, I don't mind. Who did you have in mind?'

'There's a young lady about your age whose father as we know has made her homeless. She is from a very good family; her mother died a while back and she was a member, so we were wondering if that would be all right with you.'

'Yes, that would be fine. When do I get to meet her?'

'This afternoon.'

'When are the people upstairs leaving?'

'This weekend. Now, I must get on.'

Milly sat looking at her desk. She wanted to dance round the room. She couldn't believe that she had been given another chance to better herself. She thought about her family. What would they do without her? She knew it was selfish, but she had to take the moment. Her mind was churning over and over. They didn't know where she was working; they had never been interested just as long as she brought in the money. She wouldn't give them her address but she would send them money now and again.

As usual when anything good was offered to Milly, her thoughts always went to Jane. If she hadn't taken me off the streets and educated me, where would I be now? She knew she would never forget her friend and would be grateful to her for the rest of her life.

★   ★   ★

It was late in the afternoon when Elizabeth Phillips walked into the office. She was a small, thin girl with large blue eyes and mousy-coloured wavy hair that peeped out from under her lovely fur hat. She glanced quickly round the room and smiled at Milly. 'Hello, I'm Lizzie Phillips.'

Milly jumped up and held out her hand. 'I'm Milly Ash.'

'Are you the one I'm going share these rooms with?'

Milly nodded. 'Please take a seat.'

Ada came over smiling. 'I'm going to leave you two to have a chat. Lizzie, would you like a cup of tea?'

'Yes please.'

Milly suddenly felt very shy and scruffy, even though she always wore a nice skirt and blouse for work. Lizzie, who was wearing a beautiful brown coat, sat down and placed her brown leather handbag on her lap and removed her matching leather gloves. Milly could see that everything about her was expensive.

'I hope you don't mind me sharing with you, but you see, my father doesn't approve of women getting the vote. He's in government, so it means he has to be against us, even though secretly he's quite supportive really. I'm not a very active member, it's just that Mother was and I feel that in part I should try to keep up her work.'

Milly sat listening to the lovely way Lizzie spoke. 'No. No, I don't mind. In fact I shall rather like it. I've never lived on my own before.'

Lizzie giggled. 'Neither have I. I'm sure we shall muddle along together.'

Milly smiled. Somehow she knew she was going to like Lizzie and enjoy this new life.

* * *

On Saturday, once the tenants had moved out, Milly and Lizzie went upstairs to check out the rooms. They were like a couple of children laughing and giggling at their newfound freedom.

There was a bedroom, a dining-cum-sitting room, a very small kitchen and a toilet.

'Thank goodness for that,' said Lizzie as she opened the door that led to the toilet. 'I couldn't face having to go to that one in the yard.

'We must get some new furniture,' she continued. 'Tomorrow we can make a list. Can you come here tomorrow?'

'Yes.'

'Good. Look at the state of that fireplace. I'm

not very good at cleaning, are you?'

'I'm good at cleaning, but Lizzie, I can't afford to buy any furniture.'

'Don't worry about that,' she said dismissively, waving her hand. 'I expect my father will help; besides, I get a very generous allowance and we can go shopping together.'

Milly couldn't believe her luck. In some ways Lizzie was a bit like Jane, always with a ready smile and full of life. This was going to be a new start, and Milly was very happy with that.

★　★　★

Milly had a job to keep her excitement to herself when she arrived home that evening.

'Where is everybody?' she asked Pammy as she took off her coat and hat.

'All out scrounging. Why?'

'Nothing. I've got us some beef for tomorrow, so we can have a nice roast dinner.'

'Cor, you come inter a fortune then?' asked Pammy, who was sitting at the table feeding Freddie.

'No. I was lucky, the butcher was just closing up and was selling his meat off cheap.'

'I dunno what we'd do without yer now, Mil,' said Pammy, smiling. 'I can't believe how good you are to us. And it was you what paid Bert's fine, wasn't it? Where did yer git that sort a money from? I know yer wouldn't pinch it; did yer borrow it?'

Milly swallowed hard and just smiled. They could think what they liked. Her big worry now was that in a week or two she would have to tell them she was leaving again.

'So, where d'yer work now? It must be a nice clean place, as yer always look really nice when yer goes orf.'

She quickly changed the subject. 'Pammy, I know it's none of my business, but I do wish you wouldn't sleep with Dad.'

'Don't start on that again.'

'I'm worried at what he does to you.'

'He don't do nuffink.'

'Now that you're thirteen, you'll be starting your monthlies soon.'

'I told yer before, he just cuddles me, that's all. He don't do what uvver blokes do.'

'Why don't you go and sleep in with the others?'

'I told yer. I like being wiv Dad and in a proper bed. Don't keep on about it.'

Milly sat down. She had been over and over this conversation with her sister many times. She knew it was useless trying to make Pammy see the danger, but the poor girl wanted some love in her sad life and didn't care who gave it. But what if she became pregnant? How would they manage then?

* * *

'I might be late back this morning,' said Milly on Sunday as she adjusted her hat in front of the mirror. 'I've done the potatoes and the veg, and Pammy, can you put the meat in the oven about ten?'

236

'You wanna tell that vicar bloke not ter keep yer, we want our dinner,' said Bert.

Milly didn't answer, and left without telling them that she wasn't going to church. She was meeting Lizzie at the flat.

When she arrived, she was surprised to find Lizzie already going round making a list.

'Now, we need two beds and a dressing table. We can hang our clothes behind the door for now, and we can put a lot of things in that big cupboard next to the fireplace.'

Milly was impressed with her efficiency as she followed her around.

'In this room we need a sofa and a table, it can't be very big, and we shall have to have two dining chairs. Then there's cutlery, curtains, china and bedding, of course. Can you think of anything else?'

Milly was dumbfounded. 'I can go to the market and see what I can pick up on the second-hand stalls.'

Lizzie looked shocked. 'I don't want second-hand.'

'But Lizzie, we can't afford all that.'

'We can't, but my father can. He's lovely and I know you'll like him.'

Milly still couldn't believe her luck. How could she be given two chances in her life? What had she done to deserve this? She still had this fear that she would have to pay again with some terrible consequence for any happiness that came her way.

27

Milly and Lizzie decided they would wait till after Christmas to move into their new home.

'That will give us time to get together the last few things we need,' said Lizzie, bubbling with enthusiasm.

One morning, only a few days after they had looked at the flat, Milly was surprised when furniture and various other goods arrived for upstairs.

When Lizzie came in, she told Milly that most of the furniture had come from her house. 'I hope you don't mind?'

Milly was speechless as she admired the quality. She was beginning to get really excited about the move. Never in her wildest dreams had she even begun to think that once again she would be sleeping in a bed and sitting on expensive furniture, and she couldn't wait for the big day.

On the Saturday morning before Christmas, Ada said they could go upstairs and hang the curtains that had arrived.

'That way the place will look as if people have moved in.' After the shop had had its window broken, she was always concerned about reprisals.

'These are so lovely,' said Milly as she arranged the beautiful rust-coloured brocade curtains. She stood back to admire her work. 'They're a bit long, but I can soon sort that out when we've moved in.'

'You are so clever. Now, as I don't know what else you need in the kitchen, could you get what you want?' Lizzie handed her a five-pound note. 'After all, you're the one who will be doing the cooking and the like.'

Milly gasped. She had never even seen a five-pound note before. From the beginning she had told Lizzie that she was more than happy to do the cooking and cleaning, while Lizzie had insisted on paying the lion's share of the rent. 'You have been more than generous. There are just a few things I shall want, and I certainly won't need all this.' She held out the money.

'No, please take it,' Lizzie said. 'So, what are you doing for Christmas?'

'I shall be with my family,' replied Milly.

'I was going to ask you if you would like to spend it with us. Father said he'd love to meet you.'

'That's very kind of you, but . . . '

'I can understand.'

Milly wasn't really sure about Lizzie's background — she knew she worked for her father but had decided to move away because of his strong views on women's suffrage. She'd told Milly that she didn't want her father to lose his position because of her. Milly noted that she was very cagey about what she said.

* * *

Later that afternoon Milly was busy at the market buying goods for the kitchen. The place was buzzing as usual and she always loved the happy atmosphere among the people who had nothing but who could still enjoy a laugh and a joke with the stallholders.

She wasn't surprised to see her brother hanging around, and when he spotted her, he came marching up. 'Cor, Mil. Is all that stuff fer us?'

'No. It's for someone I work with.'

'Couldn't yer pinch a bit? They wouldn't know what yer got.'

'I could do no such thing. These people trust me.'

'D'yer know, yer a silly cow at times.'

'Thanks.'

Milly took the stuff back to the flat. As she began hurrying home, the fog started to slowly descend, enveloping everything like a thick yellow blanket. How long would this one last? she wondered. Some fogs could last for days, and that would mean her father wouldn't be able to get any casual work. The thought of him being in the house for all that time caused her to shudder.

When she got home, her father was sitting in his chair. He put his newspaper on the floor.

'Wot's this I hear about yer buying stuff fer some nobs?'

Milly slowly took off her hat. 'Yes, that's right.' Bert certainly hadn't wasted any time in getting home and telling their father.

'So where is it then?'

'In their flat, I expect.'

'Bert reckons yer should 'ave given us some of it; they wouldn't miss it, not if they've sent you out ter do their shopping. Who d'yer work for anyway?'

'It's a office that sends out letters.' That was all Milly could think of to say.

He went back to his paper.

'Where's Pammy?' she asked.

'In the bog,' came the reply.

After a while Pammy came into the kitchen. She looked terrible.

'Whatever's wrong?' asked Milly.

'I don't feel very well.'

'Sit down, I'll make a cup of tea.'

In the scullery, Milly wondered what was wrong with her sister. Only one thing was filling her mind. But that couldn't happen, could it?

★ ★ ★

All over Christmas Pammy was very sick. Milly was left to clean up after her and look after Freddie. Rosie said she didn't like Pammy so she wasn't going to help. Neither Bert nor Iris would put themselves out to lend a hand, and Milly was at her wits' end running around after Pammy and trying to comfort Freddie.

'Please, Rosie, help me,' pleaded Milly as she once again emptied the bucket Pammy had been sick in.

'Why should I? You never take me out.'

This upset Milly. How could Rosie be so offhand? 'Is that why you were nice to me when I came back. You thought I'd take you out?'

'Yer.' She went back to sorting her buttons. ''Sides, Pammy went an' pawned me nice coat and shoes. That's why I don't like 'er, and you didn't get 'em back, did yer?'

241

Milly couldn't answer that. She had been aware the coat was missing. She had asked where it had gone and Pammy had told her that she had pawned it. She'd also said that if Milly redeemed it, it would go back again. So Milly gave up.

Christmas was a sad, miserable time. The fog persisted and everywhere was dark and dreary. The only thing Milly had to look forward to was going back to work on Saturday. But when that day came, she couldn't leave Pammy.

'Look, I should be at work. One of you will have to take Freddie out while I do the washing.' Milly was beside herself.

'Yer seem ter be coping all right,' said her father, sitting back in his chair, rolling a cigarette.

'I am not coping. And what is wrong with Pammy? Don't you care?

'She'll be all right.'

'Well I think you should get a doctor.'

'What? And whose gonna pay fer that?'

Milly put on her coat and picked up her handbag. 'I won't be long.'

'Where yer going?' asked her father.

'To get a doctor.'

He stood up and barred her way. 'I told yer, we don't need no doctor.'

'Why not? Are you frightened of what he's going to say?'

'No. Why should I be?'

'Because I think she's going to have a baby, and if she is, then it's yours and you should be ashamed of yourself.'

242

He sat down again and began laughing. 'Is that wot yer fink?'

'Yes.' With that she left the room.

Thankfully the fog had lifted a little, and as she hurried along the road she wondered if she was right. If Pammy was expecting, how would they manage? Why did this have to happen now?

★　★　★

The doctor came and examined Pammy. Milly picked up her bag, as she knew she had to pay him. Outside she asked, 'Is she expecting?'

'No, my dear, she's not. It must have been something she ate. Why did you think she was pregnant?'

'It was like when Mum was going to have a baby.'

'I thought at first she might have been, but she said she doesn't have a boyfriend.'

'It doesn't have to be a boy, does it?'

'What are you saying?'

'She sleeps with my father.'

'She did tell me. I think it's very unhealthy, but he assured me that he would never touch her in that way.'

'And you believe him?' Milly was getting angry.

'Only time will tell, my dear. Now that will be four shillings, please.'

'Four shillings! It only used to be three and six.'

He held out his hand. 'It is Christmas, and a Saturday. You should have taken her to the free hospital if you wanted charity. Good day.'

Fuming, Milly went inside.

'So how much did he sting yer for?' asked her father grinning.

'What do you care?'

'Anyway, wot's wrong wiv 'er?'

'He reckons it's something she's eaten.'

'Could be.' He lay back grinning.

Milly wanted to throw something at him but knew that wouldn't help, and took her anger out on the washing instead, scrubbing it up and down the washboard.

★　★　★

It was two days before she could get away. Pammy was feeling a little better, and although she pleaded with Milly not to leave her, Milly had to go to work to see Lizzie and explain.

'Don't worry about it,' said Lizzie in her usual cheerful way. 'I wasn't here anyway; I didn't go out at all, not in that fog. It was a real peasouper. Daddy was supposed to be taking me to a ball, but we had to stay at home. I can tell you, it was all very boring.'

'That's good. Not that you were bored,' said Milly quickly. 'It's just that I had visions of you walking around the flat with your coat on.'

'No. Anyway, how is your sister?'

'She's a lot better now. The doctor thinks she may have eaten something.'

'Well, all the rich food over Christmas can play havoc with your insides.'

Milly smiled at that. Rich food was something

her family had never known.

'When shall we move in?' asked Lizzie.

'Whenever it suits you.'

'Shall we wait till the weather gets better?'

'If you want.' Milly was disappointed at that.

'You could move in before that if you want.'

'No.' Milly smiled. 'I'll wait till you're ready to move in too.' It was a good thing she hadn't mentioned it to her family. Did Lizzie really want to move out of her grand house?

28

At the beginning of 1914, Milly and Lizzie decided that they would move into the flat in the spring.

'It'll be better when the weather's a little warmer,' said Lizzie.

Milly knew that Lizzie didn't really want to leave her comfortable lifestyle. She didn't blame her — after all, Lizzie had everything she needed at home — but she did wish she could move in. However, she had promised Lizzie she would wait and they would start afresh together. There was still a lot about the girl that Milly didn't understand. As the weeks passed, Pammy said she was feeling a lot better, but Milly continued to eye her suspiciously.

At last spring began to show itself and the time had come. Tomorrow, Saturday, Milly was moving out, and now she had to tell her family. As she walked home, her thoughts were everywhere. Was she being fair to the family? After all, they relied on her money, but she would send them some now and again. Many times since she'd come back home she'd asked Pammy to show her where her mother was buried, but Pammy always claimed to have forgotten. Milly had just wanted to be near her mother, to talk to her, but instead she'd sit quietly in the scullery and silently ask her for her help.

After they had finished their meal, Milly got up, cleared the table and did the washing-up as usual. Then, wiping her hands on the bottom of her pinny, she went back into the kitchen. She was very nervous. Should she tell them, or just go and leave a note?

Bert was sitting at the table making a paper boat. Iris was playing on the floor. Freddie was in bed and Rosie was as usual sorting out her buttons. 'Where's Pammy?' asked Milly.

'In bed,' said her father. 'She's gone fer a lay-down. Why?'

'Iris, could you go and get her?'

'Leave the poor cow be. She's been up half the night with that little sod. Dunno what's wrong wiv 'im. I told her we should chuck 'im in with the others.'

'We don't want 'im in wiv us. He stinks,' said Bert.

'If I say he's going in wiv yer, then 'e is, savvy?' Their father glared at Bert.

'I'll go and see Pammy,' said Milly.

In the darkened room she could make out her sister's back. Pammy was curled up like a small child. Milly sat on the side of the bed and remembered the last time she'd sat here, comforting her mother when Helen had died. That was a lifetime ago.

'Pammy?'

'Go away.'

'What's wrong with you?'

'I dunno.'

'Please turn over.'

'Why?

'I've got something to tell you.'

'You can tell it to me back.'

'No I can't.'

Slowly Pammy turned over. 'Well?'

'I won't be coming back here tomorrow. I'm moving in with a friend.'

Pammy burst into tears. 'I knew you'd go away one day.'

'I didn't intend to stay this long, but, well, it just happened.'

'Will you be far away?' she said pathetically.

'A fair way.'

'What we gonna do wivout yer?'

'You'll be fine. I'll send money when I can.'

'Does Dad know?'

'Not yet. Not that he cares.'

'He does.'

'He's only interested in the money I bring in.'

Pammy turned over again and Milly left the room. Although she was full of guilt, she couldn't let this opportunity pass her by. She wanted to get away. She should never have come back.

'Well?' asked her father. 'She coming out?'

'No.'

'What did yer want her for?'

Milly's courage left her. She looked round the room. How could she leave them? 'It wasn't important,' she said softly.

'I'll 'ave me cuppa now,' said her father.

In the scullery she put the kettle on the stove, then sat on the upturned box that was always there. 'Mum, what should I do?' she whispered. She desperately wanted to get away. She remembered the last time she'd left home. If only Billy and Dan were here. She missed them so much. Would she ever see them again? She wanted to talk to someone, but who? Could she leave now? What if something happened to Pammy, how would the children cope? People had died because of her. Was she cursed? The kettle's lid bobbed up and down. She wiped her eyes on the bottom of her pinny and set to and made the tea. She would wait and see what happened tomorrow.

★ ★ ★

The next morning Milly was getting ready for work when her father stormed into the kitchen.

'What's all this about?'

'What?' asked Milly, trying to act innocent.

'Pammy said yer leaving.'

'I might be. Pammy still in bed?'

'Yer fink yer very clever, don't yer? Well this is yer family, and families should stick tergevver and look after each other.'

Milly laughed. 'The way you looked after me, you mean? I remember the hidings you used to give me.'

'And yer ain't too big and mighty fer me ter give yer another.'

'What for?'

'Leaving us in the lurch.'

'You should try and do more for your family. I can't stay here for ever.'

'Yer will if I give yer a thrashing yer won't fergit.'

She ignored the threat. 'I'm going to work.'

Her father went to stand in her way, but she was quicker than him. She picked up her bag, then stopped at the open door.

'D'you know, I had second thoughts about leaving today, but what you have just said has made up my mind. You are a bully and a wastrel and you deserve all you get. It's the kids I feel sorry for. They'd be better off in a home.' She watched her father's face turn almost purple with rage and hastily left the room. As she hurried down the passage and out of the house, she could still hear him yelling. She was shaking as she walked to the bus. She had really done it now. There was no way she could ever go back.

* * *

Milly had calmed down by the time she reached the office. When she walked in, she couldn't believe the lovely vase of flowers that stood in the middle of her desk. 'Who bought these?' she asked Eve.

'Ada.'

'They are so lovely.'

'They're for you and Lizzie, to welcome you to your new home. You can take them upstairs when we close.'

Milly swallowed back a sob. Nobody had ever bought her flowers before in the whole of her life.

That evening, after they had finished their meal, Lizzie said, 'That was really nice. I had no idea you were so clever.'

250

'Thank you.'

'I'm useless at almost everything. I can dance and hold a conversation, but I think that's as far as I go.'

'I'm sure you must have some hidden talent.'

'I don't think so.'

When Lizzie picked up a book and settled herself on the sofa with her feet on a stool, Milly knew that she would be doing the washing-up alone.

* * *

At the beginning of May there was great excitement at the office. The women were being urged to attend a rally at Buckingham Palace to present a petition to the King. Ada was busy organising everyone, making sure they knew where to meet up. Lizzie was thrilled at the idea of them all marching together, but Milly was more cautious. Even after all this time she was always worried about getting arrested.

That morning as they went on their way, they met up with other groups and they all held their banners proudly up high as their numbers increased. Although Milly was very nervous, she was also exhilarated. This was wonderful, being with all these women marching together for one cause. She didn't think the King would come out and greet them, but he would know they were outside his home.

At the palace gates, the police were out in force to meet them. As the women drew nearer, the police began to move slowly forward. Some were on horseback, with their truncheons drawn. The horses looked restless, large and menacing. Lizzie had linked arms with Milly and was forging ahead. The foot police with their batons raised moved forward to meet the women. There was some screaming and yelling, and several of the women began to fight back as batons came down. Milly could see marchers wielding umbrellas and bats as well as other weapons. Women were falling all around her. There was a lot of noise and shouting. She tried to hang back, but Lizzie was dragging her forward.

A policeman's baton hit Lizzie on the side of the head and she fell to the ground. Her hat was askew, but was still held firm by her hatpins. Milly screamed and tried to pull her away as the crowd surged forward. She was terrified of the horse's hooves as they pounded the ground. Lizzie was unconscious and her head was bleeding. As Milly knelt over her, someone trod on her hand and another woman fell over them. With a great deal of effort, Milly managed to get to her feet and drag Lizzie further along the road, out of the way of the horses and the crowd. Lizzie lay in the gutter and Milly sat on the kerb. They must have looked a sorry pair, dirty and crumpled, but at least they were safe for the moment. Further along the road Milly could see women being thrown into the back of a Black Maria. Lizzie began to groan.

'My head. What happened?'

'You've been hit.'

Lizzie felt her head and looked at her gloved

hand. 'Look. Look, I'm bleeding.'

'Yes, I know. And if I hadn't dragged you away, you might have been trampled.'

'Help me up. I can't stay here in this filthy gutter.'

A policeman came and stood over them. 'Are you with that lot?' He pointed his baton at the crowd of milling women.

'Yes,' said Lizzie defiantly.

'Well you ought to get yourself along to the hospital with that cut.'

'Why? Are you afraid I might show the press and complain about police brutality?'

'No. It's just that it needs looking at, that's all.' With that he walked away.

'I agree with him,' said Milly. 'It does look rather deep.'

With blood slowly running down her face, Lizzie tried to stand up, but slumped to the ground again. 'I feel dizzy.'

'Just sit here for a while.'

'I'm cold.'

Milly looked about her, bewildered. What could she do? 'Look, if I help you, do you think you could stand?'

'I don't know.'

Milly was filled with fear. Lizzie's face was deathly white and the side of her head was covered with blood; the skin around the gash was slowly turning back and blue. 'Come on, hold on to me. I'll try and find us one of these new taxi cabs and get you to the hospital.'

Slowly she got Lizzie to her feet and they staggered away from the noisy crowd. As she looked back, Milly could see dirty, dishevelled and bloodied women sitting on the kerb and on the monument. They all looked dazed. Around them, a number of men were laughing, shouting and generally enjoying the spectacle.

29

As they approached the taxi rank, Milly could see the drivers talking. Would one of them be willing to take them? 'The hospital, please,' she said in a voice she hoped sounded full of confidence.

'Can't say I want the likes of you in me taxi,' said the first man in the rank. 'But a fare's a fare. Git in.'

As they settled down, Milly couldn't believe she was sitting in one of these new-fangled taxi cabs. She glanced at Lizzie, who sat with her head drooping forward, looking very unwell. Milly held her hand. 'You'll be fine as soon as we get that cut seen to.'

Lizzie didn't reply; she just sat back with her eyes closed.

'Right, 'ere yer are, miss,' said the cab driver as he pulled in to the entrance to the hospital and reached behind him to open the door.

Milly was worried how much he would charge them, but as they got out, Lizzie handed him her purse. He took some money and gave the purse back.

'Thank you kindly, miss.' He touched his cap.

As they made their way slowly inside, a nurse approached them. 'Come with me.' She ushered them into a small room. Lizzie's blood had seeped into her pretty fawn hat and down on to her coat. She looked a very sad sight. 'Sit here. A doctor will be with you soon.'

Lizzie slumped into the chair and Milly hovered over her.

The door opened and a doctor appeared. 'Now, what's the problem?' He moved towards Lizzie. 'Well, young lady, what have you been up to?'

'We were at a rally,' Milly began softly.

'Women's suffrage?'

Milly nodded. Would he treat Lizzie?

He turned to the nurse. 'That means we could be in for a busy time.' He returned his attention to Lizzie. 'You've taken a bit of a blow, by the look of it.' He touched her head and she winced. 'This certainly needs a stitch or two. I'll get Nurse to get you cleaned up, then we'll see where we go from there.' He left just as quickly as he'd appeared.

The nurse turned to Milly. 'I think you had better wait outside for your friend.'

Milly went and sat outside, and after a while the nurse came out and hurried along the corridor.

The doctor returned. A few minutes later the nurse reappeared and bustled down the corridor again. When a man wheeling a trolley went into the room, Milly began to sense that something was wrong.

It was a while before the door opened again. This time Lizzie was wheeled out on the trolley.

'What's happened?' asked Milly as she walked alongside the doctor.

'The young lady has had a nasty bump and lost a lot of blood, so I'm keeping her in overnight just for observation. Now be a good girl and give the nurse all her particulars, then go on home and get yourself cleaned up.'

Milly looked down at her dirty, dishevelled clothes. She looked a very sorry sight.

* * *

It was late afternoon when Milly arrived home. She wasn't surprised to see that the office was still closed. She prayed that nothing had happened to Ada, Pat, Eve or any of the other volunteers. She wandered around the flat feeling very sad and lonely. She couldn't believe that this morning they had all set off with such high hopes. Why couldn't the government just give them the vote? So many of these women were intelligent and well educated, and willing to go to prison for what they believed was their right. Milly knew she couldn't do that. She sighed. Perhaps one day women would have their say.

* * *

After a restless night, Milly could hear that some-one was in the office, so she hurried downstairs.

'Good morning, Milly,' said Ada very cheer-fully when she opened the door. 'And how are you this fine morning?'

'I'm very well, but I'm afraid Lizzie is in hospital.'

Ada put her hand to her mouth. 'Oh my dear, what happened? Is she all right? Is she badly hurt?'

'I don't know. She was hit on the head with a truncheon. I took her to the hospital and then I was asked to leave.'

'We will have to go along to the hospital later on to see how she is, and if they will let her come home.'

'Are you all right?' asked Milly.

'Yes thank you, my dear. And what about you?'

'A bit shaken, but nothing to worry about.'

'Good. A few did get themselves arrested, including Mrs Pankhurst, and I think some have been injured, but at least the press was there in force, so we are well and truly filling the papers this morning. I think I've bought most of them, so we can start cutting out the articles for our scrapbook. And don't forget, we must always remember our slogan, 'Deeds Not Words'. I think we proved that point yesterday.'

Milly was a little upset that Ada wasn't too concerned about her friend. 'Would you like me to go to the hospital to see if Lizzie will be allowed home today?'

'Leave it till this afternoon. After all, doctors don't usually do their rounds till late morning.'

Ada seemed to know the hospital routine, but then again, Milly guessed she had been through this before.

'Did you see how many women were at the palace? It was a wonderful turnout.' Ada was full of enthusiasm. 'I do hope that we disturbed the King.'

★ ★ ★

258

It was late afternoon when Lizzie, a large bandage wrapped round her head, walked into the office.

Milly rushed up to her. 'How are you? What was wrong?' She led her to a chair. 'Why did they keep you in overnight?'

Lizzie gave her a weak smile. 'I'm fine. I think I fainted, and that's why they kept me in. It was dreadful, all those people screaming out all night, and those uncomfortable beds. I didn't sleep a wink and I feel so tired.'

'Milly, take Lizzie upstairs, make her a cup of tea and see that she rests.' Ada was in control of the situation.

Once they were in the flat, Milly asked Lizzie if she wanted anything.

'Just to get out of these filthy clothes. You should have seen the state of my hat and gloves; I've thrown them away. And I can't see me wearing this coat again.' She threw the coat on to the floor.

Milly picked it up. It was beautiful brown velour and must have cost a fortune. She knew so many people who would love to have a warm coat like this, even if it was dirty and bloodied. 'I'll boil a kettle and you can have a nice wash; that will help you to feel better.'

Lizzie half smiled. 'Thank you. I knew you would look after me.'

'Would you like me to tell your father?'

'Good heavens, no. I don't want him round here fussing over me.'

When Milly returned to the flat later that evening, Lizzie was sitting on the sofa wearing her lovely dark red housecoat. She looked very pale, but relaxed.

'Milly, come and sit with me.' She patted the sofa. 'What have you been up to?'

'Not a lot really.'

'That was certainly some rally.'

'Yes, it was. Mrs Pankhurst has got herself arrested again.'

'You really do have to admire that woman, and her daughters. Now, what have we got for dinner tonight?'

The last thing on Milly's mind had been dinner. 'I don't know. I'll go out and find something.'

'Good girl.'

As Milly wandered to the shops, she thought about yesterday. It was certainly something she would never forget. She knew she couldn't be as dedicated as some of the women, but she did believe in their rights.

★ ★ ★

The following afternoon, Milly was downstairs making tea. When she came in from the tiny kitchen, she was surprised to see Tom standing in the office. 'Dr Walsh,' she said formally.

'Hello.' He turned his black trilby round and round in his hands. 'I've come to see the patient we had in yesterday. Is Miss Phillips around?'

'She's upstairs,' said Milly.

Ada came in from outside.

'Miss Roberts, and how are you? I trust the arm is in working order?'

260

'Yes thank you. My goodness, fancy you remembering me after all this time.'

'I never forget a pretty lady or her assistant.' He smiled at Milly, making her blush.

'Milly, take the doctor up,' said Ada, smiling broadly.

'This way,' said Milly. She was shaking. Had he come back into her life?

'Well I never thought I'd be back here to look at another of the walking wounded,' he said as he followed her up the stairs. 'How are you, Milly?'

'I'm very well, thank you.'

At the top of the stairs he stopped and took her arm. 'I've been thinking about you a lot. I was very sad when you said you didn't want to see me, you know.'

Milly didn't answer. She couldn't. She was still in awe of him. 'Lizzie's in here.' She pushed open the door. 'Lizzie, I hope you're decent. There's someone here to see you.'

Lizzie was stretched out on the sofa. She looked up from her book as they walked in. 'And you are?'

'Dr Walsh. I was told that a young lady had been injured yesterday, and I was sent to follow it up.'

Lizzie smiled. 'I didn't know doctors did this sort of thing. I always thought you were too busy to leave your domain.'

'We are allowed some time off, and it's just that I know some of the women here and I wanted to make sure it wasn't one of my previous patients.'

Lizzie swung her legs off the sofa. 'Please, come and sit down.' She patted the seat.

'I'll get back to work,' said Milly, closing the door as she left.

He was such a good-looking, polite man. He said he'd been thinking about her and was upset when she wouldn't go out with him. But how could she? Not with her background.

★　★　★

It was a while before Tom came back down into the shop. 'Well, everything seems to be fine with Miss Phillips,' he said, slowly pulling on his gloves.

'Is your mother well?' asked Ada.

'Yes, she is. She didn't go to the rally as she's having problems with her leg.'

'Not too bad, I hope.'

'No, but she must take it easy, so I made her promise to stay home.'

'It might have been just as well. It did get a little out of hand.'

'So I believe. We had a few come to the hospital, and I understand that Mrs Pankhurst got herself arrested again. That woman will go down in history.'

'Yes, she will, and hopefully we shall see her in Parliament one of these days.'

Milly was standing listening to this conversation. Tom had told her that his mother believed in their cause, but she hadn't realised that Ada knew her, or that she was an active member.

As Tom moved towards the door, he put his trilby on and with a slight bow said, 'Goodbye, ladies.'

'Goodbye,' said Ada and Milly together.

Once he had left, Ada turned to Milly. 'His mother is a lovely woman. She belongs to one of the other groups, but she's not very active these days.'

Milly smiled. She knew that her son was also lovely. If only she could be honest with him and tell him all about herself.

30

Milly wasn't surprised when Lizzie told her that Dr Walsh was taking her to the hospital to have her stitches out, as on Sunday afternoon he'd come and taken her for a walk round the park. Lizzie was thrilled, and seemed so happy that Milly felt a little jealous. But it was her own fault that it wasn't her in his arms. If she had felt that strongly about Tom, she would have told him about herself and her past and let him make up his own mind.

'He's so handsome,' said Lizzie. 'D'you know, I'm really pleased in a way that I had a bang on the head now that I've met Tom. I hope I shall see him again after I've had these horrid things out.' She gently touched her head.

'I'm sure you will, and he does seem very nice.' Milly hadn't told Lizzie about how well she knew him, and as far as she knew, he'd told Lizzie only that he'd met Milly when Ada had her accident.

'Oh Milly, do you think so? I've never felt like this before. I've met a lot of Daddy's friends' sons, but they are all so silly and full of themselves. That was one of the reasons I joined the suffrage movement, to give them something to think about and show them that women do have a voice and are not just pretty things to take to dinners and the like. They needed to be taken down a peg or two. But Tom is different.'

Milly was always surprised when she heard other women's reasons for joining the movement. For some it was to get at their husbands or their fathers. But some were genuinely devoted to the cause of getting women the vote and were determined that they should have a voice in Parliament.

★   ★   ★

For months there had been rumours about a war in Europe, but to most it was something that was happening very far away. At the end of June, Archduke Franz Ferdinand, heir to the Austro-Hungarian throne, and his wife were shot and killed. According to the papers, things were now beginning to look very uncomfortable for Europe.

'Tom said that could open up a whole can of worms,' said Lizzie when she came into the room and pointed to the headline of the newspaper Milly was reading. Tom had taken Lizzie out to one of the new picture houses that showed moving pictures; he hadn't come up to the flat, as he had to get back to the hospital for his night shift.

'What did he mean, a whole can of worms?' asked Milly as Lizzie sat next to her.

'I don't really know. Anyway, let me tell you about the film we saw this evening. It was so exciting, and very funny. It was that silly little man Charlie Chaplin. I did get a bit cross with Tom once or twice. Do you know, he was laughing so loud he almost drowned out the pianist. I told him to be quiet, and he didn't like that. I can't have him showing me up. Everybody was turning round to look at us. I wanted to die.'

Milly didn't say anything. She only knew that she would have laughed with Tom, not told him to be quiet.

★　★　★

As the weeks went by, Lizzie and Tom often went out together to the cinema or the music hall. Lizzie got very angry if he didn't turn up. She would stamp about the flat, throwing her hat and gloves on a chair.

'He does have to work,' said Milly.

'I know that, but he could let me know.'

Milly decided not to pursue this argument when Lizzie was in a bad mood. But after they had been out, she was all smiles and very happy.

'I'm going to take Tom to meet my father,' she said one evening when she got back.

'Could this be serious?' asked Milly.

Lizzie smiled. 'It could be.'

'So when are you planning this outing?'

'Tom will let me know when he has a day off. You know, I should ask him to bring along a friend one evening. I don't like the idea of you sitting here alone while I'm enjoying myself. Besides, it would be nice to go out in a foursome.'

Although Milly smiled and agreed, she knew that that wasn't for her. She could get very fond of Tom, but she didn't want him to know her background. Every time he came to take Lizzie out, he always spoke to Milly and made her feel special, but she knew he must never come back into her life. 'I'll make some tea,' she said. She needed something else to think about.

* * *

On August bank holiday Monday, everybody would be having the day off. For weeks there had been unrest about news from Belgium and France, but most people thought it would all blow over and were determined to enjoy the holiday.

'What are you planning to do, Milly?' asked Ada on the Friday evening as they were putting the goods away.

'Nothing. What about you?'

'I thought I would go and visit my sister. I don't see her very often, but Mother wants to go and see the children.'

Milly knew that Ada lived with her mother. 'Is that very far?'

'No, just the other side of London. I must say, I don't really enjoy going there, as my sister's husband doesn't approve of what we are trying to achieve. I have to be very careful what I say, as it can sometimes lead to words, and that upsets Mother.'

Milly thought of her own family. In some ways she would like to go and see them, but she knew that if she did, she would once again get involved. She knew that was very selfish of her. She often wondered how they were getting on, and sometimes she would send them money, but never said who it was from.

'Is Lizzie going out with the doctor today?' Ada asked.

'Yes. She's taking him to meet her father.'

'Oh dear. That sounds very serious. Is it?'

Milly smiled. 'I think it could be.'

'I only hope they know what they're doing.'

'I think Lizzie does.'

★ ★ ★

On Monday the weather was beautiful, and Milly decided to take a walk along the Thames. After a while she sat and watched the people pass by. The women looked lovely in their big hats and pretty frocks. There was an air of excitement everywhere, and she noticed that people walking along the Embankment were beginning to hurry in the direction of the Houses of Parliament. She decided to join them. There had been talk of going to war, but surely the government wouldn't do that, not today.

She was swept along with the crowd as they moved towards Downing Street, which was packed with people. Everybody was singing the national anthem, and when the prime minister came out, the noise was deafening. It took a while for the crowd to quieten down, and when he announced that he had given Germany an ultimatum, the noise and cheering was unbelievable.

'Does that mean we're at war?' asked a woman close to Milly.

'Could be, love,' said her husband.

'Will you have ter go and fight?'

'If they'll 'ave me.'

'But what about me?'

'I daresay you'll be looked after.'

Milly stood dreamlike. What was going to happen to everybody now?

* * *

It wasn't till Milly was sitting quietly in the flat that she tried to imagine what would happen. Would the men all be sent to fight? But this war was far away, in a different country. She suddenly thought of her brothers. Would this affect them? And what of Richard? Dear, dear Richard. He must hold a very high rank by now. What would a war mean to her and the people she knew?

She was in bed when Lizzie came in.

'Milly, have you heard the news?'

Milly sat up.

'Isn't it exciting? We are at war with Germany. My father reckons it will only last a few months. Tom said he's volunteering to join up. I am so excited about it. He will look so handsome in uniform.'

Milly couldn't see that there was anything to get excited about. People could be killed. 'Did you have a nice day?'

'Yes thank you. Daddy likes Tom.'

Milly lay back down again. She let her thoughts drift. Tom was a very easy person to like.

* * *

As the week went on, men were rushing to join the army.

'What's going to happen to us?' asked Pat. She was looking at the paper and pictures of men queuing outside the recruitment office. 'What will it mean for the cause? We were making so much progress.'

'I really don't know,' said Ada. 'I'm sure we shall hear very soon.'

Milly was printing out the newsletter. She hadn't thought about what would happen to her. She could be out of a job and a home. She suddenly felt very sad. Where could she go and where could she live? The thought of going back home filled her with horror.

'Milly, you're very quiet,' said Ada. 'Is anything wrong?'

'It's just that if we disband, I shall be out of a job *and* a home.'

'I'm sure it won't come to that,' said Ada. 'After all, the papers are saying it will all be over by Christmas. We shall just have to wait and see, so don't you go worrying yourself unnecessarily.'

Milly gave her a weak smile and continued turning the handle of the printing machine.

* * *

As the month drew to an end, everybody knew that this could be a long and bloody war. It wasn't going the way people had hoped, and many men had already been killed and wounded.

One evening Lizzie came in and announced that she was moving back home.

270

'I'm sorry, Milly. I have really enjoyed living here with you. But Daddy needs me to be with him. I know I work in his office and see him most days, but he says I should come home.'

Milly was taken aback, though in her heart she'd known that this wonderful life wouldn't last for ever. 'I shall miss you,' she said softly.

Lizzie hugged her. 'And I shall miss you. You must come and see us any time.'

Milly nodded. Although Lizzie had said many times that she would take Milly to her father's house, Milly had always found an excuse. She knew it was silly, but she was frightened that there might be somebody there who knew the Greens and would recognise her.

By the end of the week, Ada and Milly were the only ones left in the office. The rest of the staff had gone and it was very quiet and lonely. Milly looked out at the leaves, which had started to change colour. Autumn and then winter would be on them, and where would she be?

Eve had gone to be a conductress on the trams, and Pat said she would probably have to work in a factory. Milly knew that that was the way she would have to go too, but the thought of it made her feel very sad.

Ada looked at her. 'What are you going to do now we've had the orders to disband?'

'I don't know. I don't want to go back home. I'll have to find a job, but even so I don't think I could afford to pay rent. I haven't been trained for anything, so I expect I shall have to do the same as Pat.' She had been worrying about this for days.

'I wish I could help you. You are such a good, enthusiastic worker. I'm going to try and get an office job.' Ada gave Milly a warm smile. 'Mother is pleased that I won't be out smashing windows and chaining myself to railings.'

'Those days are all over now. The soldiers need us to help them.'

'Yes, they do.'

For the rest of the day they quietly went about their task of clearing and boxing up their past. It was getting dark when the door opened and Tom walked in.

'Dr Walsh. To what do we owe this honour?' said Ada. 'Miss Phillips doesn't live here any more.'

'I know,' he said, looking at Milly.

'I thought you were going into the army,' she said, wondering what he wanted.

'I was, but I've been told to stay here.' He looked round the room. 'This all seems very empty and sad.'

'It is,' said Ada. 'And we never achieved what we set out to do.'

'With what all the women and young girls are doing to help the war effort, I'm sure that day is very near.'

'We shall see,' said Ada sagely. 'Anyway. How can we help you?'

31

Milly was taken aback and embarrassed when Tom asked her if he could talk to her alone.

'Do you mind, Ada?' he asked.

'I'm sure what you have to say can be said in front of Ada.' Milly didn't like being the centre of attention.

'Come now, Milly, Dr Walsh must have something very private to talk to you about.' Ada smiled at the doctor. 'So many young people are getting married now, with all the problems this war is bringing. I do hope you and Miss Phillips will be very happy.'

Tom looked astonished.

'Look, why don't you go upstairs?' said Ada.

Tom followed Milly up the stairs. Once inside the tiny flat, he said, 'I'm not here to talk about a wedding. I came to see you.'

Milly stood looking at him.

'You see . . . ' He was twisting his trilby round and round in his hands. 'Could I sit down?'

'Yes, of course. *Are* you going to marry Lizzie?'

'I don't think so.' He sat on the sofa and Milly remained standing by the door. 'Oh, don't get me wrong, she is very nice and we do laugh a lot together, but she likes her own way and . . . I'm sorry, I shouldn't talk about your friend like that. After all, she is very caring towards the people she likes. You see, she told me that you will be out of a job and a home now that women's suffrage has disbanded, and she's worried about you.'

Milly smiled.

'She asked me if I could find you a job at the hospital.'

'What!' Milly sat down next to Tom and began to laugh.

'What's so funny?'

'Ada thinking you were going to tell me you're marrying Lizzie.'

Tom just smiled and said, 'If you came to the hospital you would be helping the war effort, and you could probably share rooms with another nurse.'

'But I can't. I've not had any training.'

'I think that now Queen Mary has started her Women to Work campaign, that should help.'

'I don't know.'

'I've been told that you are very good at what you do and are always willing to learn. Please, Milly, think about it. I can't bear the thought of you moving away.'

'Why aren't you joining up?'

'The hospital has advised me to stay for a while, just to see how things progress. We have started to receive some of the casualties. I don't think it will be over by Christmas, not from what some of these young men are telling us.'

'According to the papers there does seem to have been a lot of casualties.'

'Yes, and at the hospital we are busy preparing for them, as I expect a lot more will arrive here.' He smiled. 'So you see, like the posters with

Lord Kitchener saying that the country needs you, the hospital will need you.'

Milly shuddered. She was thinking of her brothers and of Richard.

Tom took hold of her hand. 'Please, Milly, think about it. You don't seem to have a family to go back to.'

Milly quickly pulled her hand away. 'You know nothing about me.'

'I know, I'm sorry.'

'Why are you doing this for me?'

'Lizzie feels she has let you down, and we both want to see you happy.'

'I am happy,' she said softly.

'But where will you go from here?'

'I don't know.'

'Please think about it. Come along to the hospital and talk it over with someone.'

She stood up. 'Thank you. I will.' She opened the door, waiting for Tom to leave.

When he got to the door he said, 'You know, you have a lovely nature. We will be glad of people like you as this war goes on.'

What would he say if he knew that she had killed someone?

Ada was still smiling as they came down into the shop.

'Well,' she said, once Tom had left. 'Was that about a wedding?'

Milly shook her head. 'He asked me to go to the hospital to see about a job.'

'Oh, how kind. I really thought that he was going to tell you he was marrying Lizzie.'

'I think he will.'

'What are you going to do? Will you go along to the hospital?'

'I don't know.'

'I think it's a good idea, especially if you get somewhere to live as well.'

'I couldn't be a nurse, that takes years of training.'

'No. But there must be other jobs, and you are very good at taking charge of things. You can type, and you are always willing to help.'

Milly knew she had come a long way since she first walked into this office two and a half years ago.

'You know I would be more than willing to give you a glowing reference.'

Milly smiled. 'Thank you.'

'I would like to see you settled before I leave. I've always been very fond of you.' Ada hugged her. 'We have been through a lot together over the years.'

Milly swallowed hard. 'Yes, we have.'

That night Milly tossed and turned. What should she do? She had to find a job and somewhere to live. Could the hospital be the answer? She would be happy helping people, she knew, but she would be near Tom, though that shouldn't bother her as long as he was with Lizzie.

★   ★   ★

The following morning Milly told Ada that she was going along to the hospital.

'I'm so pleased you've made up your mind,'

said Ada. 'Let me type out that reference for you.'

'I only hope they have a job for me.'

Later that morning Milly made her way nervously to the hospital.

'Excuse me,' she said to a young nurse sitting at a desk. 'Could you tell me who I have to see about getting a job here?'

'Matron.'

'Is it possible for me to see her?'

'Who shall I say wishes to speak to her?'

'Millicent Ash.'

'Take a seat and wait here. She's ever so busy, so it might take a while.'

Milly gave her a smile. 'That's all right.'

The nurse came quickly from behind her desk and walked swiftly down the corridor.

When she returned, Milly stood up.

'She's sending her secretary along to get you.'

'Thank you.' Milly sat down again on the hard wooden chair.

For what seemed hours she sat and watched the comings and goings of the hospital. People with blood running down their faces, women with small children and babies crying out in pain. One man came in holding his arm and weeping. The nurse was very efficient, sending them all along to the right department. Milly thought this was something she would love to do.

When the matron's secretary came to her, she quickly stood up.

'Miss Millicent Ash?'

'Yes.'

'Follow me.'

As she walked behind the woman, she wondered whether this was going to be the beginning of another chapter in her life.

'Please sit down,' said Matron when Milly entered her office.

Milly did as she was told.

Matron put her hands together on top of her desk. 'Now, Miss Ash, what can I do for you?'

Milly was very nervous. She cleared her throat. She knew she had to tell the matron about her previous employment. 'I have a reference from the office of the Women's Suffrage Movement, where I have been working for almost three years. Although I'm not a nurse, I am very willing to learn and do whatever you want me to. Queen Mary is asking all of us young women to help with the war effort, and Dr Walsh thought I might be of use to you.'

'You know Dr Walsh?'

'Only because he has been to look after some of the casualties from our campaign.'

Matron didn't reply to that, and Milly could see from the look on her face that she didn't approve.

Milly gathered her handbag to her. Had she said too much? Should she go?

'If you leave your address with my secretary, I will let you know.'

'Thank you.' Milly stood up. Somehow she knew then that she hadn't got a job. What should she do now?

As she sat on the bus, Milly's thoughts were all over the place. Finding a job shouldn't be hard, now that women were wanted in the munitions factories. Finding somewhere to live would be more difficult. The only place she could think of was back home, but would they want her? She shuddered. This wasn't how she wanted to live. But there was a war on, and everybody had to make sacrifices and do their bit.

32

Ada had decided to close everything up at the end of the month.

'I'm so sorry, Milly. What are you going to do?'

'I expect I shall go back home.'

Ada hugged her. 'I wish my mother had enough room for you, but her house is very small and she can be funny at times.' She brushed away a tear. 'I'm so sorry.'

'Please don't worry about me. It has given me so much pleasure working here. I'll get my belongings together.'

'We have a week to go yet before I hand the keys back to the landlord.'

'What about Lizzie's furniture?'

'I'll get in touch with her.'

They sat in silence for a moment or two, each with their own thoughts. They remembered the laughter and sadness they had shared. Now a new chapter was beginning for both of them.

⋆   ⋆   ⋆

A week later, on Milly's nineteenth birthday, she received two letters. One was from Lizzie wishing her a happy birthday and asking whether she would like to meet her for tea on Saturday afternoon. The other was from the hospital asking her to come and see Matron again on Monday at nine o'clock.

Milly was shaking with excitement. 'Do you think I've got a job?' she asked Ada.

'I would think so. Oh Milly, I'm so happy for you.'

'What should I wear?'

'What you wore for your interview.'

Milly gave Ada Lizzie's card to read.

'She wants to see you on Saturday at the Lyons Corner House.'

Milly smiled. 'She loves to go there.'

'You'll be able to tell her your good news.'

'But I won't really know for sure.'

'I think we can safely say that it's all right.'

'I hope so.'

★　★　★

On Saturday Lizzie was bubbling with excitement as she sat waiting eagerly for Milly to arrive. When she caught sight of her, she jumped up and hugged her. 'I've missed you so much.'

'And I've missed you.'

Milly sat down. 'Now what have you been up to?'

'Not a lot really. What about you? Found anywhere to live?'

'No, not yet.'

The waitress came up and took their order.

'I told you you could come and stay with me and Daddy, we have plenty of room.'

'I know. And it's very kind of you, but I have to stand on my own two feet.'

'Always Miss Independent.'

'So what's life like at home?'

281

Lizzie screwed up her nose. 'A bit boring. Daddy's out at meetings most evenings. This blessed war is making everyone very miserable, and so many music halls have closed down.'

Milly smiled. Although she loved Lizzie, her friend only really thought about herself. 'What should we do about the furniture at the flat?' she asked.

'I've paid the rent till Christmas, so you can still live there till then, and hopefully you should have heard from the hospital by then.'

'So Tom told you I went for an interview?'

'Yes, he did. Have you got a job?'

'I don't know. I have got to go back and see the matron on Monday.'

'Oh Milly, I'm so pleased.' Lizzie jumped up and ran round to Milly's chair and hugged her.

The people round them stopped their conversations and looked. Most of them had smiles on their faces and Milly was blushing at being the centre of attention.

The waitress put the tea and cakes on the table and Milly straightened her hat, which had been knocked askew. 'I don't know for sure if I have a job or not.'

'Believe me, that matron wouldn't call you back if it wasn't good news.'

Milly looked at her friend. Did she know more than she was letting on? 'Has Tom told you I've got the job?'

'Yes, he has. Now come on, drink up and let's have one of these delicious-looking cakes.'

Milly felt delighted. 'So how's things between you and Tom?'

'I don't see that much of him now. He seems to be very busy. They are getting a lot of soldiers in the hospital. I'm thinking of doing something useful to help the war effort myself.'

'What did you have in mind?'

'Don't really know. I quite fancy driving a tram.'

Milly laughed. 'Good job they're on rails, otherwise you would be heading off with your passengers to the nearest shops.'

They laughed and giggled together until they had finished all the cakes, then Lizzie said she had to go.

As they held each other close, Milly tried hard not to shed a tear. She loved Lizzie. She was a real ray of sunshine in her life.

'Please,' said Lizzie. 'Keep in touch. You have been a true friend to me.'

Milly choked back a sob. She had been called a true friend once before.

★ ★ ★

First thing Monday morning, Milly was waiting to see the matron. Somehow she didn't feel so nervous. She was confident now that this was a day when her life would be taking a very different direction.

'Come in,' said Matron's secretary. 'Take a seat. Matron will be here in a moment or two. She has to do her tour of the wards and check that the nurses are all clean and proper.'

When the secretary had left, Milly looked around the room. There were many framed certificates on the wall. She remembered when she got her own certificate from Miss Dance. That was something she was very proud of and would treasure for ever.

The door opened and Matron walked in. Milly quickly stood up.

'Please, Miss Ash, sit down.'

Milly did as she was told.

'Now, as you know, the war is beginning to take its toll on the young men of this country, and we have started to get many casualties sent to us. The Red Cross is now helping out, and I have spoken to them and they are willing to teach you first aid. When you are experienced, you will be able to help my nurses. Would that be satisfactory for you?'

Milly nodded. This was far better than she'd expected.

'You will of course be paid, though I don't think it will be a great deal. Are you happy with that?'

'Yes thank you.' Milly's brain was rushing along. She wasn't worried about money at the moment, as she had been able to save most of her wages, except for the bits and pieces she had sent to her family. She would be living at the flat till Christmas, and then she would worry about everything.

Matron stood up. 'If you have any questions, you can ask my secretary.' She held out her hand and a smile lifted her stern face. 'I think you will be among the first of the many young ladies who will be joining us as things go on.'

Milly shook her hand. 'Thank you so much for

giving me this chance.'

'It's hard work, but I hope you'll be happy here.'

'I'm sure I will.'

'We will see you here next Monday at seven o'clock. Goodbye.'

Milly left the matron's office and almost skipped into her secretary's room.

'Hello,' she said. 'I start work here on Monday. Perhaps you could tell me where I will have to go and what I wear.'

'You have to meet the other Red Cross workers at reception, where you will be given your instructions. What you wear isn't relevant as long as it's clean; you will be given a uniform.'

'Thank you.'

Milly was almost beside herself. There would be other girls there, so she wouldn't be alone. This must be almost the best job in the world. She wanted to dance all the way along the corridor. This was going to be another life-changing experience for her.

33

Although Milly was finding the work hard, it was also fascinating and very rewarding. She was learning so much. She had finished her first-aid course and was helping out on the wards. She was only emptying bedpans and bottles and holding dishes for men to vomit into, but she felt she was really contributing to the war effort. To see some of the injuries that these brave men had sustained was heartbreaking. She had been told to be kind but firm and carry on about her business in an orderly and helpful way.

As the weeks went on, she was given more and more jobs to do. At the end of her shift she was thoroughly exhausted, as she had sometimes been on her feet all day. But she didn't mind, she loved her job. There had been a great many casualties at Mons, and when things were very busy the workers were hardly able to pass the time of day. There was certainly no time to socialise. The only person over the weeks who seemed to be on the same shifts as her was another Red Cross girl, whose name Milly found out was June.

There had been a lull in the amount of casualties coming in, and one afternoon Milly was sitting with June rolling bandages.

'Don't often get a chance to sit down like this,' said June. She was very pretty, with fair hair, blue eyes, and dimpled cheeks when she smiled.

Milly had noticed how some of the young patients sat up when June came on the ward.

'That's true,' Milly agreed.

'You're Milly, aren't you?'

Milly nodded.

'I've seen you rushing about. You're always very willing to do any jobs.'

'I hope so. These poor lads need all the help we can give them.'

'That's true. Some of them have been through such a lot.'

'I hope this war doesn't go on for too long,' Milly said fervently.

'Have you anyone close in the army?'

'Not that I know of. My brother left home years ago and he could have joined up. He always wanted to be a soldier.'

'I'm sorry.'

'That's all right. It's just that I don't like to see all these terrible injuries on such young men.' The thoughts that had been in Milly's mind from the first were for Dan and Richard. What would she do if, God forbid, either one of them came into her care?

'Have you anyone still at home?' asked June.

'No. I live alone.'

'How do you manage? I'm absolutely exhausted at the end of my shift. Thank goodness I live at home and my mother feeds me and does my washing.'

'You are very lucky.'

'Yes, I know. Do you live far?'

'Not really, but I shall have to look for digs or something soon.'

'Why's that?'

'After Christmas the lease is up on the flat I used to share with a friend.'

'That's a shame. What will you do?'

'I don't know. Hopefully I can find somewhere cheap nearly.'

'We don't exactly get a fortune doing this job.'

'I know. We could have gone into a factory, that way we would have earned a fortune.'

'That's if we didn't get blown up or turn yellow.'

Milly smiled. 'That's true. Mind you, I love this job.'

'What sort of accommodation are you looking for?'

'Just one room or something like that. Nothing too expensive.'

'Look, I've got a lot of relatives who live round this way. If you like, I could have a word with them over Christmas see if any of them have a room you can have. It won't be all that posh, but it'll be a place till you find something.'

Milly wanted to jump up and kiss her. She was so lucky. She must have a guardian angel who really did look after her. 'Thank you. That would be wonderful.'

'Don't get your hopes up too high; wait till I've seen them first.'

They put the last roll in the box and June stood up.

'Right, that's another batch finished. Let's go and see if they can find us something else to do.'

Milly walked out of the room a very happy person.

Although Milly would be out of her flat after Christmas, she was determined to enjoy being at work on Christmas Day. The week before, all the Red Cross girls had put up paper chains to decorate the wards. In the morning, a choir from the local church came and sang to the patients. It was very moving, and many of the young men tried to hide the tears that trickled down their faces. Milly had tears too as she remembered the wonderful midnight masses she'd shared with Jane and Richard.

Milly went up to one young man who looked distressed. 'Can I get you anything?' she asked.

He smiled at her and shook his head. 'I did ask Santa for a new pair of legs, but I didn't get 'em.'

Milly held back a sob. Some of these boys were only about the same age as her. For the past week she had been writing cards and letters for those who had bandages on their hands or found it difficult to write, and she'd found it hard putting their feelings down on paper.

'Sorry, miss. I didn't mean ter upset yer.'

'That's all right.' She gently tapped the back of his hand. 'I'll bring you some extra Christmas pud.'

He gave her a thumbs-up sign.

Like the rest of the staff, Milly was wearing a red paper hat as she helped to dish up the dinners, and the laughter in the wards was wonderful. One or two of the young doctors had some mistletoe and were running after the nurses. At times the noise was unbelievable.

Milly had never enjoyed herself so much. She even caught sight of Matron walking down the corridor with flushed cheeks.

She was leaning over a bed trying to straighten a patient's bedclothes when she saw Tom striding down the ward towards her. She stood up, surprised. This wasn't his ward.

'Merry Christmas, Milly,' he said softly, and plonked a kiss on her cheek.

There was a whoop from the lads near them.

Milly straightened her hat. 'And a merry Christmas to you too, Dr Walsh.'

As he continued down the ward, Milly noticed that he kissed June as well.

She touched her own cheek. Was she reading too much into this?

★ ★ ★

It was late as Milly made her way home, exhausted but very happy. It was one of the best Christmases she had ever had since running away from the Greens. Back in the flat, she lit the gas lamp, kicked off her shoes and sat on the sofa. She would make a well-earned cup of tea later. She looked round the room. The sofa, along with all the rest of the furniture, was going back to Lizzie's house in the new year. She knew she would be very sorry to leave here; it had been lovely to be so independent, and this place had so many memories. The office and Ada and the efforts of the women hoping to get the vote. Now she didn't know where she would finish up. I mustn't get down, she said to herself; I know something will turn up.

She put her feet up and began to reflect on past Christmases. Some were good and some were very bad. What kind of Christmas had her family had? She tried to send as much money home as she could, but what would happen when she had to find rent? Whenever she thought about the family and about what she had, she felt very guilty. Perhaps she should go and see them in the new year? Her thoughts went to Jane. If it hadn't been for the Greens educating her, she would probably still be living in Winter Street. She thought about the lovely Christmases she'd had with the Greens and Betty. She would always be grateful to Jane for showing her a new life. If only things had been different. Milly knew that for the rest of her life she would be haunted by that dreadful day in the park. A tear slid down her cheek and the knocking on the downstairs door made her jump. She sat up and looked at the clock. It was ten o'clock. Who was coming here at this time of night? Whoever it was was very persistent. They knocked again, this time much harder. Milly stood at the top of the stairs.

'Milly! Milly!' It was Lizzie's voice. 'Open the door.'

'Lizzie!' screamed Milly and ran down the stairs.

She threw open the door and threw her arms round her friend. Over Lizzie's shoulder she saw Tom, and she stepped back.

'Look what we've brought round.' He held up a bottle.

'It's Daddy's finest champagne. We thought you might be lonely, so we decided to come and see you. I know it's late,' said Lizzie as she pushed passed Milly and made her way upstairs. 'But we will only stay for a while.'

Tom shrugged as he followed Lizzie.

Upstairs, Lizzie stood in the doorway. 'My God. Where is everything?'

'Packed up ready for me to move.'

Lizzie walked in and took off her gloves and scarf. 'Have you got somewhere to live?'

Milly shook her head.

'Well don't worry for now. I'll pay the next month's rent. How would that suit you? In fact I'll make it two, you don't want to be flat-hunting in the winter.' She plonked herself on the sofa.

'I can't let you do that.'

'Why not?'

'I don't know. It's not right.'

Tom had put the bottle on the table and was hunting around in the cupboard. 'Where are all the glasses, Milly?'

'Packed away.'

'Well you had better unpack them,' said Lizzie, smiling.

'How much have you had to drink?' asked Milly, getting a cardboard box from the dresser.

'A lot. And I was so pleased to see Tom. I've had such a boring evening, all I could do was drink till he arrived, and then he suggested we come and see you.' Lizzie began giggling. 'So here we are.'

Milly looked at Tom, who just smiled. So this was his idea.

The cork popped very loudly and Tom expertly poured out the champagne.

'I've never had champagne before,' said Milly, screwing up her nose as the bubbles tickled it.

'Well you deserve it. From what Tom's been telling me, you are one of the most efficient nurses they have.'

'I'm not a nurse.' Milly wanted to add that she didn't even work with Tom, but when she looked over at him he quickly shook his head.

'What about you, my little tram-driver?' said Milly.

'I can't drive a tram but as a conductress I'm having a lot of fun. I don't see the horrors of this damn war.'

For a moment the conversation stopped as their thoughts went to the men at the front.

Suddenly Lizzie said, 'Pour us another drink, Tom.'

He did as he was told.

* * *

After a while, Lizzie began to doze. To Milly's relief she was sitting in the middle, between Tom and herself. They began talking quietly.

'So where are you going to live?' he asked.

'I'm sure I can find somewhere. June at the hospital said she might be able to help me out.'

'That's wonderful. I was worried that you might be leaving us.'

'No. And I never really thanked you for helping me get it.'

'I just made a suggestion to Matron, that was all.'

Lizzie started to groan.

'I think I'd better get this young lady home,' said Tom, sitting her up.

'She could stay here,' said Milly.

'No, I'd better get her home. I don't want her father thinking I've taken advantage of her.'

Milly stood up and wobbled a bit. She giggled. The drink was affecting her. 'I'm not used to drinking,' she said sheepishly. 'I'll help you put her coat on.'

They helped Lizzie to stand up, and put her coat on her. 'It was lovely seeing you again, Milly,' she said without opening her eyes.

'And it was lovely seeing you again.'

They held each other close.

'Come on, young lady. Home for you.'

'I love it when he's so forceful.'

'Will you be able to manage?' said Milly.

'The fresh air will help. Besides, I've got her father's car outside.'

'You didn't tell me you could drive.'

'Lizzie's father taught me, so we'll be fine. Good night, Milly.' He leant across Lizzie and kissed Milly's cheek. 'See you at work.'

Milly stood and watched them leave.

Once she was sitting on the sofa again, she began to cry. The drink was making her melancholy, but she wasn't sad. Lizzie was going to pay her rent and June might be finding her somewhere to live. Why was everybody so nice to her? What would they all say if they knew what she had done?

34

The next morning Milly was looking out for Tom. She wanted to know if he'd got Lizzie home safely.

She was walking through the ward when June smiled at her.

'What you doing round here?' she asked.

'I'm looking for Dr Walsh.'

'Are you indeed? You know we're not allowed to fraternise with the doctors or the patients.'

'Of course I do. Have you seen him?'

'Not yet, I've just come on duty. I'd like to talk to you sometime.' June looked round her and said quickly, 'I'll see you lunchtime.'

'I'd better get back to my ward.'

Milly was apprehensive. Had June got some good news for her?

She missed June at lunchtime, as they had a new intake of soldiers. It wasn't till she was leaving that June came up to her.

'Milly, my Auntie Lil said she's got a room you can have, and you can go round any time and have a look.'

Milly wanted to hug June, but she knew that wasn't the right thing to do when they were in uniform. 'Thank you. Where does your aunt live?'

'Not too far away. Here's the address.' She handed Milly a piece of paper.

'I'll go round at the weekend.'

'That'll be fine. Good night.' June left Milly staring at the address. She knew where this was. It wasn't too far away, and not too near Winter Street either.

* * *

On Sunday afternoon Milly went to see Aunt Lil.

'Hello, I hope I'm not disturbing you,' said Milly when a small woman wearing a clean wrap-round floral overall opened the door. Her grey hair had been neatly cut and she had a ready smile

'No, love. You must be Milly. Come on in. It's a bit chilly out there.'

Milly walked straight from the street into a cosy, warm room.

'Sit yourself down. Cuppa?'

'Yes please.'

Aunt Lil went into the kitchen and quickly came back with a tray that held two cups and saucers, a plate of biscuits, milk jug and sugar bowl. It looked as if it had been set ready. 'The kettle won't be a jiffy. I thought you might be round today. Young June told me what shifts you'd be on. Nice kid, our June.'

'Yes, she is. Although I don't see a lot of her.'

'It's a good job you young girls are doing.'

'We hope so.'

Lil jumped up as the kettle began its shrill whistle.

Milly looked round this nicely furnished room. There was a table and two chairs, and an ornate pot that held an aspidistra was sitting in the

296

middle of the table. Two fireside chairs were drawn up beside a glowing fire that warmed the room. The fireplace had been black-leaded and was a complete contrast to the white hearth; a well-polished brass fender stood in front. Everywhere seemed sparkling and clean.

'This is a lovely warm room,' said Milly, as Lil appeared carrying a teapot covered with a multicoloured crocheted cosy. She sat down at the table.

'I try. It's been hard since my Stan died.' She jumped up again and took a photograph off the cluttered mantelpiece. 'This is my Stan,' she said proudly, handing Milly the photograph.

'He was very handsome.'

Lil smiled. 'Yes, he was. June loved him; always playing about, them two was.'

Milly smiled back. She knew she could be very happy living here.

'Do you take sugar?'

'Yes please. One.'

Lil pushed her tea towards her. 'Help yourself to biscuits.'

'Aunt Lil . . . can I call you that?'

Her face lit up. 'I'd love it.'

'How much would you charge me for a room?'

'Finish your tea first, and then we'll go and have a look, shall we?'

*   *   *

As Milly made her way back to her old flat, she still couldn't believe her luck. Aunt Lil was really lovely and said she wanted company. The bedroom was small and sparsely furnished, but Milly didn't mind. It was clean and cheap, and Lil was going to feed her and do her washing as well, all for only five shillings a week. Milly couldn't believe her luck. Once again the future was very bright for her. As she pottered about the flat, she wondered if there were going to be bad times ahead for her. She wondered why she was so blessed.

She had told Aunt Lil that she would like to move in after the new year. That would give her a chance to write to Lizzie and tell her of her plans, and then Lizzie could see about taking the furniture away.

That evening she decided to start putting a few of the very personal bits she had collected over the years into a cardboard box. There was her certificate, and the hair slide that Richard had bought her all those years ago. There was a necklace from Lizzie and a brooch from Ada. But the thing she treasured more than anything was the bracelet that Richard had given her. She sat fondling it. After she had pawned it to stop Bert from going to prison, she had been determined to retrieve it and had saved every penny she had. She recalled vividly the day she'd gone to the pawnbroker's. She had been very apprehensive. What if he'd sold it?

When she'd pushed open the door, the tinny bell rang aggressively. It wasn't a Monday morning, so the shop was empty, not like before. The man had recognised her right away.

'I know what you've come for. Got yer ticket?'

Milly nodded. She had kept the pawn ticket

298

with her all the time. She never wanted to lose it.

'That's good. Can't part with the goods without a ticket.'

Placing the ticket on the counter, she'd looked round the empty shop. In some ways she wished there had been other women there. This man made her feel afraid. 'Have you still got it?' she asked.

'Might have.'

She knew this was just a game to him.

'You know it'll cost yer more ter get it back?' He took a book out from under the counter and began leafing through it. 'What did I give yer?'

'Ten shillings.'

'It'll cost yer fifteen ter git it back.'

She took a sharp breath. 'That's a lot of money.'

'Please yerself.'

'Could I see it, just to make sure it's mine?'

He shut the book and went to a set of drawers behind him, and brought out her precious bracelet. It was wrapped in tissue paper. 'This is it.' He placed it on the glass counter.

She wanted to hold it and run away with it.

'It'll cost you fifteen bob ter get it back,' he repeated.

Milly stood looking at her treasure. 'I don't have fifteen shillings,' she said sadly.

He began wrapping the bracelet up again. 'Come back when yer have.' He turned to put it back in the drawer.

'Just a minute.'

He gave her a toothless grin. 'I knew yer had the dosh.'

Milly opened her bag and counted out fifteen shillings on to the counter.

He grabbed the money and gave her the bracelet. 'Ta. See yer again.'

As Milly left the shop she said, 'I don't think so.'

★ ★ ★

Now she sat on the bed and gently put the bracelet on her wrist. Thoughts of Richard and Jane came flooding back, and so did the tears.

35

It must have been after Lizzie got Milly's letter telling her she was moving that Tom came looking for her.

She was walking down the corridor when he caught up with her.

'Milly. Are you avoiding me?'

'No. Why?'

'I don't see a lot of you these days,'

'Well we are all rather busy.'

'That's true. Lizzie tells me you're moving.'

'Yes.'

'Where are you going?'

'I'm moving in with June's aunt.'

'Where's that?'

'Quite near.' Milly wasn't prepared to give him her address.

'What are you doing New Year's Eve?' he asked as he kept pace alongside her.

She stopped. 'Nothing. Why?'

'I'm hoping to have the evening off, and I'd like to spend it with you.'

'What about Lizzie?'

'Now that all the music halls and dance halls are closed and she has to stay at home, she gets very miserable; that's of course if she isn't working.'

'And what do you intend to do with me?'

'I thought we might go and have a meal somewhere. The best restaurants are still open.'

'Tom, you should be taking Lizzie, not me.'

'But what if we have to work? You'll understand, but Lizzie won't.'

'I don't believe that for one moment. And no, I won't go with you. I shall always be grateful to you for my job here, but I won't go out with you.' She continued walking. Inside she was very angry. Why was he doing this to her? He belonged to Lizzie, and Milly knew that she could never be with him if she didn't trust him. What if he always wanted someone he couldn't have? She wanted to turn and look when she reached the end of the corridor, but decided that would make him think she cared.

She made up her mind that she would volunteer to work on New Year's Eve and let someone else have the evening off to celebrate with their loved ones.

★ ★ ★

Milly was waiting for the removal men to come and take the furniture. When they arrived, there was a woman helping.

'Hello,' said Milly.

'Hello, miss. This lot ter go?' she asked, lifting a chair.

'Yes please, everything.' Milly smiled to herself. Women were doing so many jobs now that were once considered men's work. How different from when the Women's Suffrage Movement were trying to make themselves heard and were told by many that a woman's place was in the home. They would have to give women the vote after this.

After work that evening Milly moved in with Aunt Lil. It was the start of a new year, and once again a new start for Milly. Somehow she knew that this was going to be a very happy place for her.

★　★　★

The war was gathering pace. U-boats were sinking British ships and the east coast was being shelled. What really brought home the horrors of war to the ordinary people was that the Germans were using Zeppelins to drop bombs. This outrage caused many people to turn on the Germans living in London, smashing windows and setting fire to shops they thought were owned by Germans.

Milly was pleased that she had Aunt Lil to come home to. Sometimes she needed someone to talk to about the things she'd seen. The people turning on the Germans living in Britain had really upset her.

'These people have lived here all their lives. One woman was crying. Her little girl was badly cut with glass after their shop window was smashed. They're not German; they were born here. It's just they've got a German name over their shop.'

'That's terrible,' said Aunt Lil.

'I know.'

'Is the little girl gonna be all right?' she asked.

Milly nodded. 'Yes, thank goodness.'

'What's gonna happen to 'em when this lot is over?' asked Aunt Lil.

'I don't know. What's going to happen to any of us?'

* * *

At the end of April, the newspapers reported that the Germans were using gas on British troops. One morning Matron called the Red Cross workers to a meeting.

There was a lot of babble as they sat waiting, but when she entered the room silence fell and they quickly stood up.

'Please be seated. Now, I've called you all here this morning because a new batch of soldiers will be arriving shortly. I know this is nothing new, but these young men are different; these are men who have been affected by the dreadful poison gas.'

There was a sharp intake a breath from all who were gathered there.

Matron went on, 'The doctors, ward sisters and nurses have all been informed and are getting the wards ready now. Are there any questions?'

A young woman at the back of the room put her hand up.

'Yes, Miss Wallis.'

'Please, Matron, are these men blind?'

'Some are, and some have breathing problems. You must just go about your duties in your normal efficient way as you always do. Thank you. That is all.'

As Milly walked from the room, June came up to her.

'I hate it when I see these young lads suffering,' she said, falling into step.

'I know what you mean, but we're here to do a job.'

'I know. I might try and get round to see you this weekend. We might need a bit of time together.'

'That'll be lovely.' Milly liked June and enjoyed her company when she came to see her aunt.

Later that day the ambulances began to arrive, and everybody helped to push the wheelchairs to the wards and put the young men into beds. Many of them had bandages round their eyes. Some were waving their arms around, trying to catch hold of something. A nurse's hand seemed to comfort them.

'Hello, love,' said a young man, taking hold of Milly's hand. 'Where are we?'

'In London.'

He laid his head back on the crisp white pillow. 'Thank God for that.'

'Sarge, is that you? Is that Sergeant George Johnson?' shouted a soldier in the bed opposite.

'Yes. Who's that?'

'Reg Warren.'

'Reg Warren. How you doing?'

'Not bad. I bet these nurses are pretty.'

'They certainly sound it.'

'I fer one can't wait ter see 'em.'

'Reg Warren, just you remember where you are.'

'Yes, Sarge. We're back in dear old Blighty and the best place in the world, London.'

Most of the nurses had stopped what they were doing and were listening to this banter. Some even wiped a solitary forbidden tear away. Most of these soldiers were just boys.

The ward sister came down the room. 'Now come on, ladies,' she said softly. 'We have a job to do.'

'Yes, Sister,' they all murmured, and quickly went about their work.

When Milly finally got home that evening, she was thoroughly exhausted, but she had to tell Aunt Lil about some of the young men who had arrived that day.

'They've only just got back, and to be blind must be really awful. We have been told to try and help as much as we can. I did ask a few if they would like me to write letters to the people at home, but they don't want that. They said they didn't want to worry them.'

'It must be very hard for them. Give 'em time to adjust, love.'

⋆　⋆　⋆

For weeks Milly and her fellow workers attended the men, and some who hadn't been in the thick of the gas seemed to be getting their sight back.

Milly had been looking after Reg. When she started writing letters for him, he told her all about his wife and two children.

'When I went in the army, she went back up ter Scotland ter be with her family. Said she couldn't stand the dirt and noise in London. She should have been where we was. Talk about dirt and noise. D'yer know, some of our lot went a bit funny with the constant bombardment, it was so bloody loud. As fer the dirt and mud, I tell yer, girl, don't go over there fer the sunshine, cos they don't get a lot.'

'Did you manage to keep a photo of your family?'

'No. They got lost in the mud.'

'Perhaps I could ask your wife to send you another one.'

'Not much point if I can't see it.'

'Reg, you mustn't give up hope. The doctors can do such wonderful things these days.'

'Can't work bloody miracles though, can they?'

'Now come on, Reg, this is not like you. We rely on you to keep everybody cheerful.'

'Leave me be.'

He turned over and Milly left him. She knew that was the best thing to do when they got down.

A few days later Reg was back to his old self and Milly was pleased to tell him he had a letter from his wife. She was beginning to recognise the wives' and mothers' handwriting. 'Reg, you've got a letter from Kate. Shall I read it to you?'

'Yes please.'

When she'd finished, she said, 'She sounds lovely, and at the bottom is a kiss from Jimmy and one from Connie.'

'That's a bit daft. She knows I can't bloody see 'em.'

'But we can tell you about them.'

'S'pose so.'

'Right, it's time to change your bandages.

She took the old bandage off, and turned to take a fresh one from the trolley.

'Milly,' Reg said. 'Have you got a red cross on the front of your apron?'

'You know I have.'

Reg sat up and put his hand out. 'I think I can see me fingers.'

Milly looked at him sitting with his eyes screwed up. 'Are you sure?'

He only nodded.

'Just a minute. Nurse!' Milly hurried down the ward. 'Please, Nurse, get the sister.'

'Miss Ash, please control yourself. Now what seems to be the problem?'

'No problem. Private Warren thinks he can see.'

'I'll get Sister.' She hurried away.

Milly went back to Reg and took hold of his hand. Perhaps miracles did happen after all.

'I hope I'm not just imagining this,' he said quietly.

'We shall soon find out. The doctor's on his way.'

36

A doctor came hurrying into the ward and the staff nurse took him to Reg's bed. There was an air of anticipation as the curtains were pulled round and Milly and the other nurses went about their duties.

'What's happened to Reg?' asked another patient with bandaged eyes.

'We don't know,' said a nurse.

'I can tell there's something,' said the man. 'We can pick up on the slightest sound that's unusual.'

'So?' asked the nurse. 'What's so unusual?'

'Footsteps. One lot was the staff nurse's, and she don't usually rush about, and the other lot was a man's, so I suspect it was a doctor.'

'And what conclusion did you come to?'

'They stopped at Reg's bed so something's wrong with him.'

The nurse went up to the patient and touched his hand. 'I can tell you, there is nothing to worry about.'

'You know we all worry about each other in here.'

'I know, and I can tell you honestly that everything is fine.'

'I hope so.' He settled back on his pillows again.

Milly was watching and waiting for the curtains to open. She too was worried about

Reg. It would be wonderful if his sight had come back, even if it was only partially.

Eventually the curtains were pulled back, and Milly waited until the doctor and staff nurse had gone to her desk before she ventured over. 'Everything all right then, Reg?' she asked as she went about tidying his bed.

'Milly.' He clasped her hand. 'I can see a bit. It's very blurred, but I can just about make out shapes and bright colours.'

'I'm so happy for you, Reg. What's going to happen now?'

'The doctor said I shall be here for a bit, to make sure it's not just temporary. Then if it carries on improving, I can go to one of these houses that's being set up for us.'

Milly squeezed his hand lightly. 'I'm really pleased for you.'

'I'm looking forward to seeing if you're as pretty as you sound.'

'I can see I'll have to watch you when you start running round the ward.'

He laughed. To Milly, it was one of the nicest sounds, and now Reg really did have something to laugh about.

Reg had mentioned the houses that were being set up as places for soldiers to convalesce and adjust to the outside world. The nurses and Red Cross workers had been talking about them too. Although it was still a new idea, some wanted to go and work in these places, but others, including Milly and June, weren't so sure. They were very happy at the hospital.

'That lad must be over the moon,' said Aunt Lil when Milly told her about Reg. 'Sit yourself down, love, and I'll get you a cuppa. I expect you could do with one.'

'Yes please.'

'June was telling me about some of the lads in her ward. Got a lot of problems with their lungs.'

'I know. They will never get better.'

'Neither will a lot of your lads.'

'That's true.'

'Terrible stuff, that gas. Let's hope they don't drop it on us.'

'Please don't say that,' said Milly.

'So where's these new places June was talking about?'

'Don't know. They're calling them auxiliary hospitals, but they might only be a rumour.'

'June don't want to go.'

'Neither do I.'

'But if you're told to go, you'll have to.'

'I know.' Milly didn't want to leave Aunt Lil. She was so very happy here.

★ ★ ★

It was late spring, and Milly knew she had to call on her family. It was something she had been meaning to do for months, and when she had told Aunt Lil about them, she had encouraged her to go. So one Sunday afternoon she found herself knocking on the front door of the house in Winter Street.

Pammy opened the door and stood looking at her. 'What d'yer want?'

'Nothing. I just came to see that you were all right.'

'No thanks to you we're fine. Mind you, we could 'ave all bin dead and buried for all you care.'

'Please, Pammy, I do care.'

'Not enough to visit.'

'So how are you managing?' Milly could see that Pammy was looking a lot smarter. 'I'm sorry I've not been able to send you much money lately, as I work for the Red Cross now and we don't get a lot.'

'Don't worry about us. This war's been a godsend. I work in a factory and get good money, and Dad's got work as there's plenty of fings he can git hold of and sell. So yer see, we're doing all right.' She went to shut the door.

Milly put out her hand to stop her. 'Can I come in?'

'No.'

'How are Freddie and Iris and Rosie?'

'All right. Now bugger orf. We can manage without you.'

'But Pammy, please . . .'

'I said go. Now clear orf.' She shut the door.

Milly stood on the doorstep. She felt utterly rejected, but it was all her own fault. She should have kept in touch. Slowly she walked away, without looking back. She knew they were all watching her from the window.

★ ★ ★

In the summer, some of the men were being moved to one of the auxiliary hospitals that were being set up. Sergeant Johnson was one of the men who were going. Milly had grown fond of him and was sorry to see him leave.

'I shall miss you,' he said.

'And I shall miss you,' she replied.

'Mind you, the ward's not been the same since Reg left us.'

'That's very true. It is a lot quieter.'

'It was nice of his wife to write to us,' he said.

'Yes, it was. And you must get someone to write to us for you, just to let us know how you are getting on.'

'I will.'

'You never know, you might finish up in the same house as Reg.'

'That would be great.'

'Sergeant Johnson, your carriage awaits,' said the old porter who wheeled the lads around.

'Ready and waiting, James.' He turned to Milly and held out his hand. 'Bye, Milly, and thank you.'

'Look after yourself.'

'I will.'

Milly swallowed hard as she helped him into the chair, then stood with a few of the nurses and watched as he was wheeled away. It wasn't any good waving; he couldn't see. Like all the men in the hospital he was wearing the blue uniform that told everybody he had been injured. At least he'd never get one of those terrible white feathers that were being sent to some young men.

It wasn't long before the beds were full again. The war had been going on for over a year now, and more and more young men were being killed and injured.

'I'm sure they're getting younger,' said Milly one evening as she sat with Aunt Lil, who was busy knitting socks for the soldiers. 'Either that or I'm getting older.'

'I'm always surprised that young girls like you and June haven't been snapped up by some nice young man.'

Milly smiled. 'Not allowed to fraternise.'

'What about a doctor? Any of them you like?'

'No, most of them are old; they've been called out of retirement to help out, as a lot of the young ones are at the front.'

'That must a terrible job.'

'Yes, I expect it is.' Milly was thinking about Tom. He had told her he was going to France, and Lizzie was beside herself. There had been a lot of tears. Lizzie had told her that as soon as he got back to England they were to be married. Milly was pleased about that. She hoped that Tom had got her out of his system, and genuinely hoped that he and Lizzie would be happy.

★　★　★

A few days before Christmas, Milly was called to the matron's office. She knew what was coming, as some of the other Red Cross women had been sent away to one of the auxiliary hospitals.

'Please, Miss Ash, sit down.'

Milly did as she was told.

'I have been more than pleased with your work here.'

'Thank you.'

'As you know, we are sending some of our nurses to these new hospitals that are more like convalescent homes. They help the men to adjust to the outside world. Although they are run by doctors and nurses and the VAD ladies, we have been asked to send a few Red Cross workers, as they are known for being very efficient in helping nurses. I think you would be able to cope very well, and you will be going in the new year.'

Milly tried hard not to let her face show her feelings. She was happy here, but there was a war on.

'I know it will be hard for you to leave, but I'm sure you are more than capable of adjusting. That's all. I will give you more information nearer the time.' She stood up.

'Thank you,' said Milly, and left the room.

That evening as she told Aunt Lil her news, she felt like crying. 'I've been so happy here.'

'I know, love, and I've enjoyed having you here.'

'I'd better write to Lizzie and tell her where I'm going.'

37

It was a beautiful spring morning when Milly arrived at Waterloo station. She looked about her and saw two other women in Red Cross uniform talking to a man.

'Excuse me, is this where we have to meet?'

'Miss Ash?' asked the man.

Milly nodded. 'Yes.'

'Good, now you are all here. You are going to Billington.'

'Where's that?' asked the older of the two women.

'It's in Surrey. Here are your train tickets.' He handed out the third-class tickets. 'There should be someone at the station to meet you. Hope you enjoy your new location. Goodbye.'

'Goodbye,' they all said together, and made their way to the train.

Milly put her small suitcase on the rack above her head and settled down.

'I'm Nancy Stevens,' said the older woman. She leant forward and shook hands with Milly and the other young woman.

'Gertrude Collins, but I prefer to be called Trudy.'

'I'm Millicent Ash, but I like to be called Milly.'

They were all smiling broadly.

They told each other where they had been working, and found that they had all come from different hospitals. Trudy, who was about the same age as Milly, had a ready smile and appeared to be enjoying this journey as much as Milly.

'I've never been this far away from London before,' she said.

'Neither have I,' said Milly.

'Surrey is very nice. I wonder what sort of transport will be waiting for us,' said Nancy.

'I hope it's not a horse and cart,' said Trudy.

That statement made them laugh.

'Can't say I fancy wandering around the countryside looking for this place,' commented Nancy, glancing out of the window.

They settled back and let the gentle rhythm of the train take them to their new life.

★   ★   ★

When the train pulled into Billington, the three of them were ready and waiting to open the door.

A car was outside and the driver came up to them. 'I'm to take you to Seatly Manor.'

'That sounds very grand,' said Trudy.

'It is,' said the driver, holding the doors open for them.

As they drove through the countryside, Milly was enthralled. It was all so lovely, and you could almost forget the horrors of war. There were cows in the fields as well as sheep, and everywhere looked so fresh and green. She knew then that she was going to enjoy her time here.

The large house was set in its own grounds

and looked very peaceful.

'This is nice,' said Nancy as she stepped out of the car.

When the driver pushed open the huge wooden front door, all Milly could do was stand and stare. She had never seen anything so lovely. In the middle of the hall was a well-polished table, on top of which stood a vase holding a huge arrangement of flowers. Behind that was a wide staircase that rose up to a gallery.

'This is very grand,' said Nancy.

'It's beautiful,' said Trudy, who was looking all around her. 'I've only ever seen places like this in picture books.'

'Me too,' said Milly.

'I'm sure you'll be very happy here,' said the driver, and he left them, closing the front door behind him.

They stepped inside on to black and white tiles. As soon as the front door was closed, one of the doors in the hall opened and a tall, stately woman came over to them. 'Welcome, ladies. I'm Matron. I'm so pleased to see you. I'll get someone to show you to your room. But for now, please follow me. You can leave your cases here.'

They trooped behind Matron to her office. 'Please take a seat. This place is for some of the young men who have been injured and still need medical treatment, but it is also a place where they can adjust before they are sent home. Some are badly scarred, some are blind and some have shell shock. I know that you are all familiar with various types of patients.' She looked at some papers that were in front of her. 'Miss Ash, I see

318

you have been with the blind.'

'Yes, Matron.'

'And Miss Collins, you have been helping the shell-shocked.'

'Yes, I have.'

Nancy it seemed had been with the badly burned and injured.

There was a knock on the door. 'Come in.'

A tall nurse came into the room and nodded to Matron. 'I see our young ladies have arrived.'

'Yes. Nurse Webb, could you take them to their accommodation.'

'Of course. Follow me.'

As they made their way up the grand staircase, Nurse Webb addressed them over her shoulder. 'You will be sharing. As soon as you've seen your room I will take you on a tour. This is a lovely place to work in and our patients are so nice, but they do need our help.'

Once again Milly was amazed at the grandeur of the place she was now going to call home.

There were four beds in the room, with cupboards and a dressing table and two large chests of drawers.

'This part of the house is the staff quarters, and there is a bathroom along the corridor.'

As they were shown around the house, they passed many men in the hospital blue uniform. Some of them gave them a wave, and others just sat with a blank look on their face. A few were feeling their way round the room.

'Now that summer is almost here, the garden is very popular,' said Nurse Webb as she pushed open one of the two glass doors that led out on to a beautiful green lawn with chairs and a few tables dotted around. There were many men sitting in the chairs, and Milly visibly shuddered when she saw two patients being pushed round the grounds in wheelchairs on the lovely green grass. Thoughts of the happy times she'd had with Jane came flooding back.

'Miss Ash, are you cold?' asked Nurse Webb.

'No. Sorry. I think someone must have just walked over my grave.'

'Don't say things like that. I'll show you the rest of the house, then after tea we can visit the hospital.'

'Is it near here?' asked Nancy.

'It's just at the back of the house.'

As they made their way round the garden, Milly saw more men in wheelchairs. She just prayed that there wasn't a lake here. She knew she would never, ever forget that dreadful day.

Two men started to walk towards them.

'Are you the new girls?' asked one soldier who had a very badly scarred face; Milly guessed he'd been burnt.

'Yes, we are,' said Nancy.

'Now come on, Roger,' said Nurse Webb. 'I don't want you playing any of your tricks with these young women.'

'As if we would. Pleased to meet you, ladies,' said Roger, bowing low.

'I'm Peter,' said the other one, who was leaning on a stick. 'Roger thinks he's a bit of a ladies' man, and I'm the one who has to keep him in check.'

'Pleased to meet you,' said Nancy.

Trudy and Milly both smiled and nodded.

They made their way back to the house, where Nurse Webb told them about mealtimes and anything else she thought they should know. She looked at her watch. 'The gong for tea will be sounding soon; we can carry on with our tour afterwards. And please don't hesitate to ask any of us if you need help.'

When they were back in their room, Trudy said, 'I have never been in such a lovely place as this.'

'Neither have I,' said Milly.

'I must admit it is rather grand,' said Nancy. 'I wonder what we are expected to do.'

* * *

The babble in the dining room was unbelievable. The men were very noisy.

'Come and sit with me,' said one man to Milly. 'You can sit on my other side,' he added to Trudy. 'Look, lads, I've got two of the new intake.'

A young soldier holding on to another man's arm came and sat on Milly's other side. 'Trust you, Robbo,' he said.

Milly touched his hand. 'Don't worry. I'm sitting next to you.'

'That's good.'

Milly watched as his friend passed him his tea and a plate with sandwiches on. 'What's your name?' she asked the first man.

'Andrew. Although everybody calls me Robbo on account of my surname being Robinson. And yours?'

'I'm not sure if we are allowed to use our Christian names,' she said.

He smiled. 'Whisper it to me and I promise not to tell.'

Milly laughed. 'I'm Milly.'

He held out his hand. 'Pleased to meet you, Milly.'

'And I'm pleased to meet you, Andrew.'

38

As the months passed by, Milly was very happy. She even managed to overcome her fear of pushing a wheelchair again, although it was very hard at first and she had to keep her feelings to herself. She found out that most of the men here were officers of some sort, so the possibility of seeing either of her brothers vanished, as she didn't think they could be officers. You never knew, though. Who would have thought that she would have got an education and gone into the nursing profession? Perhaps Billy and Dan were still well and healthy. She didn't want to think of the alternative.

Sometimes Milly was in the hospital helping the new patients try to come to terms with their blindness; other times she was reading or writing letters. Like Trudy and Nancy, she also helped the doctors and nurses. They were always ready to do anything that was asked of them.

One afternoon she was sitting reading to Major Robinson. They had become great friends, although Nurse Webb had told the Red Cross girls that they must be very professional at all times and not fraternise with the men.

He had laughed when she told him that. 'I'm twice as old as you, and I have a wife, and daughters as old as you.'

'I know that. I read and write all your letters for you, remember.'

'You're a good girl, Milly, and I'm very fond of you.'

She patted the back of his hand. 'Don't tell anyone, but I'm very fond of you.'

They laughed together.

Milly was pleased when Lizzie wrote and told her all her news. It seemed that Tom had been very busy at the front and was now coming back home to work at the hospital for a while. Lizzie was also talking about setting a date for the wedding and asked Milly if she would be able to attend. Although Milly was very fond of Lizzie, she wasn't sure if she would be able to go. Matron was very reluctant for her girls to leave, even if it was only for a weekend.

★ ★ ★

It was a Monday morning and some of their patients had left. It was always a sad time when they had to say goodbye. A few of the men were frightened of leaving the security of the hospital and didn't want to go home, and some even invented curious symptoms, but Matron could always see through them. Now they were waiting for new arrivals.

Matron was there as always to talk to them about the new patients. 'We are going to have more men than usual this time and some will just have to go where we have room. Most of these men have been badly injured. Although they were treated in the field hospital, some were injured again before they were shipped back. I am given to understand that some of them are very traumatised, and I don't have to remind you that we have to treat minds and well as bodies. Now they should be here about midday.'

They all went about their duties in a professional way. Beds were prepared and everything was ready as they waited for the new arrivals.

When the ambulances drove up, Milly, Trudy and Helen were there with the porters and wheelchairs. Gradually the men were helped into the chairs and taken to their wards.

'Looks like we've got quite a few burns victims this time,' said Trudy late that evening as the girls were getting ready for bed.

'I've got some very traumatised lads,' said Nancy. 'And a few who will be moved to your part of the building, Milly, when they've been assessed.'

'This part of the job always upsets me,' said Milly. 'Seeing the new ones for the first time.'

'I know, and some are so traumatised that it takes a while to get them to speak,' said Nancy as she sat on her bed and combed out her long dark hair, which she always wore in a bun.

'It doesn't matter how many times we see it, it's still wrong that young men are suffering like this,' said Trudy, who was sitting up in bed.

'I'm afraid that's war,' said Nancy.

They were all used to each other now. Nancy was tall, and when her hair was pulled back she always looked stern, although she was very nice and gentle and always had a shoulder for the soldiers to cry on when it was needed.

Milly climbed into bed and looked across at

Trudy. She was very gentle with her patients, and according to the men, nobody could dress burns like she could. That might be because they liked this small, willowy blue-eyed blonde hovering over them.

Milly sat up and hugged her knees. 'I thought I saw enough trouble when I was a suffragette before the war.'

'I was in the movement as well,' said Nancy.

This was one of the few times they could talk among themselves. Often they didn't work the same shifts.

'Did you go on marches?' asked Trudy.

'Yes,' they both said together.

'I think the saddest one was at Emily Davison's funeral,' said Nancy.

'Yes, it was,' said Milly. 'That all seems a lifetime ago.'

'It is for some.'

'True,' said Milly as she settled down to prepare herself for another long day tomorrow.

* * *

A week later, Nancy was pushing a young man along the corridor when she saw Milly. 'Ash,' she called. They had to call each other by their surname in front of the patients. 'You can take over from me. Lieutenant Green is to go into your ward.'

Milly stood still as she looked at the man in the wheelchair.

'Ash, are you all right?' Nancy came up close to her and whispered, 'Milly, what is it? You look like you've just seen a ghost.'

'Is everything all right?' asked the young man.

'Yes. Yes. Everything is fine,' said Nancy. 'Milly,' she hissed, beginning to get cross. 'Pull yourself together.'

'Sorry,' Milly said softly, taking hold of the handles of the wheelchair. She felt sick. How could this happen? Why was Richard sent here? She would have to go and see Matron and tell her she had to leave. She couldn't stay here. Not now.

In the ward, she silently helped him into a bed.

'Is that you, Ash?' asked the man in the next bed.

'Yes,' she said quickly and quietly.

'You're quiet today,' he said.

She didn't want to speak in case Richard recognised her voice. Blind men were able to pick up on every little sound.

'She's normally such a chatterbox.' The man was talking to Richard now.

'Must be my good looks have left her speechless.'

She looked at Richard's once handsome face. He had a terrible red, angry-looking scar right across his left eye and down his cheek; the other eye had a dead look about it. His beautiful grey-blue eyes. Milly wanted to hold him and kiss him. She knew then that she had never stopped loving him. But what about him? He couldn't possibly love her, because he must blame her for Jane's death. She had to get away. She couldn't bear to be so near to him and not

327

be in his arms. What would he do if he found out she was standing next to him?

'Were you gassed, mate?' asked the man in the next bed.

'No. Caught in the blast of a gun that got hit. What about you?'

'That bloody gas. Didn't do my lungs much good either.'

'Sorry to hear that. I'm Richard Green, and you are . . . ?'

'Frank Miller.'

'Pleased to meet you, Frank. As soon as I'm on my feet I'll come and shake your hand.'

'You'll be up and about with our little Red Cross nurse in no time. Ash is our guardian angel. And according to my wife she writes lovely letters. Have you got a wife?'

'No.'

'What about mother and father; she'll write to them.'

'They were both interned in Germany. I haven't heard from them for a long while.'

'Sorry to hear that.'

'That's all right. It was just one of those things. Father was working over there. I just hope they're all right. Mother was a bit poorly the last time I heard.'

Milly couldn't believe that in that short space of time she had found out all about Richard's parents and that he hadn't married. That was the thing with these men; they would tell anyone all about themselves if they found a willing ear.

39

For the rest of the day Milly tried to stay away from the ward that Richard was in. She was worried that if he heard her voice he might recognise her.

That night Trudy was working. Milly was in bed when Nancy came into their room.

'What was wrong with you this morning? I've never seen you like that before.'

Milly let a tear run down her cheek. 'I'm sorry,' she said.

Nancy came and sat on her bed. 'You don't have to be sorry. What was it? What upset you?'

'Nancy, I've got to leave here.'

'What? Why?'

'It's very difficult.'

'But I thought you loved it here.'

'I do, but . . . '

'It was that patient, what was his name?'

'Richard.'

'That's it. That's the problem. You know him, don't you?'

Milly nodded and wiped away a tear. 'What can I do?'

'How well did you know him?'

'Very well.' Milly wasn't prepared to tell her friend anything more. What would Nancy say if she found out that Milly was responsible for his sister's death.

'You'll have to have a word with Matron. Go

and see her in the morning.'

'Thanks. Nancy, please don't say anything to Trudy.'

'Nothing to tell, is there?'

Milly knew as she settled down that her thoughts would be on Richard. She knew from reading his notes that he would never be able to see her. Who would look after him when he was able to leave here? She desperately wanted to hold him and be there for him, but she knew that he had loved Jane and would never forgive her. She turned over. Sleep was going to be hard to come by tonight, and tomorrow could be another turning point in her life.

★ ★ ★

Milly knocked on Matron's door.

'Come.' She looked up from her desk. 'Ash. What can I do for you?'

Milly looked at the chair. She wanted to collapse on to it, but they had to stand till they were told to sit. 'Please, Matron, I wish to be transferred.'

'Please sit down and tell me what has suddenly brought this on. I thought you were very happy here?'

'I am.'

'So what seems to be the trouble?'

'I know one of the new patients.'

'Which one is that?'

'Lieutenant Green.'

'And does he know you?'

'I haven't told him who I am.'

'He's not recognised your voice?'

'I have been very careful not to speak in front of him.'

'I see.'

Milly looked at her hands.

'Was this a love affair that went wrong?'

'In a way. We were both very young.'

'Have you looked at his notes and found that he's married?'

'He's not married.'

'I scc. And you think that you both being here could start the relationship again?'

Milly nodded.

'Well, you know the rules.'

'Yes, Matron.'

'As you know, although we look after the men, we're not like a hospital; we are here to help them learn to live with their disabilities, and because of that we become involved less in a clinical way and more in a social way. I like to think that we are one big happy family.'

Milly wanted to smile at that remark. She didn't look on Matron as a motherly figure.

'Leave this with me and I'll let you know.'

Milly left Matron's office with a heavy heart. She loved this job and the camaraderie with the men. Sometimes as she read their letters and wrote their replies, she almost felt she was part of their family.

★　★　★

Later that afternoon Milly took a letter out to Major Robinson, who was sitting in the garden.

'It's from your wife,' she told him.

'Wonderful. Will you read it for me?'

'Of course.' She settled herself in a chair close to him and began reading the letter. When she'd finished, she said, 'She sounds very well, doesn't she?'

'Yes. In some ways I wish she could come and see me.'

'Would you like me to talk to Matron about a visit?'

'Could you. I know it's a bit of a way for her to come, but I'm sure she'd be happy to make the journey.'

'Would you be happy for her to see you?' She knew that some of the men had had their wives to visit, and that one or two had found it very hard to come to terms with the situation.

'I think so. She knows it's going to be hard when I'm sent home, and if she saw how well I was managing, I'm sure that would help to put her mind at rest.'

Milly touched his hand. 'I'm sure it will. She sounds a lovely woman.'

She looked up and saw a nurse pushing Richard towards them.

'I have to go,' she said and quickly walked away.

Was this how it was going to be every time she saw him?

*　*　*

A week later Matron called Milly to her office.

'Please take a seat. I've had a letter from

332

Major Robinson's wife. She is coming to see him at the weekend and she has asked to meet you. I am still waiting to hear about your transfer.' She folded the letter she had been holding. 'Have you managed to avoid talking to Lieutenant Green?'

'Yes, Matron.'

'So he still doesn't know you're here?'

'No.'

'Well, go along and tell Major Robinson the good news.'

Milly left the office.

Major Robinson was over the moon. 'How do I look? Do I need a haircut? I'm getting better at shaving, but will you look at me on Saturday just to make sure I haven't missed a bit?'

'Of course I will, and I'll make sure you're turned out spick and span.'

'Thank you. You're a good girl, Milly, and I know Frances is going to love you.'

* * *

On Saturday afternoon, Major Robinson was very happy and talked continually to anybody who would listen.

Milly knew what time Frances Robinson was arriving, and when the taxi pulled up outside the house, she went to meet her. 'I'm Milly Ash. Pleased to meet you.' She held out her hand.

'May I call you Milly? I feel we know each other through your letters.'

'Please do,' Milly said with a smile. 'Andrew is in the garden.'

She went to lead the way, but Frances held her

arm. 'Please. Tell me, is he very bad?'

'Not physically, but he can't see at all.'

'Will he ever regain his sight?'

'That's hard to say. I have known some gas victims to see again even if everything is a blur, but I shouldn't hold out too much hope.'

'He shouldn't even have been in the trenches. He was just visiting his men. He's always been the same, always has to poke his nose in.' Frances took a pretty lace handkerchief from her handbag and dabbed at her eyes. 'I'm sorry.'

'That's all right. Now, are you ready?'

She stood up straight. 'Yes.'

They made their way across the beautifully kept lawn to a group of men sitting under a tree. Among them were Major Robinson and Richard. Milly was cross with herself. She should have got the major to wait up near the door.

She went over to him and whispered, 'I've got someone to see you.'

Frances went to him and kissed his cheek.

'Frances. Let me touch you.'

She bent down, and he ran his fingers over her face.

Milly could see that Frances was crying, and she started to walk away.

'Just a minute, Milly,' called Frances.

Milly was in her own world and didn't hear her name being called.

'Milly. Milly Ash.'

She stopped and turned.

There was a crash of a glass being dropped. Richard was trying to get out of his wheelchair. She rushed over to him, afraid that he would fall or bump into something.

He held on to her. 'Please say you are my Milly Ash.'

'Yes, I am, Richard.'

Tears fell from their eyes as they stood locked in each other's arms.

'What's going on?' asked the major.

'I don't know,' said Frances. 'But it looks beautiful.'

* * *

Milly helped Richard back into his chair and wheeled him to a secluded corner of the garden. There she sat on a seat with Richard at her side.

'Why did you run away?' he asked, holding out his hand for her to hold.

'Because of Jane. I had to,' she said softly, taking his hand.

'Milly, no one blamed you. It was an accident. If anyone was to blame it was me, for starting all that in the first place.'

'But what did your mother and father think?'

'We tried to find you. We didn't know where you lived. We even tried to find your Aunt Doris.'

'You did all that?'

'You had become part of our family and I have never stopped loving you. I just wanted you back again.' He kissed her hand. 'Why didn't you talk to me when I first arrived here?'

'I thought you would be angry with me.'

'But now I've found you and we can be together. You're not engaged or married?'

'No.'

He kissed her hand again. 'Please kiss me.'

'Richard, I can't. I shouldn't even be holding hands with you.'

'I've loved you all this time. What about you? Did you ever think of me?'

'Richard, I have always loved you. Every time I feel a little down, I look at my lovely bracelet and think of you.'

'You still have that bracelet? I would have thought you'd have sold it by now.'

'It's been a close call at times.'

'Milly, I still love you. Could you feel the same way about me, even if I am scared and blind?'

She choked back a sob. 'Richard,' she said softly, 'I've never stopped loving you, but I never thought I'd ever see you again. I thought you would hate me for what happened to Jane.'

'We knew you would never hurt her.'

'She was my best friend and I loved her.'

'I know.' Richard kissed her fingers. 'Please say you'll never leave me and that you will be my wife.'

'I will, Richard. I will.' Milly wiped the tears from her eyes, then held him close and kissed him. She couldn't believe this was happening to her.

'We should be married as soon as we can,' Richard said softly.

The gong sounded for tea.

'We must go.' Milly stood up and turned his wheelchair round. 'As you can see, I'm better at handling these now.'

'Please don't think about that.'

'It's something I shall never forget.'

As they got nearer to the house, Richard said, 'Can we talk after tea? We have a lot of catching up to do and a lot of plans to make.'

'I would love that.'

As she pushed him up the ramp, she turned and looked at the sky. It was just starting to turn a lovely shade of pink, heralding a new day tomorrow. Milly knew at that moment that she had found her true love at last, and that from now on, all her tomorrows would be wonderful.

We do hope that you have enjoyed reading this large print book.

Did you know that all of our titles are available for purchase?

We publish a wide range of high quality large print books including:
Romances, Mysteries, Classics
General Fiction
Non Fiction and Westerns

Special interest titles available in large print are:
The Little Oxford Dictionary
Music Book
Song Book
Hymn Book
Service Book

Also available from us courtesy of Oxford University Press:
Young Readers' Dictionary
(large print edition)
Young Readers' Thesaurus
(large print edition)

For further information or a free brochure, please contact us at:
Ulverscroft Large Print Books Ltd.,
The Green, Bradgate Road, Anstey,
Leicester, LE7 7FU, England.
Tel: (00 44) **0116 236 4325**
Fax: (00 44) **0116 234 0205**

THIS TIME FOR KEEPS

Dee Williams

It's 1943. When Babs Scott is left homeless, after losing her beloved parents in an air raid, The Land Army offers her a new life away from the bombed streets of Rotherhithe. Working on a farm in Sussex, with the support of fellow Land Girl Lydi Wells, Babs starts to heal. But the arrival of Gino and Demetrio, two Italian prisoners of war, undermines her safe world. And then Pete, an RAF rear gunner, whom she has fallen in love with, dies and Babs is once again grief-stricken. Back in Rotherhithe after the war, a foolish mistake one night changes Babs' life for ever. She fears she has lost her one chance of happiness, but a letter from abroad offers an unexpected ray of hope . . .

ALL THAT JAZZ

Dee Williams

February 1921. When influenza claims the life of their mother, Daisy Cooper and her younger sister Mary are suddenly alone in the world. Daisy works long hours to keep a roof over their heads, but worries she's neglecting Mary. Mary is thrilled when the moving pictures come to Rotherhithe, but for Daisy, the magic really begins when the glamorous dancing girls perform. When one of the dancers suggests that Daisy should try out a routine, she discovers she is a natural and is soon offered a place at a dancing school. Her teacher thinks she has what it takes to hit the big time, and Daisy hopes she can make a better life for her sister. But then the little girl disappears . . .

AFTER THE DANCE

Dee Williams

It's late 1935 and Sue Reed is living with her parents in Rotherhithe, working in the office of local car dealer Fred Hunt. Pretty and vivacious, Sue has many admirers, including her best friend Jane's brother, Ron. But her main love is dancing, and Sue and Jane are always to be found at the local dance hall. When one night the band has a new singer, Cy Taylor, Sue can't help falling for him. Handsome Cy invites her to visit him in his hotel room . . . Afterwards, however, reality hits hard. For Cy has neglected to tell Sue he is married. And, just when she thinks life couldn't be worse, tragedy strikes. Will Sue ever find the love and happiness she craves?

SUNSHINE AFTER RAIN

Dee Williams

Sisters Connie and Jenny Dalton have always taken their comfortable lives for granted. They are sheltered from the deprivation which their housemaid Molly and her family endure in nearby Rotherhithe. But, in April 1912, their father leaves for a business trip to America — on the new ship *Titanic* . . . Within days William Dalton is resting in a watery grave. And, with his death, his widow and daughters learn that they have inherited only debt, with their home soon to be taken from them. As war approaches, it seems that the sisters' dreams for the future are to be snatched away. Yet new doors are about to open, behind which lie dangers and many changes — but also the possibility of happiness for both.